electric 2

Also Edited by Nicole Foster

Awakening the Virgin: True Tales of Seduction
Electric: Best Lesbian Erotic Fiction
Skin Deep: Real-life Lesbian Sex Stories
Body Check: Erotic Lesbian Sports Stories
Wet: True Lesbian Sex Stories

electric 2

Best Lesbian Erotic Fiction

Edited by Nicole Foster

alyson books
los angeles

MANUFACTURED IN THE UNITED STATES OF AMERICA.

THIS TRADE PAPERBACK ORIGINAL IS PUBLISHED BY ALYSON PUBLICATIONS,
P.O. BOX 4371, LOS ANGELES, CALIFORNIA 90078-4371.
DISTRIBUTION IN THE UNITED KINGDOM BY TURNAROUND PUBLISHER SERVICES LTD.,
UNIT 3, OLYMPIA TRADING ESTATE, COBURG ROAD, WOOD GREEN,
LONDON N22 6TZ ENGLAND.

FIRST EDITION: APRIL 2003

03 04 05 06 07 a 10 9 8 7 6 5 4 3 2 1

ISBN 1-55583-796-4

LIBRARY OF CONGRESS CATALOGING-IN-PUBLICATION DATA

ELECTRIC 2 : BEST LESBIAN EROTIC FICTION / EDITED BY NICOLE FOSTER.—1ST ED.
    ISBN 1-55583-796-4
    1. LESBIANS—FICTION. 2. AMERICAN FICTION—WOMEN AUTHORS. 3. EROTIC STORIES, AMERICAN. I. FOSTER, NICOLE.
PS648.L47E433 2003
813'01083538—DC21   2002043930

COVER PHOTOGRAPHY BY DIGITAL VISION.

For Becky,
who keeps me rolling in the aisles

Contents

Introduction

*T*hree years ago I put together a fantastically fun anthology called *Electric: Best Lesbian Erotic Fiction*. In the introduction to that book I claimed that the stories inside were "the *steamiest, spiciest, loveliest, sizzlingest,* and *funnest.*" Well, I didn't think it was possible, but I was wrong. The book you're *now* holding in your hands, volume 2 in the Electric series, beats the first volume hands down. These stories are so hot, I'm surprised you're not scorching your hands right now. (Quick! Run into the kitchen and grab some oven mitts!)

A quick glance through these pages will give you a taste of what I'm talking about. Take Rosalind Christine Lloyd's sultry "subway ride 4 play," for example. Girls, if you've ever been on a packed New York City subway and wondered what it would be like to rub up against a certain hottie, wonder no more. Ms. Lloyd explains it all for you—in very graphic and sexy terms. And then there's the studly convict in Julie Lieber's "Lock Bend Exodus" who breaks loose and breaks in a sweet Southern girl. In Sacchi Green's "Riding the Rails," a hot bodyguard and the wife of an Arabian sultan mix it up on a speeding train, while a cabin "boy" and her beautiful captain give new meaning to the phrase "all hands on deck" in Catherine Lundoff's sassy yet hard-driving "On the Spanish Main."

I hand-picked these terrific stories from the dozens of lesbian erotic stories published by Alyson Publications over the past three years. I've read many of these stories over and over, and each time, every one of them makes me break into a sweat. But hold on, these stories aren't just sexy—they're all well-crafted pieces of fiction, with exciting characters and plotlines that push the definition of erotica.

I feel privileged to have my name associated with the group of fine writers who contributed to this volume, including such well-known talents as Lesléa Newman, Patrick Califia, Linnea Due, Anne Seale, Wendy Caster, and Carol Queen, as well as up-and-coming writers such as Renee Hawkins, Raphaela Crown, and Julie Lieber. Thank you all for making this such a wonderful book.

Thanks also to my friends and colleagues who constantly support me, even when they're positive I've got "erotica on the brain." Thank you for keeping me sane.

—Nicole Foster

Burning Zozobra
Renee Hawkins

*W*e may be setting Old Man Gloom on fire tonight, I told myself, but if I'm not careful, I'll get burned right along with that overgrown puppet. I shook my head and wondered what was going to happen.

I was driving from Albuquerque to Santa Fe, on my way to meet the girls at Fort Marcy Park. Tonight was the burning of Zozobra, or "Old Man Gloom," as he was affectionately called. Zozobra is a larger-than-life papier-mâché marionette. Every year he is burned at the stake as part of Fiestas de Santa Fe, a time-honored New Mexican tradition celebrating the anniversary of the city's settlement. Burning Zozobra is also a great excuse for a party.

Normally I would be in the best of moods. Zozobra meant the beginning of autumn, my favorite time of year, but right then I was not up for the celebration. My head was in a permanent fog, for all I could do was think about my friend Sharon. I don't know how, but it happened. Suddenly I had a crush on her.

The past few months had been hell. I agonized about

telling her, weighing the cost. What if I revealed my feelings and lost her as a friend? I went crazy every time I was around her and even crazier when I wasn't. I told myself that if it didn't work out, I'd just forget about her.

I wasn't sure how I was going to accomplish that, especially since we all hung out together. We called ourselves Sisters in Black, the SiBs. We were all African-American, all lesbian, and we were inseparable. We went to the movies, shopping, the bar. We'd have breakfast, lunch, and dinner together. Tonight it was an excursion to Santa Fe. It would be Sharon's first Fiesta, and we couldn't wait to show her what it was all about.

Sharon had been in town almost a year. She was in the military, stationed in Albuquerque at Kirtland Air Force Base. I had seen her in uniform only a couple of times, but that was enough for me. I had fantasies about making her scream. We made love on my imaginary movie set—on the kitchen table, out camping, in the bathtub, and on the hood of my car. Hot nasty fantasies that left me wet, no matter where I was or what I was doing. I played them over and over in my mind until I could think about nothing else.

I couldn't stand it anymore. I was losing sleep and was sick of worrying about losing my friends. These women were my support system, my family. If I told Sharon I had feelings for her and it didn't work out, what would happen to the dynamics of our group? Fuck that. *What about the dynamics of my life?* I asked myself.

For the past two weeks, I had stayed close to home, trying to figure things out, and it got me nowhere. I missed everyone, especially Sharon.

Then came the phone call last night. I thought it would be Gina, one of the SiBs, calling to firm up plans for Zozobra.

"Hello?"

"Hey, girl, what's up?"

It was Sharon! "Where you been? Why haven't we seen you lately?" she asked.

It took several minutes and some of my best acting, but I finally convinced her I was just "laying low." When she was satisfied there was nothing wrong with me and that I would still be going to Santa Fe with the group, the interrogation took an unexpected turn.

"Let me ask you a question. How come you haven't settled down with anyone yet?" she asked.

"I don't know."

"That's all you gonna say?"

"Why you all in my business? I could ask the same thing about you," I said, feeling defensive.

"Don't get upset. Just answer the question."

"Girl, I'm too busy worrying about me."

"Why is that?" Sharon asked. "As long as I've known you, you've never been with anybody."

Because all I can do is think about you. "You haven't known me all that long," I said.

"Answer the question."

"OK! Hell, I don't know. They say you find the one you're supposed to be with when you aren't looking. And what about you?" I asked. "Why haven't you found the right one?"

"I guess I'm picky."

"About?"

"Mainly about the sex."

"Sex? I guess that's honest."

"Hey," she said, "I know you need to be friends and work on a relationship and all that, but good sex is just as important. To get with me, you gotta be special."

I could hear the smile in her voice. Sharon could be mischievous, and that's part of the reason I was so attracted to her. I relaxed, since the focus was off me. "Special," I said. "You sounding pretty bold, girl."

"I speak from experience."

"Oh, really?"

"Hey, it's all good."

Yeah, I knew it would be, if I'd only speak up. I wondered what Sharon was wearing right then. I pictured her on the couch in just a T-shirt, legs propped on the coffee table. I leaned back on my own couch and closed my eyes. "So what makes for good sex?" I asked.

"It has to be memorable."

"What does that mean?"

She laughed. "Honey, I want the kind of coochie you can call up from memory like the taste of your mama's peach cobbler."

I laughed too. "You don't know anything about my mom's peach cobbler."

"Yeah, I do. I likes to get all in it, have it all over me."

"The cobbler or the coochie?"

There was a pause. "Well, to tell you the truth," Sharon's voice dropped low, "I've been thinking a helluva lot about pussy."

The word jarred me. Maybe because I couldn't remember the last time I'd heard it said like that. Or maybe because I'd never heard her say anything like that. I cleared my throat. "Go on."

"Hey, you know, I've been single a long time," she said.

"Yeah. And of course your last girlfriend was the bomb in bed, huh?"

"Oh, yeah, we had mad sex, bumpin' pussies like bunnies."

"And what made it so good?" I asked.

"My girl put me through a lot of shit but knew some things

in bed. She could make me come just by playing with my nipples. Have you ever been that sensitive? With someone just sucking on them?"

"No, I—I can't say I have," I stammered. I could think of nothing else to say, but she had my attention. Every bit of it.

Her voice grew sexier, more intimate. "Don't you love it when you put your head between a woman's legs and she's already wetter than your tongue could make her?"

"Well—"

"And it's not just all over your mouth. It's on your cheeks and chin and eyelashes too."

I couldn't believe what I was hearing. "Eyelashes?" I said.

"Mm-hmm."

I laughed. "You're crazy."

"I miss working my tongue on a woman's clit and looking up and watching her titties heave up and down."

Did she really say that? Suddenly, I realized my clit was asking for attention. This pillow talk was getting to me. I couldn't help it—my hand found its way between my legs. Damn, I was wet! I let out a small groan. Did she catch it? I swiveled the phone's mouthpiece to the top of my head to keep her from hearing what I was doing.

"What gets you excited?" she asked.

It took a second to get out the answer. My hand was feverishly working on my cunt, and I could barely keep my voice even. "Me?" I managed to say.

"Yeah, you. Tell me what you like." I heard rustling on the line. Did Sharon just switch ears, or was she getting as comfortable as I was?

"I forget."

"What kinda answer is that? Come on," she coaxed, "give it up, girl."

Was it my imagination? Or was her breathing a little errat-ic too? My hand slowed, but it didn't stop. "All right," I finally said. "I like it outdoors, OK? Especially when I'm camping. You can be as naked as you want, and nobody's around."

"Outdoors, huh? I stop when the pavement does. Camping is not for me."

"But you're the big bad army girl. Don't they make you go out on maneuvers or whatever it's called?"

"Yeah, and that's part of the reason I don't like being out there unless I have to," she said.

"Well, one day you should try it out there."

"Well, maybe one day I'll get the opportunity. Tell me how wild it gets when you go camping."

Just then my call-waiting clicked in. Not now! The only person I knew who would call this late was Gina. As usual, her timing was the worst. Maybe it was a wrong number and I could just ignore it. The phone beeped again. It had to be her; I'd bet my last dollar on it. "Sharon, I have to get the other line," I said. "I'm sure it's Gina."

"No, you don't. Get on with the camping story."

"You know how she is. We won't get any peace."

Sharon sighed. "Let her call back!"

"It'll just take a minute."

"Look—"

"Hang on," I interrupted, and clicked over to the other line. Sure enough, it was Gina, wanting to finalize our Santa Fe plans. Since I was working so late, I'd join the group later. We would check out Zozobra, then head to the bar and go dancing. I quickly worked out the details with Gina and went back to Sharon.

"Well, that was convenient," she said.

"Hey, I didn't do it on purpose. I haven't talked to Gina all week, and we needed to figure out where we should all hook up tomorrow."

"I forgive you. Now finish."

"Finish what?"

"Don't let me hang like this! You owe me a story!"

"I'll finish the story tomorrow," I said.

"Oh, hell no!" Sharon wailed. "Finish what you started!"

Gina's interruption had definitely changed my mood. And the reflection in the mirror with my shorts around my ankles didn't help either. "Girl, it's late. I'm going to bed."

"I can't believe you're gonna hang up!" Sharon protested.

"I'll tell you tomorrow, I promise. In fact, I have a lot to tell you."

"Tell me now!"

My mind was made up. I was done for the night. "You can wait one day," I told her.

"No, I can't."

"Well, you have to. I'm hanging up."

All day, I obsessed about our conversation. Over and over I wondered what would have happened if we hadn't been interrupted, although I had no way of knowing whether our little chat had affected her the same way it had me. Sharon was used to getting her way and definitely knew what she wanted. The question was, would she want me? I was making myself crazy. I had to make that move, and it had to be tonight. *This shit's gone too far*, I told myself. *If she kicks me to the curb, so be it.*

The plan was to meet the girls just inside the main entrance at Fort Marcy Park, then settle in to watch the burning of Zozobra. Fort Marcy could hold about 20,000 bodies, but it sorely lacked parking space. Most people left their vehicles downtown on the Plaza and hiked the mile or so to the celebration. I took a chance and looked for something closer. I finally found a road on a hill above the park that ended in a new cul-de-sac. There were several houses under construction and a few cars on the street. I thought it would be safe enough. I could even see Fort Marcy below.

I got out of my Honda and hesitated. On the one hand, I couldn't wait to see Sharon. On the other, I was afraid of what was going to happen when I did. *Just don't freak her out,* I told myself. How I was going to accomplish that was beyond me. I was freaked out. For a moment, I thought about just staying put and watching the fireworks from my car, but I forced myself to begin the trek to the park.

The entrance teemed with people trying to get through the gate at the same time. Many young children were dressed as little "glooms," racing through the crowd in ghost-like costumes and makeup, playing pranks as part of the festivities. There were souvenir and food booths, a mariachi band, and, of course, Zozobra.

He stood silent for now but would later come alive, moaning and thrashing about at the bidding of his puppeteers, then become engulfed in flames until there was nothing left of him. And there was a lot to burn. Old Man Gloom towered more than 50 feet. He was dressed in his usual bright red gown, buttoned from head to toe. On top of his long body sat an over-sized head with saucer-like eyes that were supposed to look scary, but his wide mouth, crooked nose, and cauliflower ears made him appear comical. I smiled, forgetting about my queasy stomach.

"Hey, girl!" Gina pulled me from my thoughts. She, along with Tami, Vida, Janelle, and Sharon, was waiting just inside the gate, food and beverages in hand.

"Y'all couldn't even get a drink for me?" I asked.

"You just mad 'cause you gotta catch up," said Vida.

Sharon offered me some of her beer. "You ready to get into a little somethin'-somethin'?"

"Oh, yeah!" I sang.

At least we were speaking. After the way I got off the phone last night, I wasn't sure how she would act around me.

Sharon was actually in a great mood, laughing and joking as always. I couldn't help checking her out. Her short, curly hair was pulled tightly back in a ponytail, with bangs above her almond eyes. She was wearing jeans and a yellow sweatshirt that set off her mahogany skin. Her jacket was tied around her waist, outlining that sweet ass of hers. Damn, she looked good. I had to stop staring at her, so I craned my neck upward and took another look at Zozobra.

Sharon stood next to me and looked up too. "I didn't think he'd be that big. Tell me about this shit."

"I will as soon as I get something to eat," I told her. Instinctively, I reached for my fanny pack and realized I had left it on my dashboard. I was so nervous about Sharon, it was a wonder I'd made it to the park at all. "Damn! I gotta go back to my car, y'all."

I felt like an idiot in front of Sharon. What would she think of me now? My friends chided me, but there was no way I could enjoy myself wondering if someone was gonna walk off with my shit, especially since I had left the invitation of cash and credit cards in plain view.

"I'll go back with you," Sharon offered. "Then you can tell me about Zozobra."

I didn't know what to say. And I was so surprised she volunteered to leave with me, I had to think hard about exactly where I'd left my car.

Sharon took charge and suggested everyone meet later at the bar. It was obvious we wouldn't be able to find one another again in the sea of people, especially after the sun went down. We said our goodbyes and began the long walk back to the cul-de-sac.

I was grateful to be alone with Sharon, although I couldn't stop my stomach from churning. I quickly began telling her about Fiestas de Santa Fe to hide my nervousness. "Back in the late 1600s, a Conquistador named De Vargas conquered this part of New Mexico. Folks have been celebrating ever since."

"I bet not everybody wanted to celebrate."

"I hear ya. But there's a Fiesta anyway."

"And Zozobra?"

"Invented to help with the party. They set Old Man Gloom on fire every year," I said.

"So what does he have to do with anything?"

"Part of Fiesta is letting go of past bullshit. And the way to do that is to burn Zozobra."

"I don't get it," Sharon said.

"The official story is he's been running around all year spreading doom and gloom. We put a stop to him and start fresh. A new beginning."

"But why burn the man? Can't they just tell him to lighten the fuck up?"

"Hey, he was actin' a fool all year. He had his chance to chill."

"So it's death by fire."

"Zozobra's the bogeyman. You gotta burn him. Besides, how else are they gonna light all the fireworks?"

"I get fireworks with this too? Viva la Fiesta!"

I laughed. Sharon's mood was light, but something was not quite right. She seemed preoccupied. Maybe it was my imagination. And after last night's conversation I couldn't find the courage to bring anything up. I had no idea when or how I was going to tell her how I felt. "We'd better hurry," I said. "It's gonna be dark soon."

"Damn, girl, where'd you park? Egypt?"

"We're almost there."

My little Honda was right where I had left it, valuables still inside. A few more cars had found their way to my secret parking spot, but no one else was in sight. I grabbed my fanny pack, extracted a couple of 20s, then shoved the bag under the seat. "Let's hit it," I told her.

Sharon didn't move. "You know, you got off the phone at a bad time last night," she said.

My stomach did a back flip. "Yeah, why is that?"

"'Cause we were just getting started. I couldn't believe you wanted to get off—the phone, that is." With a knowing smile on her face, she moved toward me.

She took my hand and leaned in to kiss me. I had always pictured our first lip lock as sweet and sensual, but this was neither. We were rough and hungry as we explored each other. I finally pulled away. "I've wanted this for a long time, but I wasn't sure."

She kissed my collarbone, and as she moved up my neck I felt a surge of electricity concentrated in the small of my back. "I wanted you too," she breathed in my ear, "but I wasn't sure either. And after last night…you got off the phone so quick."

All my fear and doubt melted away. I lightly brushed my lips on her face, then parted her mouth with my tongue. Finally! I turned her against the car, grinding my crotch against hers. My hands wouldn't keep still. I touched her everywhere at once.

Wanting more than just her clothes rubbing against me, I moved her hand to the top of my jeans, and she yanked at the buttons. I leaned against the car and supported myself with both hands but continued to explore her mouth.

Sharon's hands slipped inside my panties, and I felt them

slide down my thighs, exposing my skin to the night air. I felt the warm breeze against my wetness and across my ass, making me even hotter.

I finally pulled away from her mouth and looked into her eyes. I couldn't explain what I was searching for, but with the look she returned I somehow got the right answer.

She held my gaze while continuing to tease me. My clit now had a pulse of its own, the blood simmering just below boil. "Touch me," I pleaded. I concentrated on the feel of her hands, needing more.

In response, she ran her finger the full length of my crack but stopped just short, taking her hand away. "Tell me what you want," she said.

"Why you makin' me beg? You're driving me crazy."

"That's the idea."

I moved my hips, trying to catch up to her hands, but she kept one step ahead. "I can't take much more of this."

"Gimme some titty," she said.

I took a step back to open my shirt and unhook the front of my bra. I was just the right height to feed Sharon one of my swollen nipples.

My breath caught in my throat as she put her mouth on me. She took in as much of my breast as she could and greedily began sucking. I felt a jolt as her hand finally gave me the release I needed. She slid her fingers in and began to move inside me. I thought my knees would buckle, but her other hand moved around my waist and held me tightly.

My moist cunt made noises as I fucked her hand, hips moving along with my ragged breathing. I was surprised at how quickly I came, the orgasm rolling over me in wave after wave.

It took me a minute to recover, but I wanted to make love to her as much as I had needed her touch. "Your turn," I told her.

I took Sharon's jacket from around her waist and put it on the hood of the car. I turned back to her and kissed her long and hard while I unbuckled her belt.

"God, you feel good," she whispered.

"You too." With trembling hands I fumbled with her jeans. They did not come down as easily as mine, but I finally managed to get them over her ass. I picked her up and put her on the car. We locked eyes as she moved the jacket underneath her.

I kissed her again as I pushed her backward. I took one of the legs of her jeans and pulled it all the way off. To my delight, Sharon wasn't wearing any underwear. She lay back against the windshield, head cradled in her arm. "Come here," she said.

I put a knee between her legs and leaned over to kiss her. Taking her tongue in my mouth, I sucked gently as my hand wandered across her belly, then down to her thighs.

My mouth moved from her lips to her chin, then selfishly lingered on her throat. I wanted to explore every inch of her, to know this was real, not just another one of my fantasies.

I pushed her small breasts together and tongued a figure eight between them. Moaning, she put her hands on my head and aimlessly played with my hair. I blew on her wet nipples, then began kneading them between my thumbs and forefingers. As I continued the motion, I used my tongue to make a wet trail on her torso. Every so often I retraced the pattern and blew on her skin, raising goose bumps.

I licked her belly and followed a thin line of fuzz down to the tight patch of short, curly hair between her legs.

"Hurry, baby," she whispered.

Sharon arched up to find my mouth, and I obliged her. I inhaled deeply, taking in every bit of her. Her strong legs wrapped around my shoulders, and I was pulled into her salty, moist box. My tongue flickered over her clit, and occasionally darted inside as far as it could go. She tightened her grip on my hair and undulated against my face. I continued working on her little button and roughly put two fingers inside her.

Her belt buckle played an urgent rhythm on the hood of my car, and I knew it wouldn't be long before she came. Sharon was more vocal than I had been, although I couldn't make out much of what she was saying.

Finally her body began to shudder. She cried out so loudly as she came that I was sure the entire neighborhood had heard.

I took her in my arms and held her. "I guess we'll have to head to the bar soon."

"We might not get there," she replied.

Fireworks began to fill the night sky. Zozobra was going up in flames for another year, marking a new beginning.

An Anatomy Lesson for Mary Margaret

Margaret Granite

Mary Margaret hesitantly opened the creaky door to the bar. A string of bells around the door knob jingled, and she tried not to flinch with self-conscious surprise at inadvertently announcing her own entrance. Two weathered butches in leather looked up from their game of pool and openly cruised her. Mary Margaret blushed and cast her eyes down.

"Over here!" A familiar voice called from somewhere through the smoke. Finally, Mary Margaret spotted Rose at a table in a corner. Rose took a long drag off an Export A with one hand and ushered Mary Margaret toward her with the other. Mary Margaret, with her wave of shiny black hair, intense blue eyes, and 21-year-old innocence, captured the gaze of the leather dykes as she walked past the pool table.

When she saw Rose's face light up, just for her, Mary Margaret's heart stumbled all over itself. She went to sit down on garish purple cushions next to Rose but then balked at what looked like a fresh spill of Coke. "Ew," she said, crinkling up her nose.

"Oh," said Rose, laughing. "It's not exactly the cleanest place, is it?" She arranged some paper napkins over the offensive spot. "All better?"

Mary Margaret sat down, inwardly wincing but not wanting to make a fuss.

"Hello, Mary Margaret." Mary Margaret looked up, a little startled. She had been so tortured trying to decide how much of Rose's smile she could bear to take in that she hadn't noticed Lynn and Janet. They were Rose's coworkers, fellow nurses, and they were sitting a yard away.

"Hello," said Mary Margaret.

"How was your day?" said Rose, riveting Mary Margaret's attention by stroking her hair, which fell over her generous breasts, hidden beneath a bulky sweater.

"Good. I gave a paper on camp and drag in my Theorizing Identity class. I think the professor liked it."

"You're a prodigy, honey." Rose turned to Lynn and Janet. "Did you know Mary Margaret is the youngest person in her graduate program?" It was true, but Mary Margaret didn't like attention called to the fact.

"Drag, that's like drag queens, but how exactly do you define camp?" asked Janet.

"Well, that depends on what point you're at in the historical debate about camp. Susan Sontag defined it as—"

"Look!" said Lynn, tugging on Janet's sleeve. "Those two ladies are finally done with the pool table."

"Let's get over there!" exclaimed Janet. "The blonds at the bar are eyeing the table." Lynn and Janet hurried to rack up before all was lost.

Rose put a finger on Mary Margaret's chin. "Kiss me," she breathed, turning Mary Margaret's face toward her own.

Mary Margaret hesitated. She'd never kissed in public before.

"Kiss me," Rose insisted, leaning forward to claim Mary Margaret's lips. The tidal wave of the kiss washed the room away. Somebody's breath quickened. A caress melted into a thigh. A hot flush rose from Mary Margaret's chest up into the roots of her hair. She felt an impulse to wrap her arms around Rose's waist but quelled it by planting her hands into the sticky seat cushions instead.

Finally, Rose drew back and smiled. Her dark brown eyes, almost black, now sparkled mischievously. She was Mary Margaret's first girlfriend, her first love. Her hair was close-cropped and red, and she always wore earrings and traffic-stopping lipstick, which she reapplied frequently. She was svelte. She talked like Marilyn Monroe, yet her voice was husky from smoking nearly a pack of cigarettes a day. Her facial features presented an almost comical cross between Boy George and David Bowie. She was one of the sexiest women Mary Margaret would ever meet in her life.

"I need a drink," said Mary Margaret.

↕

After rapidly siphoning a sloe gin fizz, a concoction Rose had introduced her to, Mary Margaret felt more at ease in her surroundings.

Rose was the belle of every bar she frequented. She made everyone laugh with her hospital stories.

"Guess what he had up his butt? Just try to guess. I defy you."

"I dunno," said Janet, blasé. "A hamster?"

"No, that wouldn't be terribly original, would it?"

Mary Margaret blanched. Why would somebody have a hamster up his butt? She didn't get it.

"An Easter egg," Rose said, deadpan. "One of the real ones they put chocolate in, however they manage that. The chocolate had melted, and the shell broke!"

"Ee-e-e-aah!" exclaimed Lynn.

Mary Margaret was appalled. She could imagine an Easter egg. She could imagine an Easter egg with chocolate inside. She could imagine an Easter egg with chocolate inside, broken into parts. But...a wedge of apprehension inserted itself between these images and the human anatomy.

"Doesn't surprise me," said Janet.

"The great thing is, there really isn't any excuse," continued Rose, gesturing with her cigarette. "I mean, one guy came in with a shampoo bottle up his butt once, and even though the fags in E.R. knew full well he didn't slip in the shower, at least he could have claimed that he did with some sort of plausibility!"

Rose went on to talk about how she'd determined her cat was gay, because he enjoyed getting his temperature taken rectally.

"I changed his name from Buddy to Fabulous Buddy," she told the now-small crowd of an audience, an assortment of hospital staff come to pay court to her during happy hour. She proceeded to impersonate her cat receiving this particular form of pleasure by wiggling her ass deeper into the seat cushions and caterwauling. Almost everyone burst out laughing, except Mary Margaret, who was pleased that Rose was so popular but uncomfortable about the subject of her performance.

"I have to go to the rest room," she said, close to Rose's ear.

"OK, doll." Rose stroked her lover's arm.

The touch lingered all the way to the bathroom stall, where Mary Margaret carefully arranged sheets of toilet paper over the seat. The lock on the stall door was broken, and she leaned forward, awkwardly trying to keep it shut while she went to the bathroom. She tried to relax. Sometimes she got stage fright. If she could just go before someone interrupted. A few drops came out. What if one of those butches walked in? The stream abruptly stopped before it could begin.

"Yoo-hoo!" Rose burst in and stooped down to address Mary Margaret's feet. "Darling, I freshened your drink!"

"Almost done!" Mary Margaret decided to forgo the effort and zipped up the pleated black skirt she'd worn especially for Rose, who'd said she liked it on her.

"Here, take a sip," said Rose, plying her with the drink. Mary Margaret obeyed, then Rose whisked the drink away and set it precariously on a sink top. She removed the cherry from the glass and backed Mary Margaret up against the sink.

"Eat this for me, will you?" Rose more or less commanded.

Before Mary Margaret could swallow, Rose's tongue was in her mouth, mixing and swapping maraschino cherry bits around.

"Wait!" said Mary Margaret. She swallowed. "There." She pulled Rose forward by the belt buckle and kissed her passionately. Rose groaned. Mary Margaret felt a surge of excitement and power at turning the tables on Rose, if only for a moment, and getting her to respond so intensely. She felt Rose's thighs press against her own—Rose's hands impatiently working their way under her sweater to her bare skin…caresses on either side of her spine…fingers journeying up the vertebrae…her bra unfastening.

"Not…here…" panted Mary Margaret into their kiss.

Rose slid her hands around to Mary Margaret's breasts and gently pushed them together. "You have such beautiful breasts…I'm one of the few people in the world who really knows." Rose pressed the lushness against her face and urgently dragged one cheek, her nose, the other cheek, against Mary Margaret's breasts through a now-maddening barrier of wool sweater. Mary Margaret caught her breath, closed her eyes. Rose imprinted Mary Margaret's neck with a kiss, then another and another until Mary Margaret couldn't refrain from grabbing her lover's sweet ass. So tantalizing, it came to view in Mary

Margaret's mind as she'd seen it the week before, in the hospital elevator, where she'd been flooded with stymied desire while rediscovering its full curves in khaki pants. The doors opened onto the hospital cafeteria; Mary Margaret gripped harder.

Rose put a hand on Mary Margaret's thigh, then slid it up to the crotch of her tights. "Oh, honey," she murmured.

Mary Margaret suddenly remembered where they were. "We...we can't...I want...to be in bed with you," she managed.

"You're very wet," Rose breathed. "I can tell."

"Oh, Rose, not here!"

"I've always wanted to do it in this bathroom."

"Rose!" Mary Margaret grabbed Rose by the wrists to keep her hands out of trouble. Rose rolled her eyes and smiled. She handed Mary Margaret her second sloe gin fizz. "Drink up, sweetheart."

One of the leather dykes walked in when there wasn't much to walk in on anymore. She smiled warmly at the two girls. "Ah, to be young and in love," she said before disappearing into a stall. Mary Margaret felt flustered and looked down at Rose's stylish half-boots. Rose squeezed her hand and led her out of the bar.

↕

It was a surprisingly warm night in San Francisco, almost balmy. They sailed down 18th Street, past rows of Victorians, on Rose's scooter. They rode without helmets. With her hands clasped around Rose's waist, Mary Margaret got whiffs of hair gel and Aussie shampoo mingled with the cheap men's cologne Rose liked to wear, Eau Sauvage. It was a divine smell. Utterly divine. Mary Margaret wished she could loosen up and meet Rose's spirit, but she was too painfully and awkwardly in love.

an anatomy lesson for mary margaret

How she would have liked to tease Rose the way Rose sometimes teased her. Oh, Nurse Rose, take my pulse! Nurse Rose, my forehead is burning up. Feel! Nurse Rose, I cra-a-ave your attention. It was hopeless...you couldn't rehearse in your head how to tease someone, how to flirt with them. You just did it, spontaneously, as Rose seemed to do everything.

↕

Back at Rose's apartment, with the tap water running, Mary Margaret managed to empty her bladder. She breathed a sigh of relief and gazed up past the bunched-up tights around her ankles to take in the sights of the bathroom with pleasure. On the sink top, Rose kept a ceramic dish filled with soap in the shape of little scallops. Next to the soap dish was a glass jar filled with brightly colored bath beads, and a basket overflowing with toiletries. Mary Margaret was fond of the tile, robin's-egg blue. There was a large old-fashioned tub with claw feet, where she had taken baths with Rose, who sometimes shaved her legs for her. "Trust me," said Rose, the first time. "I won't cut you."

"Sister Mary Margaret! Come to bed!"

Rose had taken off her clothes and lay propped up on one elbow. Mary Margaret stopped when she came in the room, uncertain whether to take off her clothes first or just get into bed. The graceful curve of Rose's hip fixed her gaze.

"Undress," said Rose. Mary Margaret unzipped her skirt, folded it, and placed it on the seat of a chair. She likewise removed her tights and sweater and folded them. She tried to concentrate on folding. She made a neat pile of clothes on the chair.

"Look at me," said Rose. Her eyes were shining with desire.

21

Mary Margaret unhooked her bra and slowly took it off. Rose took a sharp intake of breath as Mary Margaret's breasts came into view.

"Come here," said Rose, who with one swift movement sat up on the edge of the bed and held out her arms. Mary Margaret walked into them, and Rose, making a sound somewhere between a sigh of satisfaction and a groan of impatience, kissed her hungrily on the inside of her left breast. Mary Margaret could remember this. Rose slid her fingers beneath the elastic of Mary Margaret's cotton underwear. For a moment, everything became a teasing touch at some magical juncture between spine and ass.

Mary Margaret's breath came quickly as Rose cupped her lover's breasts together and circled her tongue around and around the pink nipples, surprisingly small and delicate, like an adolescent's. Through half-closed eyes, Mary Margaret watched her lover kiss and suck the treasure kept hidden beneath bulky sweaters. Their swell, their heft, their soft generosity all seemed meant for this. The hunger welled up hot into her pussy, surged into her fingertips.

Rose pulled Mary Margaret onto the bed and shifted to her preferred place on top. Now, finally, for Mary Margaret, Rose's weight, the length of the woman was fully upon her. She entwined a leg around Rose's and gripped Rose's ass, each finger claiming its own indentation. Rose gently sunk her teeth into Mary Margaret's shoulder, gripped her ass tight in return, and began to bump and grind. The first time Rose introduced her to this motion, Mary Margaret had been a little taken aback. But now she met Rose's thrusts with her own, angling for the tantalizing brush of pelvic bone against clit, a special challenge through underwear. A neighbor might have heard the sound of dueling girlish moans and sighs through the bedroom wall, mounting in volume and intensity, but neither Rose nor Mary Margaret cared.

Yes, Rose liked to be on top, but Mary Margaret felt impatient to kiss from that vantage. She shifted her weight out from underneath Rose, and they wrestled a little for dominance. Mary Margaret gained victory and straddled her lover, pinned her wrists to the bed. Rose looked up at her with longing. "I want you," she breathed. "I can't stand it."

Mary Margaret slowly leaned down, pressing her nipples against Rose's. "Unmmnh!" someone exclaimed. Mary Margaret kissed Rose lightly, then drew back as Rose tried to kiss her back. She kissed Rose again, flicking her tongue briefly into the corner of Rose's lips. She drew away. She kissed Rose lightly again, then caught her lower lip and sucked, let go. Rose groaned, plunged her hands in Mary Margaret's hair, and drew her down for a long, fierce kiss that left both breathing like sprinters. As they kissed more gently, Rose worked her hand between their bodies and into Mary Margaret's panties.

"Mmm, what are these doing on?" Rose murmured.

Before Mary Margaret could decide whether to reply, Rose had melted her fingers into the luscious folds of Mary Margaret's pussy, which greedily took in the attention. Mary Margaret cried out. Rose lightly stroked Mary Margaret's clit with one hand while making caressing circles on her ass with the other. "Say yes," Rose urged. "Tell me yes." Mary Margaret kissed Rose's cheek, her neck, breathed *yes* into her ear.

At first with just a dip, Rose entered Mary Margaret. Then came a very shallow rapid fucking, until Mary Margaret couldn't refrain from thrusting forward to try to take in more of Rose's finger. Rose withheld it, and her lover, straining in frustration, felt a finger travel gingerly down the crack of her ass and then stop at the entrance no one's finger had ever come near. Rose continued to teasingly fuck her lover to distraction with one hand, then experimentally worked her middle finger into Mary Margaret's anus.

Mary Margaret drew away. "No, not that!" she exclaimed.

"What?" Rose asked with mock innocence.

"You know," insisted Mary Margaret. Really, it was unthinkable.

"OK, honey," said Rose gently, flipping Mary Margaret onto her back, taking her face between her hands, and softly kissing her. She kissed her way down between Mary Margaret's breasts, briefly delved her tongue into Mary Margaret's belly button, then impatiently pulled off the panties and threw them into a corner. Rose traveled along the inside of Mary Margaret's thighs, grazing them with her lips. She burrowed her fingers into Mary Margaret's pubic hair and traced around its perimeter with precise brush strokes of the tongue.

Mary Margaret relaxed and sighed, whimpered as Rose's tongue finally made its way into the secrets of her cunt, then began teasing her clit, flicking it back and forth. The heat fanned out in waves from Rose's tongue, coursing through Mary Margaret's veins. Rose gripped her lover's hips and felt them thrust forward, ever so slightly now. Mary Margaret's moans, like caresses on a much-neglected expanse of flesh, made Rose even wetter. As Rose started slowly fucking Mary Margaret with a finger, she humped the bed a little, never ceasing the movements of her avid tongue.

Mary Margaret felt she was melting into a molten pool of pleasure. Her pelvis shuddered once, strained. Rose started finger-fucking her swiftly now. Mary Margaret moaned over and over. As wave upon wave of hot pleasure crested near the high-water mark of complete ecstasy, Rose worked another finger into Mary Margaret's asshole and began to move it in and out slowly. Mary Margaret bucked with orgasm, plunging Rose's finger deeper into her ass with the motion. But oh, how she wanted her ass worked now. How good it was! Her cunt and ass filled and overflowed with an overwhelming satisfaction that blotted out everything but itself.

Rose knew well enough to remove the otherwise marauding finger just as Mary Margaret began sliding down the slope of her climax into quiescence. When Mary Margaret lay on her back, still and panting, Rose kissed her stomach, then caressed it. Mary Margaret's hairline was wet with sweat. She sighed, opened her eyes, and turned on her side to smile at Rose. She felt an urge to put the giddy euphoria into words.

She couldn't. The feeling turned back on itself and lodged in her chest. Trapped there, it made her want Rose badly, so much that she could cry.

"How was that?" asked Rose.

"That was…not what I'd expected," said Mary Margaret.

Rose threw her head back and laughed, an intoxication. "The best things are never what we'd expect," she said. Mary Margaret pulled Rose to her. Her mouth descended on Rose's breasts, which in contrast to hers were small, like a Grecian statue's. Rose surprised her by evading her grasp and jumping out of bed. "Always wash your hands!" she exclaimed.

"Oh," said Mary Margaret, embarrassed.

Mary Margaret waited impatiently as the water in the bathroom ran. She thought about what she might say—teasing, clever things—if only she were the playful somebody else she kept locked up inside herself.

↕

The next evening Rose came home from work to find the bed she had reluctantly left at dawn—then disordered, harboring a sleeping lover—now carefully made. This came as no surprise, but the note she discovered on top of the pillows did. "Nurse Rose," she read, "thank you for the lovely anatomy lesson. Love, Mary Margaret." As she laughed and laughed with delight and dialed the phone, Rose had no idea how many crumpled-up, scratched-out, ripped-apart drafts had been removed from the site of composition, nor did she know how eagerly, and with what suspense, the author awaited a response.

A Show for a Showgirl

Carol Queen

*I*n the early '50s I roomed with a lovely blond starlet who had just gotten her first break. They'd changed her name and her hair color, but she didn't care when I slipped up and called her Norma Jean. When you got hooked up with a studio in those days, sometimes all you had left when they got done with you was your own tits. (Of course, these days you can't even count on that.) Marilyn had nice tits. They were actually the first thing I noticed about her when I met her at a party at Lillian Hellman's house, but then she was wearing a real summery dress—it was hard not to notice them.

Lillian sure knew a lot of dykes. This Norma Jean gal was surrounded by nice-looking women, and she was laughing and talking with them, but it turned out she needed a roommate, and I was looking for a place, so I was the one who went home with her number. I don't mind telling you that we sometimes shared more than the rent, though it was never anything really serious.

Our biggest adventure started the day she came running home from the studio all excited, saying, "Lili St. Cyr is coming to town! She's doing her show at that big burlesque place! We've got to go see her!"

Marilyn kept up with all the shows in town. It was more than keeping up with opportunities for work—she was already signed. It was as likely to be Shakespeare as burlesque. Sure, we'd both done our share of things to pay the rent. Marilyn even made a movie—I mean a nudie one—and I'm sure I'd have done the same thing if I was broke and an opportunity came along. But going for the burlesque circuit—that was a real commitment. Usually if a girl did that, people whispered behind her back that she'd failed—because everyone knew you could never get respectable work again. But no one said anything like that about Lili St. Cyr. She was the tops, a class act.

Marilyn went to work at the studio the next morning looking especially swell. She put on lots of extra makeup and a very tight sweater. She came home grinning and waving tickets to the show.

"How did you get those?" I asked, laughing, because I was pretty sure I knew the answer.

"Got 'em from Darryl," she said. "Only took a minute," and she made an O with her mouth and wiggled her tongue around. Giggling, I slapped her butt.

A week later, dressed to the nines, we presented the tickets to the doorman at the big fancy burlesque house that hosted the best shows. We'd been there before, double-dating with a couple of nice young actors who roomed together down the street. They never laid a hand on us, though I thought the show was plenty sexy. Marilyn and I ran off to the powder room together when we saw we weren't going to get any action from the boys. We didn't come back to the table for quite a while, though they never said anything about missing us!

"Welcome, ladies," said the doorman, with a little leer. I

guess it wasn't too common for women to come to shows without men. But Marilyn had some big plans for the evening, and fellows would just get in the way. She wanted to get backstage to meet Lili St. Cyr. I'd heard there were burlesque clubs in Paris where only women went. I whispered this to Marilyn as we found a table. "Maybe you'll get work on a movie in Paris someday," I said to her wistfully, "and I can come visit you, and we can go to one. Then the guys won't be around to bother us."

She squeezed my hand, but I knew what she was thinking: She didn't much mind being bothered by fellows. She could almost always turn it around to her own advantage. I had seen her coo at those big producer types and wrap them around her finger. I had a feeling she was going to go far. I was so excited for her that it almost didn't matter that someday she'd be moving on and would never look back at me. A burst of applause cut off my train of thought. The show was starting, though it would be a while till Lili St. Cyr came on; she was the headliner, and there were always several acts that preceded the big show. The idea was to warm up the audience, but Marilyn didn't need to get any warmer. She was on the edge of her seat, waiting eagerly for Lili to come out from between the spangled red-velvet curtains. "I've just gotta meet her!" she was saying, barely audible beneath the applause. "I have a feeling she's gonna be very important to me!" Marilyn was like that in those days—very self-centered as far as her career went. She was sweet and loving too, but she wanted to be a big star more than anything. She hadn't gotten any really good parts yet, but I knew she would. I just wasn't sure how she thought the Queen of Burlesque could help her. One after another the girls appeared onstage. They were beautiful—blonds and redheads and brunettes—and their costumes were sparkling and opulent, if a bit skimpy! One pretty redhead did a fan dance; the

MC said the fan dance had been a staple of burlesque acts "for thousands of years!" I thought that was pretty funny because I knew burlesque dancing wasn't nearly that old.

During the intermission Marilyn got up and ran to find the cigarette girl. In lots of places the cigarette girl only sells smokes, but here she had some chocolates too—and roses. Sometimes men liked to bring their dates there to warm them up; I guess the candy and flowers were supposed to help. Marilyn had a rose when she came back to our seat, but I was pretty sure she hadn't bought it for me. "For Lili?" I asked, and she nodded, digging vigorously in her handbag for a pen and paper. I watched while she wrote, "Destiny means for me to meet you. Please invite me and my friend backstage." She wrote it in her prettiest hand. I was pleased she actually intended to invite me along—sometimes stringing along with Marilyn meant taking a taxi home. Looking back, I think destiny meant for Marilyn to meet a lot of people—some I wish I could have stood in the way of. I wonder if she knew how many important people would fall under her spell.

The lights flashed to signal the end of intermission. The band came up, and spotlights played back and forth on the deep-red curtains. Suddenly a beautiful blond head peeked out. Marilyn jumped up, screaming, and the rest of the crowd was going wild too. Lili St. Cyr revealed just about half of herself, sliding one shapely leg provocatively out from between the curtains while holding the drapery modestly to cover her body. Then she slipped back inside, the band settling into a slow swing number to accompany her show. The curtains swung open, but the stage was dark. As the lights came up, very gradually, we could see Lili herself—enclosed in an old-fashioned bathtub. You could only see her head and nude shoulders above its sides. Bubbles were piled high around her, and as the music got louder she began to play with them, mounding them up like big tits, grabbing handfuls and tossing them high in the air. The spotlights lit her up so the soapsuds sparkled. Her tub was backlit, and as the music reached a crescendo, everyone gasped. The backlights had been getting steadily brighter, and suddenly we all realized that Lili's tub was made of transparent glass. We could see her body clearly now through its walls, but because of the backlighting, we could only see its silhouette. Still, the crowd went wild as she raised her legs high and very slowly washed herself all over. When her "bath" was done, she turned away from the audience and rose out of the water. A pretty attendant ran out with a huge white Turkish towel and draped Lili, obliterating the audience's brief, tantalizing view of her shapely ass. Lili toweled dry and finally stepped out of the tub and faced the audience, her fresh-faced Nordic beauty wrapped up completely in the big white towel. Marilyn was out of her seat like a shot, down the aisle and at Lili St. Cyr's feet, holding out the rose. Lili gave a gracious bow, then took it—and its attached note. I thought I saw her smile warmly at Marilyn before she turned and sashayed offstage.

Back at our table Marilyn ordered another drink. "Now let's just wait a little while," she said, tossing back what was left of her Manhattan. But she hadn't even had time to order another before the pretty woman who'd brought out Lili's towel appeared at our table. "Hello," she said. "I'm Jeannette, Miss St. Cyr's personal assistant. Would you please follow me? She'd like to meet you backstage." My sidecar was only half finished, but I left the glass and trailed behind Marilyn and Jeannette, who was a living doll. Marilyn had turned on the charm, and at one point she even took Jeannette's arm for a second. Jeannette was a very feminine girl, but Marilyn's attentions didn't seem at all wasted on her. *Hoo boy,* I thought, *we're off on one of Marilyn's joy rides.*

Lili St. Cyr had a very luxe dressing room, and it glittered with her spangled costumes. That bathtub number was her first act; she'd go on again in an hour with a completely different show. I saw a silver tray with a bottle of nice champagne and four glasses, laid out on a low table flanked by a couple of sofas. Lili's makeup mirror was big and better lit than anything at Marilyn's studio. Lili herself was wearing an ivory silk peignoir with simple gold leather mules on her pedicured feet. Her toenails, painted a rich, deep red, peeked out of the open-toed shoes. Marilyn and I both had on red nail polish—all the girls wore it—but somehow on Lili it looked different, sexy and extra posh. Of course, she was older than we were, by maybe 10 years, and that gave her an especially sophisticated air.

Lili extended her hand when we entered the dressing room, and Marilyn ran right up to her and clasped it—she didn't let it go right away either. "Miss St. Cyr, it is such a great big honor to meet you!" Marilyn said, and Lili smiled right into her eyes. We introduced ourselves, and Lili turned that dazzling smile on me for a too-brief moment, and I thought that no matter what Marilyn was up to, I'd always love her for getting me this close to such a gorgeous lady. I'd had brushes with plenty of big stars at the studio, but few of them had what Lili St. Cyr had—so strong and self-possessed and womanly. She was just plain classy. And even in the silky robe, her figure made my head spin.

"Jeannette, darling, pour us some champagne, will you?" Lili indicated the sofas and the bottle, snug in an ice bucket.

I perched on one sofa and accepted a glass from Jeannette, whose fingers lingered a second longer on mine than was necessary, while Lili patted the sofa next to her and invited Marilyn to sit down. Marilyn wasted no time getting as close as possible to the beautiful blond dancer. She clinked glasses with Lili, her eyes bright. I wondered what kind of excitement she was feeling. Was it the thrill of the chase? Being that close to someone so famous and, in her way, powerful? Or was it just that she found Lili St. Cyr as irresistible as I did?

"So, my lovely girls, what brings you to see my show?" asked Lili, but she didn't wait for us to answer before going on to her real question. "And are you two beauties...together?"

I decided to let Marilyn answer that one. I was never sure whether to think of us as "together" or not.

"Well, in a way we are," said Marilyn diplomatically, "and in a way we're not, I guess, since we are very close, yet we don't, um, we don't—"

"Tie each other down," I finished for her. I doubted anyone could ever tie Marilyn down, except in the literal sense.

"How very modern," purred Lili. "I prefer to conduct my life in exactly that way." Her hand strayed to Marilyn's knee and stayed there. I noticed Marilyn—oh, that tart!—inching up her skirt little by imperceptible little. Jeannette noticed it too.

"Miss St. Cyr, I don't suppose you'd mind if I locked the door?" Jeannette suggested. "I suppose you'd like a bit of privacy?"

"Yes, darling Jeannette, please do see to that," said Lili, and then stroked very deliberately up Marilyn's inner thighs, high enough to reach white skin where her stockings ended. She looked deeply into Marilyn's eyes, gauging her effect. Marilyn was flushed.

"Miss St. Cyr, I've always wanted to meet you," she said breathlessly. "I've always known you were going to be important in my life somehow."

"Oh, I certainly intend to be important, my darling. Take your panties off for me, why don't you?" No bigwig at the studio could ever be half that suave. Marilyn didn't take her eyes off Lili while she stood up slowly and peeled her sheer panties off. "Marilyn, that's very lovely. Darling, I'm constantly putting on shows for other people, but so very few are ever thoughtful enough to put on a show for me."

Marilyn blushed even pinker—I often wondered if she could do that on cue, because she really wasn't an especially blushable person—and, her eyes gazing down demurely, said, "Well then, Miss St. Cyr, perhaps you wouldn't mind if I... didn't stop, you know, with my panties?" I figured if I didn't get in on this soon, I was going to be left on the sidelines, so I added, "Miss St. Cyr, we can put on any kind of show you want." Lili rewarded me with a dazzling smile. There was something a little bit predatory in it, like when Marilyn and I would do this act for the fellows Marilyn wanted to impress, but there was also a sweetness in it I had never seen in a man's eyes. *No wonder,* I thought. Lili St. Cyr was a wealthy, powerful woman because she was so successful at what she did. But what she said was true—she'd had to put on a lot of shows to get where she was. "Darlings, please call me Lili. I can see we're going to be quite friendly. Jeannette, sweetheart, top off my champagne. Yes, Marilyn, I think you should take off just as much as makes you comfortable. And give me any sort of show you'd like. Dear Jeannette may watch too, might she not?"

"Please!" Marilyn and I said it practically in unison. Jeannette was quite a doll. Marilyn's satin dress had buttons all the way up the back. If getting out of it were to be part of the show, I'd have to help—after all, I had buttoned her into it. I moved behind her and undid each sapphire-blue, satin-covered button, one by one. Marilyn edged us around so that Lili and Jeannette, who was perched on the arm of the sofa next to Lili, could see. When I'd gotten down to the very bottom button, Marilyn gave a sexy shrug of her shoulders and the dress slipped down, revealing her satiny brassiere. It was the new kind with concentric circles sewn around the nipples, and it made her breasts stand out like nobody's business. Marilyn stepped out of her dress, revealing a matching black satin garter belt holding up her silk hose. She always wore beautiful underclothes; she said you could never predict who you suddenly might want to impress. Now I certainly saw her point. Marilyn turned and helped me out of my red velvet gown. It was off the shoulders, so as soon as she'd undone the side hooks—while I held my arms up prettily so she could get at them—the gown slipped off. I had on a strapless bustier with garters attached, but it was elasticized, and Marilyn just pulled it right down off my breasts. She knelt in front of me and began to suck my nipples; she positioned herself so Lili had a perfect view of her heart-shaped ass. I ran my hands through her blond hair, thick as gold silk.

We'd hardly gotten started, but Lili obviously liked the show very much. She spread her amazingly long legs and the robe fell open, revealing her sex, and she purred, "That's so lovely, my darling girls, but come here to me now." Jeannette reached for her breasts—now her robe was fully open, Lili revealing to us the sights she'd so cleverly hidden from the audience. Her ivory skin glowed, and Jeannette's ministrations made her lovely nipples stand out from the perfect swell of her breasts. I didn't need to be asked twice. I fell to my knees before Lili St. Cyr's sex, and after only a second of gazing at the sight that everyone still in their seats outside had paid good money to catch a glimpse of, lowered my mouth to her and began to pleasure her as well as I knew how. She rewarded me at once with a voluptuous moan. When I did that to Marilyn, at home or when we were on a campaign to "impress" somebody, she always wiggled and mewed, interspersing the kittenish sounds with breathy little laughs. But Lili had her legs apart like it was her birthright as a woman to always have somebody down there between them. I'd done it to plenty of girls, I guess—even a couple of the handsome women who came to Lillian's parties—but nobody had ever made me feel like I belonged where I was the way Lili St. Cyr did. In the meantime Lili was urging Marilyn to dance for her. Jeannette hopped off the arm of the sofa and put the radio on—to a station with some nice swing music. Marilyn, never one to pass up an opportunity to get someone's attention, started to sway and step to the music. "Lovely, darlings, lovely," murmured Lili, then, "Marilyn, I know that pretty brassiere conceals even prettier breasts. Please show them to me."

Marilyn's arms curved back behind her, reaching for the clasp. When she had it, Lili said, "Now, darling, don't take it right off. Tease me a little bit. You know how to do it." And indeed, Marilyn did—her burlesque style was great! I licked Lili more and more feverishly while Marilyn performed a bump and grind that would have passed muster on Lili's own stage. But she didn't stop there. She danced right up to the sofa, kicked her pumps off, and stepped up onto the cushions, planting one foot on each side of Lili. From there she could lower her pussy right to Lili's lips. I ran my hand up her stockinged leg, so silky smooth. And Lili began to do to Marilyn what I was doing to her. From behind the sofa, Jeannette leaned over to kiss Marilyn and fondle her breasts. I couldn't believe Marilyn had been so bold! But I didn't have much room to think, what with Lili's firm, creamy thighs wrapped around my neck. I felt their long, cool weight on my back as she arched up into me, and through her body—I can't explain this very well—I felt her focus almost all her energy into Marilyn's pleasure. It was almost like I was making love to both of them at the same time, especially since I knew how it felt to have Marilyn's little bud swell between my lips. Soon Marilyn made the little mews and giggles that I knew meant she was close to climax. I could glance up and see her bottom—her gorgeous, full bottom—hovering right above me, and her cleft too, with Lili's tongue twisting like a snake being charmed. In my mouth Lili's sex was wetly succulent. I was in heaven, and I don't mind telling you I still think about that moment. Marilyn's voice got higher, till suddenly she gave out a little squeal and then her pretty mewing, the kind that signaled orgasm was upon her. With that, Lili's climax started, quaking through her body so that I had to hold on to her thighs to keep from being pushed away from the mark I had so faithfully kept to. My tongue kept working side to side on the sensitive button of flesh that held the key to her pleasure, and the sounds she made were deep yet strangely musical, maybe like the kind of chanting you'd hear in a ritual in another country.

I'm not sure how it happened that Jeannette and Marilyn wound up lying atop each other on the other sofa, because it was a few minutes before I raised my head from Lili's lap—she was stroking my hair, and she smelled so rich and salty and good, and I never wanted to leave her. But I finally took my head from the pillow of her thigh to look up at her and smile a little shyly while she smiled back and tousled my hair. The other two were going at it like cats in heat. Jeannette's nails were manicured very short—I'd noted this approvingly when she handed me my champagne—and she sure knew how to use those hands. Lili drew me up to sit beside her on the sofa, put her arm lightly across my shoulders so she could graze her fingertips across my breast, and we watched them. "This really is the loveliest show I've ever had," said Lili, reaching for her glass, which the very attentive Jeannette had left full before she started in with Marilyn.

Of course we couldn't stay very long in the secret pleasure

palace Lili's dressing room had become; she had to be back onstage in 15 minutes. But Jeannette worked fast—she was a treasure in every way!—and Lili made her next show, her own version of the Dance of the Seven Veils, right on time. Her makeup had been expertly reapplied, though her nose was still full of Marilyn's scent, and we watched her drive the crowd mad from our perch in the wings, where we sat quietly with our arms around Jeannette. During the finale, Lili, wearing an enigmatic little smile, looked right at the three of us.

That was years and years ago now, and it's hard to keep track of—much less think about—all the things that have happened in the meantime. But Marilyn was right about Lili; they saw a lot more of each other after that. Marilyn never got over feeling awestruck by Lili, and their relationship mixed up elements of mentor and protégée, lover and fan—but under her tutelage, Marilyn began to move and speak differently, and she even changed the way she chose her clothing and applied her makeup. People we knew noticed and said Marilyn had picked up a touch of class. I think it helped her when she read for parts. Sure enough, Marilyn's star rose quickly. I guess you know a lot of the rest of the story. Marilyn and I never got to Paris—well, not together. Just as I'd known, we grew apart. Before long it was one husband after the next. Me, I spent more time with a couple of the women writers I'd met at those parties at Lillian's. But Marilyn wasn't the only one who took something away from Lili St. Cyr. Just like Lili, I still love a good show.

Possibilities
Wendy Caster

Cleo took a left onto 11th Street. She could have turned right. She could have continued walking north. But she took a left. The sidewalk was jammed. A group of pierced and tattooed teenagers dressed in leather and studs pushed past two suburban couples gawking at a shop-window bondage display. As Cleo jaywalked to the food co-op, she heard one of the suburban women say, "Should we go in? We can't go in!" and giggle.

Cleo perused the food co-op bulletin board. She never actually went into the co-op—she believed that if God wanted us to eat green things, he would have made green chocolate—but she always read the notices and announcements outside. Cleo sympathized with Natalie, "single nonsmoking female college student," in search of "studio apartment, $500 a month." To achieve that goal, Natalie had two options: move a thousand miles away or go back in time 25 years.

A sign offering singing lessons caught Cleo's eye. Someday she would have the money, the time, and the nerve to take singing lessons.

An extremely cute long-haired woman came out of the co-op, lit a cigarette, and stood next to Cleo. Cleo resisted the urge to bum a smoke—after six months, she still wanted one—and got involved in reading an 11x14 handwritten tirade against "the fascist management of the food co-op."

The woman with the cigarette said, "What that jerk doesn't realize is the food co-op doesn't have a management. We have committees and boards. Fascism means saying 'yes' and something happens. The food co-op means saying 'maybe' and in six months changing the decision to 'possibly.' "

Cleo laughed. "That's why I freelance," she said.

"Lucky you. Freelance what?"

"Human resources consultant. I go in, I give a seminar, they pay me, I leave."

The woman with the cigarette examined Cleo from head to toe, taking in her high-top red Keds, faded jeans, black tank top, and close-cropped hair. Cleo explained, "I look very different in my corporate drag and makeup."

"I'd like to see that."

Was she flirting? Was she gay? It wasn't clear. Cleo remembered her "date" last year with Marion from her karate class, when she discovered—after six lovely hours of conversation and laughter—that Marion was happily, even enthusiastically, heterosexual.

The woman rubbed out her cigarette against a section of the wall speckled with ash prints. She threw the butt in a trash can, rubbed her right hand against her black slacks, then stuck it out toward Cleo. "Roxanne," she said. Cleo took her hand. It was warm, with a friendly grip.

"Cleo."

"Two more hours of work and then a hot date with my laundry. Some Saturday night, huh?"

possibilities

"Hey, clean laundry can be a beautiful thing." Cleo was embarrassed by her dumb response.

"I guess." Roxanne smiled, shrugged, and went back into the food co-op.

Tuesday morning, on the bus to Powerhouse Inc., Cleo tried to read a cutting-edge article about problem employees, but her mind kept drifting to Roxanne. Was there any possibility?

Maybe Roxanne was gay but not out yet. Yes, that could be it. Maybe Cleo could be Roxanne's first lover. That was a possibility! Maybe, Cleo thought, maybe…

I sit in my ancient faded red armchair, Roxanne on the newish faux-leather Ikea couch. Roxanne says, "I've never been involved with a woman, but I've always wondered—"

I say, my voice calmer than my heart, "Can I brush your hair?" Roxanne's hair is French-braided, thick and dark down her back.

Roxanne says yes and smiles a nervous smile. I move to the couch. Roxanne pulls a brush out of her backpack and starts undoing her hair. "No," I say. "Let me."

My hands tremble as I gently unravel the intricate braid. I can hear Roxanne breathing.

I comb Roxanne's hair with my fingers, long strokes that I feel through my own body. I brush the back of Roxanne's neck and Roxanne quivers. "Yes," I think to myself. "Yes."

I hold Roxanne's hair to one side and kiss her neck. Roxanne moans. I nibble on Roxanne's shoulder and stroke her breastbone and breasts in circles that go almost to her nipples but do not touch them. She arches her back and leans against me.

It was Cleo's bus stop. Time to be a neutered professional grown-up. Damn.

41

On Saturday, Cleo decided it wouldn't kill her to buy some broccoli.

The food co-op was dark and cool and smelled of nectarines and peaches. Cleo spotted Roxanne at the first cash register. She really was cute.

Cleo roamed the small, crowded aisles. She pondered why the world needed five different brands of veggie burgers—or one brand, really. She grabbed some broccoli, a can of soup, and a box of raisin bran, then got in Roxanne's line. Roxanne was very fast but friendly to the customers. Occasionally one of the other cashiers interrupted to have her sign something. Cleo hoped Roxanne would remember her.

"Hey, Cleo," Roxanne said, "how ya doin'?"

Cleo put her three items on the counter. "Fine," she said. "How are you?"

A muscular teenage cashier bristling with energy thrust a piece of paper in front on Roxanne. "You said it was OK on Tuesday," he said. Roxanne answered, "Don't worry. I remember," and signed the piece of paper.

"Do you live around here?" Roxanne asked. She looked Cleo right in the eyes; her voice was creamy and deep. She was flirting. Wasn't she?

"About a mile away," Cleo said.

A woman with dozens of tiny braids came over to Roxanne. "This guy's check-cashing card is out of date and he's pissed."

Roxanne said to Cleo, "Excuse me for a second."

Cleo watched Roxanne deal with the angry customer. Roxanne smiled and listened, then spoke quickly and quietly. The customer shrugged and pulled out cash. Roxanne thanked him and went back to Cleo.

"Sorry 'bout that," she said. "It gets hectic here."

Roxanne checked out Cleo's three items and Cleo paid.

possibilities

Cleo knew she needed to say goodbye and leave, but she didn't want to. What should she say next? Something, she had to say something. Preferably clever. She pointed to chocolate bars stacked next to the register. "They seem so un-food-co-op-y," she said, feeling foolish as soon as the words left her mouth.

"They're organic, made from happy cocoa beans, with no refined sugar." Roxanne grinned. "But they're still rich as hell and very fattening." Roxanne tossed a few into Cleo's bag. Cleo went to pay, but Roxanne waved her money away. "A little thank-you for being patient while I dealt with that guy." Roxanne's voice was deeper than ever. She was definitely flirting. Wasn't she?

The muscular teenager was back, asking Roxanne to OK a check, so Cleo said goodbye and left.

Roxanne had been flirting. Cleo was sure of it. Well, pretty sure.

But was she one of those women who just flirted with everyone? Or was she actually interested in Cleo? Cleo liked how Roxanne had dealt with the angry customer. Roxanne had a presence that people respected. She'd make a good butch, Cleo thought. Yes, that was a possibility. Maybe...

I say goodbye to Roxanne, glad that we had a lovely evening full of talk and laughter, but sad that neither one of us made a move. I close my door, lock it, and get ready for bed. In a few minutes, I'm in my sleeping gear—underpants and a tight red tank top. There's a knock at the door. I look through the peephole. It's Roxanne. I think of running to get a bathrobe, but I don't. I open the door. She looks me up and down, grins, and says, "Oh, my." In one quick, smooth movement, she steps in, closes the door, pushes me against the wall, and kisses me deep and hard.

"I wanted to do this all night," she says, and kisses me again,

running her hands hard over my breasts. I melt under her insistence. If I wasn't up against the wall, I would fall down.

Still kissing me, she runs circles around my nipples with her fingers. They jump up to her touch, hard and luminous. I realize that I am digging my fingers into her back.

We stagger into the bedroom, weak-kneed and panting. We fall onto the bed and she lies on top of me, her leg between mine, rocking against me as we bite each other's necks. She takes my hands and holds them against the bed next to my shoulders. She kisses me hard, then pulls away. I strain to reach her, but she keeps her mouth about an inch from mine, still rhythmically rubbing her thigh against me.

"Cleo! Cleo!" Cleo's best friend Jimmy hugged her hello. "What's with you, honey?" he said. "I've been chasing after you and calling your name since you passed my corner three blocks ago! And now you look like you have a fever. What's going on here?"

"I met this woman."

"Oh, you *do* have a fever."

They walked to the park as Cleo told Jimmy the whole story, every word she and Roxanne exchanged, every nuance, leaving out only the fantasies. When she finished, Jimmy said, "There's one way to find out. Ask her out."

"But she's always at work, and there are people around, and what if she's not even gay, or what if she is and just doesn't find me attractive? What if I make a fool of myself?"

"Join the human race, honey. We're all fools. Ask her out."

Cleo wasn't sure what to do, so she called her other best friend, Diane, and brought her up-to-date. Diane said, "Don't bother. She's straight."

Cleo called her third best friend, Leslie, and asked her advice. Leslie said, "She gave you chocolate. She wants you."

possibilities

I go to the co-op just as it's closing. Roxanne says, "I have to close up. Can you wait?" I sit on a crate near the books and magazines while she goes into a small office and works on the computer. I'm trying to figure out how the woman in a yoga magazine got her feet behind her head when I realize that Roxanne is behind me. She runs her hand across my brush cut, then grazes the back of my neck with her fingertips. She leans down and nibbles on my earlobe. The yoga magazine flutters to the floor.

I turn to face her and we taste each other's lips with delicate, lingering kisses. Her hair is down and I run my hands through its silky thickness. She kneels and kisses my nipples through my T-shirt. I figure that if I ask her out, she will probably say yes.

Cleo kept shopping at the co-op. She had even developed a taste for broccoli, but she still couldn't get up the nerve to ask Roxanne out. There were too many interruptions, not enough privacy. After all, Roxanne was at work whenever they saw each other. Cleo finally asked Jimmy if it would be too damn wimpy to ask Roxanne out by leaving a card. Jimmy laughed and said, "Honey, whatever works."

Cleo called Diane. Diane said, "Don't bother. She's straight."

Cleo called Leslie. Leslie said, "She gave you chocolate. She wants you."

Cleo found a beautiful card with a closeup of a giraffe's face. The giraffe's eyes were deep and dark and somehow sexy. She wrote, "Thanks for the chocolate bars. Can I take you out for coffee sometime?" She included her phone number and E-mail address.

Only two registers were open. A long line of people stood grumbling at each one, shooting dirty looks at Roxanne at one register and the muscular teenager at the other. The old man paying wendy caster

for his groceries at Roxanne's register pulled out his bills one at a time, straightening them and counting them over and over. The next person on line, a superthin woman in jogging clothes, radiated impatience. Roxanne smiled when she saw Cleo. Cleo handed her the card. Roxanne said, "Thanks!" then looked around her and shrugged at the chaos. Cleo smiled, and left.

Within a block, Cleo felt terribly embarrassed. What had she done? She didn't know if Roxanne was remotely interested. She didn't even know if she dated women. Cleo pictured Roxanne being pleased when she opened the card. She pictured her being annoyed.

Cleo called Jimmy. He said, "If she calls, she calls. If she doesn't, she doesn't. There are lots of fish in the sea, and you're a heck of a sexy fisherwoman!"

Cleo called Diane. Diane said, "You won't hear from her."

Cleo called Leslie. Leslie said, "She wants you. It's just a matter of time."

Roxanne lies on the bed, naked, her long hair draped across the pillows. I look up from between her legs at the landscape of her beautiful body, the rolling hills of her breasts and belly, the brush of her pubic hair. I kiss her thighs, rub my cheek against her. I'm finally going to lick her and I can't wait, yet I also want to stop time at this perfect moment of anticipation. Her lips glisten with moisture. Shall I start slow, with long, liquid licks, or quick, with the shock of the sudden? I want to have 10 first times, 20 first times, so I can try every variety, every approach.

I kiss her tenderly, slowly, all over her triangle of hair. She moans so deeply that she raises my temperature. I leisurely open her lips with the tip of my tongue. She moans again, a long, deep sound that follows my movements. She is swollen and wet and smooth and salty and sweet, and I lick her with the flat of my

46

*tongue to get as much of her as possible. And again. And again. I
want to lick her forever.*

*I slip two fingers a tiny way into her. She squeezes me hello.
I lick her clit as I stroke her opening with my fingers. Then I thrust
my fingers all the way in. She gasps. I pull out most of the way,
still licking her. I move my fingers in and out a tiny bit, a tiny bit,
in and out, a tiny bit, and then I thrust them in. Her gasp is
shocked, thrilled. I pull my fingers out again, still licking her.
Again I tease her. And again. And again. And again. I thrust my
fingers in. This time, her gasp is practically a scream.*

*Keeping my timing and pressure steady on her clit, I move my
curved fingers in and out, in and out, deep, hitting her G spot
again and again and again. When I think she is about to come, I
reach up with my other hand and roll her nipple between my fingers. Her moans quicken and deepen, and her thighs tense, and
her clit vibrates under my tongue. I suck on her clit, pulling her
orgasm into my own body. She comes for a very long time.*

A day passed, and then another. Cleo jumped every time
her phone rang. She checked her E-mail frequently, but not so
frequently that Roxanne would get a busy signal if she called.
And she talked each day to Jimmy, Diane, and Leslie, not quite
willing to admit how much she wanted Roxanne to call but not
quite able to change the subject either. She told each of them
about the note she had left, asking if it was too forward or not
forward enough, too obvious or not obvious enough. They
teased her, but they were also patient. They too had waited for
phone calls.

She ended each conversation by saying that even if
Roxanne did call, it could be to say no thanks. And each time,
Jimmy said, "Whatever happens is fine," and Diane said,
"Forget her," and Leslie said, "She wants you."

Cleo sat in her red armchair and thought about what each of her friends had said. She thought about Roxanne.

Roxanne holds her arms out to me, and I go to her. We fit perfectly, with our heads tilted to the left, our right arms around each other's necks, our left arms across each other's backs, our breasts and bellies and thighs pressed together. We hold each other for a long time. We've been together a year, a full year, and it just keeps feeling better and better.

We go into the bedroom. Roxanne lights the candles we keep on the dresser. I set up our CD changer with Bonnie Raitt and Annie Lennox and Sade and Diana Krall and press "random." On comes Diana Krall's voice singing, "They Can't Take That Away From Me."

We turn to each other and kiss. In our year together, we have developed a choreography of kissing, a dance in which no one leads and no one follows, yet the steps get more and more intricate. We're at the unhurried waltz stage now, tasting each other's lips and mouths and tongues. Each kiss melts into the next, feeding the fires in our bodies.

It strikes me that one year is the perfect moment in a relationship: new enough to be hot and surprised but old enough to know each other's desires and needs. I know that if I nibble on her ear, she will shiver with delight, but I also know that it is too soon. I want this night to take forever. So we kiss, and we kiss, and we focus on the kisses as though they are the center of the universe. Which they are.

Roxanne unbuttons my shirt. I'm not wearing a bra. She holds her hands a quarter of an inch from my nipples and heats the air around my breasts until my nipples cry out, "Touch me, touch me!" But I say nothing. She takes my shirt off and just looks at me. It is all I can do not to throw myself at her. "Beautiful," she whispers. She reaches out and strokes my left nipple, once. Both nipples jump to attention so quickly that we laugh. My laugh is half moan.

Roxanne kneels and unties my shoes. She removes my shoes and socks and kisses the tops of my feet quickly. Then she reaches up and opens my slacks and pulls them down toward her, taking my underpants too. I lift one foot and then the other as she removes my slacks, and then I am standing there naked. She is completely dressed.

I reach toward her blouse, but she shakes her head no. This is something new. I feel more naked than I have ever felt with her, and it's a delicious, slightly scary feeling.

Roxanne lowers me onto the bed. She lies on top of me and kisses me hard. I feel the buttons of her shirt, her belt buckle, the zipper of her jeans. I feel even more naked and very vulnerable and very very turned on. We kiss for a long time.

Roxanne gets up. I start to ask where she's going, but she says "Shhh" and goes into the bathroom. I'm a little cold, but I feel as though it would be wrong to get under the covers. Roxanne left me naked and waiting, and I'll stay naked and waiting. I want to touch myself and feel how wet and swollen I am, but I wait for Roxanne. Annie Lennox sings about sweet dreams.

When Roxanne comes back, I'm a little disappointed. I expected something—a change of clothing, a sex toy, something. She lies on top of me, and I realize that there's a bulge between her legs. Now I know what my anniversary gift is.

Roxanne kisses me on my neck, down my shoulder to my breasts. She blows on my nipple then licks it once, quickly, as though to see what mood it's in. My moans answer her question and she takes my nipple in her mouth and sucks it until it is a hard, happy mountain of flesh. She sucks rhythmically until my hips are following her rhythm. She moves to my other nipple with her mouth, playing with the first nipple with her fingers. My hips move faster and faster, pushing against her crotch, pushing against the surprise waiting inside. When I feel as though I might come just from what she's doing to my nipples, I reach down and unzip her pants. She reaches down and holds my hand away.

"*Do you want me inside of you?*" *she whispers.*

"*Yes!*"

"*Then ask nicely,*" *she answers.*

"*Please,*" *I moan.*

"*Please.*"

"*Please.*"

She releases my hand and I unzip her. The dildo is lavender and curved. When I realize where it will hit me inside, I moan again.

Roxanne reaches to the night table and pulls out some lube. I take it from her, pour some on my hand, and start stroking the dildo. Now we are both moaning. It is almost a flesh and blood part of her.

I wrap my legs around her and pull her into me. She tries to enter me slowly, but I push up against her. She says, "You want me, don't you?"

"*Yes,*" *I say, as I push up against her again.*

"*Yes.*"

"*Yes.*"

"*Yes.*"

We buck against each other in a frenzy of sensation. We kiss and bite each other. Our hair is matted against our heads with sweat. We stare hungrily at each other then close our eyes as emotions overtake us. Bonnie Raitt is burning down the house, and so are we.

Soon I realize that I have to come. Roxanne realizes it too and pulls out of me, slowly, tiny bit by tiny bit. My insides don't want her to leave, but I need to come. Roxanne starts to slide down my body to lick me, but I stop her. I push her on her side, facing me, then I flip over so that her mouth can go between my legs while I lick the dildo clean. When Roxanne sees what I'm doing she laughs, a husky, sexy laugh.

Roxanne starts licking me. I'm very close to coming, but somehow I manage to suck the dildo while pushing the base against her, so she'll feel the movement. We get into a rhythm of licking, the dildo in and out of my mouth, her tongue back and forth on my clit. It is only minutes until I come, a muscular orgasm that clenches my fists and curls my toes and arches my back. To my delight, I realize that Roxanne is coming too.

We lean on each other, heads on each other thighs, breathing deeply. Roxanne kisses my thighs then starts to lick me again and—

The phone rang. Cleo took a deep breath and picked it up. "Hello," she said.

"Cleo?"

"Yes."

"It's Roxanne."

Cleo took another deep breath and said, "So, Roxanne, how ya doin'?"

Now she would know.

A Religious Experience

Lesléa Newman

*M*y girlfriend, Melissa, also known as the *shayneh maidel* from Manhattan, has skin the color of a perfectly toasted bagel, lips like lox, and teeth white as cream cheese. Her eyes are two dark poppy seeds, and her hair is luscious as chocolate babka. Ooh, I could just eat her up, my little *Vildeh Chaya* with her shiksa-straight nose and *Gone With the Wind* waist, the only woman in the world who makes Vanessa Williams look like chopped liver. But I can't. Not today anyway, because today is Yom Kippur, the one day of the year my fetching femme won't let me lay a finger on her. And nothing makes a butch hornier than a slap on the wrist followed by those four little words: "Hands off the merchandise."

For those of you who have strayed from the fold as I have, let me fill you in. Yom Kippur (pronounced "Yum Kip-PAH" by us Noo Yawkers and "Yome Kip-POUR" by the rest of the world) is the most important Jewish holiday of the year. To celebrate it, we Jews refrain from eating, drinking, talking on the phone, riding in a car, working, watching TV, and making love. Some holiday. It's also the day that God (spelled "G-d" by the

52

true chosen people) opens his little black book and decides who gets to stick around for another year and who gets to kick the bucket. So all of us Yid kids put on our Sunday best (only in our case it's our Saturday best) and schlepp ourselves to shul to atone for our sins. Except for yours truly of course, who hasn't set foot in a synagogue since 1979, the year I got caught in the coat room nibbling on the neck of the rabbi's daughter, because I thought it was a sin for such a drop-dead gorgeous *girlchik* to be sweet 16 and never been kissed.

So much for religion. I don't really believe in God and all that, but Melissa does. She almost didn't even date me because she thought I was a goy. "Laurie Dellacora," she mulled my name over. "What kind of Jewish name is that?"

"My mother's maiden name is Lipshitz," I told her. "Thank God my parents didn't decide to hyphenate." Then I explained further that my mother's side of the family is Russian Jewish and my father's side is Italian Catholic, which didn't please Melissa too much because, as she said, she had her heart set on a purebred. But what could she do? Jewish butches are awfully hard to find. Plus the fact that I am quite handsome and charming, if I do say so myself, especially when I want to be. And I definitely wanted to be the day I met Melissa. Lucky for me, the Jews believe that everything is passed down through the mother's line, and any rabbi worth his weight in Manischewitz would proclaim I was one of the tribe (as would Hitler, by the way). My parents didn't care all that much about either religion, to tell you the truth, except during the month of December, when we had both a menorah and a Christmas tree in the living room, which was fine with me because it meant I got lots of presents. But other than that, I never really cared about religion one way or the other.

Until I met Melissa. Let's just put it this way: If my being a Jew makes her happy, then it makes me happy too. Melissa likes to celebrate the Sabbath by lighting candles and eating challah, which is A-OK by me. She also likes to get down and dirty on Friday nights (and Saturday mornings, too) because the Jews believe it's a mitzvah to make love on the Shabbat. Now, there's a tradition I can certainly get behind (and on top of) on a regular basis. We have a lovely little thing going on Friday nights, my Melissa and I. After work we have a nice dinner, and then while I'm doing the dishes my Sabbath bride whips up an out-of-this-world noodle kugel that she pops into the oven. It takes about an hour to bake, which is just about how long it takes for us to get cooking too. And somehow, even though we usually have a pretty big supper, an hour later we're simply starving.

But that's about as far as it goes when it comes to tradition, no matter how magnificently Zero Mostel sings about it on Melissa's *Fiddler on the Roof* album. I mean, I'll be the first to admit Melissa has me wrapped around her little pink-tipped pinkie, but the one thing she cannot do, no matter how hard she tries, is convince me to go to shul.

"Are you sure you don't want to come?" she asks this morning, sitting on the edge of our bed, pulling a sheer silk stocking over her shapely thigh.

"I never said I didn't want to *come*," I reply, sitting down next to her, but as soon as our auras touch she moves away.

"On Yom Kippur, Laurie? You should be ashamed of yourself," Melissa says, but to tell you the truth, I'm not. In fact, I'm kind of proud that even after all this time, four years, seven months, and 14 days to be exact, my beautiful babe can still drive me delirious with desire. And don't think she doesn't work it. After she's got both her stockings on, Melissa stands to slide her slip over her hips and then bends over to pour her bodacious bosom into her bra. Then she steps into her dress and turns around. "Will you zip me?" she asks, lifting a yard of hair to show off the back of her neck. Even though we're not really into S/M, I could swear Melissa is getting quite a thrill out of torturing me like this. But if she thinks her little act is going to convince me to go to synagogue and sit stone-still on a cold folding chair for hours, listening to some old guy chant in a language I don't understand while my stomach gurgles in harmony (I'm fasting along with Melissa as a sign of solidarity), she's got another think coming.

"I'm going now," Melissa says, putting on a coat since the autumn air's a little crisp. "Last call for services."

"I'll pass," I say, coming over to kiss her good-bye, but as soon as I come near her Melissa backs away.

"Unh-unh-unh," she says, wagging her finger at me. Then she flounces down the steps and, knowing I'm watching her, moons me when she reaches the bottom. Since she has nothing on underneath her holiday frock except a garter belt, I have to hang on to the banister to keep from falling down the stairs. She laughs, straightens up, and leaves, locking the door behind her.

So now what? There's nothing to do but go back to bed, since Melissa didn't have to work too hard to convince me to take the day off. "Yom Kippur is supposed to be a complete Sabbath," she said. So, fine. Just because I don't observe the religion doesn't mean I shouldn't enjoy the perks. I doze off for a while and then sit up and watch a little TV. But it's no use. All I can think about is my Melissa. Those dark, dark eyes. Those pouty pink lips. Those big, beautiful breasts. That amazing ass.

Well, why not? Here I am in bed, and I can't think of one good reason not to let my fingers do the walking. I mean, what the hell, I've got all day. And here's something I don't understand: If, as Melissa says, Yom Kippur is a complete Shabbat, the holiest day of the year, the Grand Poobah of Sabbaths, and ordinarily it's a *mitzvah* to make love on the Sabbath, then why wouldn't it be a blessing to spend all day in bed with your beloved? Like, let's be consistent here, you know what I mean?

I take off my T-shirt and boxer shorts and start by running my hands lightly up and down my body. I'm strong and in pretty good shape, if I do say so myself. I'm not doing too badly in the flab department either, except for some recent developments around my stomach area, but still, I'll be damned before I start drinking Miller Lite. I don't care if I gain a pound or two as long as I stay in shape—mostly so I can sling my zaftig sweetie over my shoulder and bundle her off to bed the way she likes. And the way I'd like to right now.

But like it or not, this is a solo performance. I rub my palms around my nipples in small circles and wait for them to get hard. It takes a while because, frankly, I don't have the kind of body I'm attracted to. I'm pretty flat, unlike Melissa, who's a 38D, which I always tell her stands for delicious. Melissa can come just from having me lick and suck her breasts, which amazes me. I, of course, can come just from making her come, which amazes Melissa, but hey, what can I say? It's a butch thing, I guess.

I'm not exactly getting turned on here, so I shut my eyes and pretend my hands are touching the body of my beloved, which means I have to leave the breast department and travel south. I move my hands down my body and start stroking the insides of my thighs, which, like Melissa's, are as smooth and silky as puppy ears. Then I start petting my pubic hair and pulling on it gently, the way that drives Melissa wild—I mean when I do it to her, of course; I would never touch myself in front of my girlfriend, though I like it when she touches herself in front of me. The first time I asked her if she'd ever do that, she just smiled and took her top off. In fact, she kind of got off on it. It's a femme thing, I guess. I actually start to get a little worked up, so I use my left hand to make small circles around my clit. Ah, instant relief, like an itch that's dying to be scratched. And then my right hand gets a little bored, I guess, because there's no other way to explain what happens next. All of a sudden, my middle finger sneaks in where no one has gone before. My snatch, the final frontier.

Wow, I'm surprised at how hot and wet and soft I am inside. *Well, what were you expecting,* I ask myself, *sandpaper?* I've never really penetrated myself before, or let Melissa, even though she tries sometimes and pouts when I say she can't. But I don't know, it seems too much of a femme thing to let some-one in like that. I almost can't stand doing it to myself, if you want to know the truth, so I make sure my eyes are shut tight and continue to pretend I'm touching my lady.

I keep the finger that's inside still, the way Melissa likes, and I keep rubbing my clit back and forth with my other hand. I'm breathing pretty heavy now, and before I even think about it I slide another finger inside. Whoa, I guess there's room at the inn, because before I even know what I'm doing, finger number three joins the rest of the crowd. Dare I go for four? No, I have a better idea. When my girl's really hot and open for me, she likes my thumb inside, all the way up to the fleshy part that joins it to my hand, and my middle finger up her butt. I go for it and before I can even say, "Come for me, baby," my hips are moving, my legs are shaking, and I'm practically drooling all over myself, but I don't care. Thank God there's no one around to see me like this. No, wait a minute. I wish there were some-one around to witness me losing total control. But not just any someone. A certain someone named Melissa. I know how much I love her when I see her giving me everything she's got.

I wonder if she would feel the same way. Or would she laugh at me and demand I turn in my butch card?

"Melissa, Melissa," I yell as I come and come and come. It takes a few minutes for me to stop shaking and a few more after that for me to catch my breath. When I'm finally my usual calm, cool, collected self, I remove my fingers and thumb from my various orifices and reach for Melissa, but of course she's not here. That's the thing about masturbation: Afterward there's no one to hold and squeeze and say I love you to while you look deep into her eyes. There's no one to stroke and pet and whisper sweet nothings to while she rests her head on your shoulder. There's no one to even say, "Wow, I never knew you could come like that," so I get out of bed and say it to myself in the bathroom mirror. "Wow, I never knew you could come like that."

"There's a lot of things about me that you don't know," I say to my reflection as I wash my hands. I mean, I've always been the one who got off on pleasing my lover, and I've never gotten any complaints. But I know Melissa wishes she could do some of the things to me that I just did to myself. I swore long ago I'd never flip. But now that I've flipped myself, who knows? After all, it is a new year. Maybe it's time for a change.

So, is Melissa going to stay in shul all day or what? It's only a little after 1 o'clock, which means I have five hours to go until the holiday is over. Officially Yom Kippur ends at sunset, but since we stopped eating at 5:30 yesterday, I convinced Melissa we could break the fast at 5:30 today. I wonder if that means we can fuck at 5:30 too. I certainly hope so. You'd think I'd have had enough for one day, but for some reason I'm hornier than ever. In fact, I can hardly wait to get my hands on that girl.

I take a shower, get dressed, make the bed, listen to some music and wait for Melissa to get home. When she finally walks in around 4:30, I go to scoop her up in my arms, but she's too excited to sit still.

"Laurie, you won't even believe what happened to me in temple today," she says, fluttering all over the room. Maybe the poor girl is delirious from lack of food—I know I am—not to mention lack of caffeine. "So, I'm sitting there, right, just minding my own business, reading along with the prayer book and everything," Melissa says, "and then like halfway through the service, the rabbi stands and the ark is open, so the whole congregation stands too. And then this new cantor goes up to the *bima,* and she starts to sing and she has the most amazing voice—I swear, it's like an angel is in the room. I was wishing you were there to hear her, Laurie, and then it was almost like you were there, right next to me. I could, like, *feel* your presence or something. And I was swaying to the cantor's voice, and then my whole body started to shake and shudder and I had to sit down even though the ark was still open because I really thought I was going to faint. My heart was beating really fast, I could barely catch my breath, and my face was all red, almost like when, almost like, well, you know." Melissa looks down demurely.

"Wait a minute, was this cantor a femme or a butch?" I fold my arms in a huff. Maybe I should have gone to synagogue with Melissa after all.

"She was a femme, silly. Anyway, that's not the point. The point is, these, like, *waves* started rippling through my body, and all I could think about was you, like I could practically hear your voice, like you were calling me or something, and then I sat back down, and I swear, my whole chest was all flushed, like it is after we make love. It was totally amazing, like some sort of religious experience or something."

Am I good or what? I think, my heart starting to beat fast too. "So, um, like what time was this?" I ask, trying to sound nonchalant.

"What time?" Melissa looks up at the clock. "I don't know. Why?"

"Just curious."

"I don't know, let me think." Melissa tilts her head. "It must have been around 1 o'clock because then the rabbi started his sermon, and he always does his sermons around 1."

"I see," I say, more to myself than to her.

"So, what did you do today?" Melissa asks, coming to sit down next to me on the couch, but not too close, since the sun has yet to set.

"Oh, not much. Just hung around. Thought about you," I say putting my arm across her shoulder.

"Lau-*rie*." Melissa rolls her eyes, but she isn't really annoyed because she doesn't pull away. "God, I'm starving, aren't you?"

"You betcha. What are you in the mood for?"

"Well, I bought a bagel-and-lox spread to break the fast with, but what I really feel like eating is a huge piece of noodle kugel. What about you?"

"I'd kill for a kugel right now," I say.

"I know," Melissa jumps up. "I'll put one in the oven, and by the time it's ready we'll be able to eat." She bustles around the kitchen, putting up water to boil for the noodles, beating eggs, melting butter, and before I can even offer to help the *Shvitzing* Gourmet, our dinner's sizzling in the oven.

"Will you help me do the dishes?" Melissa asks, wiping her hands on a dish towel.

"I have a better idea," I say, coming up behind her and putting my arms around her waist. "Let's get into bed while it's baking."

"Lau-*rie,*" Melissa says again, but I can tell she's weakening. Her eyes are all big like they are when she wants me.

"C'mon, love," I whisper in her ear, letting my tongue linger. "I've got a surprise for you."

"Ooh, what is it?" Melissa squeals. Melissa loves surprises.

"You'll see," I say taking her by the hand.

"Is it something to eat?" she asks, her stomach rumbling.

"Not really," I answer, "but it's finger-licking good."

And it is.

Riding the Rails
Sacchi Green

"*H*ey, Jo! Josie Bissette!" A voice from my past, fitting all too well with the Springfield station visible through the train's foggy windows and the blowing snow. I'd been at college not far from here, and so had that voice's perpetrator.

"If it isn't Miss Theresa," I grunted, and kept tugging at the sheepskin jacket caught behind a suitcase on the overhead rack.

"I never forget an ass," Terry said pointedly, casing mine as I reached upward.

"Sure as hell wouldn't have known yours." My jacket finally yielded. I tossed it over the voluptuous décolletage of my seated companion. A few minutes earlier Yasmin had been whining about being cold. Now, of course, for a new audience, she shrugged off the covering with an enthusiasm that threatened to shrug off her low-cut silk blouse as well. Not that it had been doing much to veil those pouting nipples.

Terry, brushing snow off her shoulders and shaking it from her hair, rightly accepted my remark as a compliment. Fourteen years ago she'd been on the lumpy side; now she was buff—and all style. Sandy hair lightened, cropped, waxed just right; multiple piercings on the left ear and eyebrow, giving her face a rakish slant; studded black leather, cut to make the best of the work she'd done on her body. I'd have felt mundane, with my straight black hair in a club and my brown uniform pants and shirt, not ironed all that well since Katzi took off—if I ever gave a damn about appearances. Which might have had something to do with why Katzi took off. Which had a whole lot to do with why I hadn't been laid in two months and wasn't in top condition to resist Yasmin's efforts.

"You just get on?" Terry asked. "Didn't see you in the station. No way I could have overlooked your little friend." Her look raked Yasmin, who practically squirmed with delight.

"Been on since White River Junction," I said shortly. It was more than clear that Terry expected an introduction. "Yasmin, Terry O'Brian. We were in college together. Terry, Princess Yasmin, fourth wife of the sultan of Isbani." It was some satisfaction to see Terry's jaw drop for an instant before her suave butch facade resurfaced.

"Ooh, Terry!" Yasmin warbled, jiggling provocatively. "I didn't know Sergeant Jo could have such nice friends!"

"The princess somehow…missed leaving New Hampshire with her husband's entourage," I said. "They'd been visiting her stepson at Dartmouth. I'm escorting her to D.C. to meet them." As far as I could tell, it had been a combination of Yasmin's laziness and the head wife's hatred that had culminated in her missing the limo caravan and her absence going unnoticed until too late. I was developing a good deal of sympathy for the head wife.

"The weather's too risky for flying or driving," I added, "but the train should make it through. Not supposed to be much snow south of Connecticut."

"Well, now," Terry said, sliding into the seat facing Yasmin. "I'll be happy to share security duty as far as New York."

"Don't get too happy." I sat beside my charge. There were suddenly more limbs between the seats than would comfortably fit; I tried to let my long legs stretch into the aisle, but that tilted my ass too close to Yasmin's, and she gave an appreciative wriggle against my holster. I straightened up. "This is official business. The last thing I need is an international incident."

I wondered why the hell I hadn't told Terry to fuck off in the first place. Did I hope she'd distract Yasmin enough to take off some of the pressure? The tension had been building all morning. Even the rhythm of the train had been driving me toward the edge with its subtle, insistent vibration. Or maybe it was just that the little bitch was too damned good at the game and too clearly driven by spite. I don't have to like a tease to call her on it; if I hadn't been on the job, I'd have given Yasmin more than she knew she was asking for, and if it left my conscience a bit scuffed, what the hell—other areas would have earned a fine, lingering glow.

But I was on duty, and she was doubly untouchable. And knew it. Seven more hours of this was going to be a particularly interesting version of hell.

"Keep it professional, Jo," Lieutenant Willey had said. "This one's a real handful."

"I noticed," I'd told her. Several handfuls, in fact, in all the right places, with all the right moves. "Don't worry. I know better than to fuck the sheep I'm herding." She should have slapped me down for that, but instead she rolled her eyes toward the door, and I saw, too late, that the troublesome sheep I had to herd had just come in. No hope that she hadn't heard me. Anger, sparked with interest, sharpened that kittenish face, segueing into challenge as she looked me up and down.

"You're off to a great start," the lieutenant said dryly. "Just bear in mind that the sultan wants her back 'untouched,' and I'd just as soon not have to argue the semantics of that with the state department." Something in her usually impassive expression made me wonder whether our charge had come on to her. If so, I was sure sorry I'd missed it.

By the time the train had crossed from Vermont into Massachusetts, I realized Yasmin would come on to any available pair of trousers, with no discrimination as to what filled them. Even the professionally affable conductor got flustered when she rubbed against him in passing, and she had a threesome of college boys so interested that I'd made the mistake of putting a proprietary arm around her shoulders and shooting them my best dyke-cop look as I yanked her back to our seats. The look worked fine, but it encouraged Yasmin to renew her attack on me.

"Ow!" she yelped when I tightened my grip on a hand that kept going where it had no business. "Why you are so mean to Yasmin?" Her coquettish pout left me cold, but a definite heat was building where her hand had trailed over my ass and nudged between my thighs, and she knew I wasn't impervious.

"Let's just stick to the business of getting you back to your husband," I said neutrally, aware of the continuing interest of the college kids three seats back. The less drama here, the better.

"Why do you worry? He can't order them to cut off your balls, the way they did to Haroun just for looking."

"Right, and you can't yank me around by them either," I muttered. The glitter of pleasurable recollection in her eyes was nauseating. What little I'd read about female genital mutilation flashed through my mind, and for a few minutes I really *was* impervious to her charms.

Terry's company, whatever the complications, might be better than being alone with Yasmin. Unless my competitive instincts reared up and made it all exponentially worse.

Terry could have been reading my mind. "Gee, Jo," she said, "remember the last time you introduced me to one of your little friends?" Her grin was demonic.

"How could I forget? You healed up pretty well, though." I stared pointedly at the scar running under her pierced eyebrow.

"Nothing like a dueling scar to intrigue the ladies," Terry said cheerfully. "You seem to have found a good dentist."

"You bet." I flashed what Katzi used to call my alpha-bitch grin.

Yasmin was practically frothing with excitement, jiggling her assets and leaning toward Terry to offer an in-depth view of her cleavage and a whiff of her insistently sensuous perfume. When she balanced herself with a far-from-accidental hand high on my thigh, I realized I'd only set her up to play us against each other.

"So, Terry," I said, firmly removing the fingers trying to make their way toward my treacherously responsive crotch. "What are you up to these days? Still living in the area?"

"I'm a paralegal in Northampton," she said. "Going to law school nights." Her gaze lingered on my badge, and for a rare instant I was hyperconscious of the breast under it. "Funny how we both got onto the straight side of the law."

"No kidding," I said. "I heard anything goes in Hamp these days, but can you go to court rigged out like that?"

"I could, but I don't." I was pleasantly surprised to see a bit of a flush rise from her neck to her jawline. "I'm on my way to New York to do a reading at a bookstore in the East Village."

"You're a writer?" My surprise was hardly flattering, and her jaw tightened even as the flush extended all the way to her hairline.

"On the side, yeah," she said brusquely. "Doesn't pay much, but the fringe benefits can be outstanding."

"Hey, I'll just bet they are, if the stories match the getup! Erotica groupies, huh?"

Terry caught the new respect in my voice and relaxed. She let her legs splay apart. I'd already noticed she was packing; now Yasmin stared at the huge bulge stretching the black leather pants along the right thigh, and her Kewpie-doll mouth formed an awestruck O.

"Loaded for bear, aren't we?" I said. "Ah, the literary life. I'll have to check out some of your stuff, maybe get you to auto-graph a book." I was more than half serious. She started to grin, and then an odd startled look swept over her face. I glanced down and saw Yasmin's stockinged foot nudging against the straining black leather.

It wasn't a big enough deal to account for my first raging impulse to break Yasmin's leg. I managed to suppress it, but by then everything seemed to be happening in slow motion except the throbbing in my crotch. Terry's presence was definitely making things worse. Much worse.

Yasmin pulled up her silk skirt so we could get the full ben-efit of the shapely leg extended between the seats and the toes caressing the leather-sheathed cock. Then she applied enough force that Terry caught her breath and automatically shifted her hips to get the most benefit, and I felt the pressure as though it were prodding against my own clit. But all I was packing was a gun, and that was on my hip.

I know from experience that you don't get the optimal angle the way Yasmin was working. But you can get damned close. Katzi used to tease me like that in restaurants—her leg up under the table, her foot in my lap, her eyes gleaming wickedly as she watched me struggle not to make the kind of sounds you can't make in public. She knew I wouldn't let myself come, because I just can't manage it without making a whole lot of noise.

The train wasn't crowded, but it was public. Terry's head was thrown back, her eyes glazing over, her hands gripping the seat hard. I was afraid my own breathing was even louder than hers, and damned sure my cunt was just as hot and wet. I had to stop the little bitch, but I was afraid if I touched her I'd do serious damage.

Then Yasmin, with a sly sidelong glance at me, unbuttoned her blouse and spread it open. As she fondled her own breasts, her rosy nipples, which had thrust against the silky fabric all morning as though permanently engorged, grew even fuller and harder. Her torso undulated as her butt squirmed against the seat. Her foot was still working Terry's equipment, but her focus had shifted.

"*Goddamn!*" came Terry's harsh whisper. Or maybe it was mine. Then Yasmin turned slightly and leaned toward me, still working her flesh, offering it to me, watching my reaction with half-closed eyes, her little pink tongue moving over her full upper lip. The tantalizing effect of her perfume was magnified by the musk of three aroused bodies.

"We're coming into Hartford." Terry's strangled words sounded far away. "We'll be at the station any minute!"

Yasmin's voice, soft, taunting, so close that I felt her breath on my throat, echoed through my head: "Sergeant Jo doesn't have the balls to fuck a sheep!"

I snapped.

I lunged.

With my right hand I clamped her wrists together above her head. With my left arm across her windpipe I pinned her to the seat back. I leaned over her, one knee between her thighs. Then I dropped my hands to her shoulders and shook her so hard that her head bobbled and her tits jiggled against my shirt front and the hard edges of my badge.

A strong hand grabbed my shoulder and yanked me back. When I resisted, something whacked me fairly hard across the back of my head. Then a soft, bulky object—my sheepskin jacket—was shoved down between us.

"Damn it, Jo, cool it!" Terry hissed. "And you," she said to Yasmin in a tone slightly less harsh, "you little slut—and I mean that, of course, in the best possible sense of the word—cover up or I'll let the sergeant toss you out onto the train platform."

I nearly turned on her, but people were moving down the aisles to get off the train, and more people would be getting on. By the time the train was rolling again I'd begun to get a grip, although I was still breathing hard and my heart, along with several other body parts, was still pounding.

"Thanks," I muttered. "I guess I needed that."

"What you need," Terry said deliberately, "is a good fucking. Jeezus, Jo, if you don't get it off pretty damn soon, you'll have not only your international incident but the mother of all lawsuits!"

She was right, which just made things worse. I glanced at Yasmin. She had stopped whimpering and sat clutching my jacket around herself, watching us with great interest.

I pushed myself up into the aisle. "Can I trust you to keep her out of trouble for a couple of minutes while I at least take a leak?"

"You can count on me," Terry said, and I had to go with it.

There was a handicapped-accessible rest room just across from us, long and roomy by Amtrak standards. I pissed, tied my long straggling hair back up as well as I could with a mirror too low to show anything above my chin, and leaned my pelvis against the rounded edge of the sink. It was cold, but not enough to do me any good. Then I shoved off and unlocked the door, knowing that nothing I could do for myself would give me enough relief to be worth the hassle.

As the door slid open, a black-clad arm came through, then a shoulder, and suddenly Terry and Yasmin were in there with me and the door was shut and locked again.

"Sudden attack of patriotism," Terry announced with a lupine grin. "Have to prevent that international incident. It's a tough job, but somebody's gotta do it."

"You and who else?" I challenged.

"Just me. Our little princess is going to keep real quiet, now and forever, in return for letting her watch. No accusations, false or otherwise."

I looked at Yasmin. Her eyes were avid. "I swear on my mother's grave!" she said, and then, as I still looked skeptical, she added, "On my sister's grave!" Somehow that was convincing. Just the same, I unhooked the cuffs from my belt and snapped them around her wrists with paper towels for padding, then pinned her to the door handle. When I turned back to Terry, the quirk of her brow made me realize I'd tacitly agreed.

To what, I wasn't sure. We sized each other up for a minute like wrestlers considering grips. Then Terry made her move, trying to press me against the wall with her body, and I reflexively raised a knee to fend her off. Her cock against my kneecap made me feel naked. I'm used to being the hardbody in these encounters. I know the steps to this dance, but I've never had to do them going backward.

She retreated a few inches. "Gonna stay in uniform?" she asked, eyeing my badge. I unpinned it, slipped it into my holster, unfastened my belt, and hung the whole deal on a coat hook. "Civilian enough for you?"

"Hell, no! The least you could do is show me your tits."

I stared her in the eyes for a second—somehow I'd never noticed how green they could get—and unbuttoned my shirt. I wasn't sure yet just where I might draw the line. "Fair enough."

I hung my shirt and sports bra over the gun and holster, even yanked my hair loose from its knot and let it flow over my shoulders. It would have come down anyway. "So how about you?" She had left her jacket behind but still wore a tight-cut leather vest over a black silk shirt.

She observed me with such interest that she might not have heard. "Breasts like pomegranates," she said softly. "Round and high and tight. Jeez, don't they have gravity in New Hampshire?"

I looked down at myself. My nipples were hardening as though under an independent impulse. I sure felt them, though. I grabbed Terry's vest and pulled her close to mash the studded leather hard against me, then eased up to rub languorously against it. The leather felt intriguing enough that I didn't push the issue of her staying dressed. And Katzi had accused me of never trying anything different!

Terry pressed closer again. I leaned my mouth against her ear. "Pomegranates? Christ, Terry, is that the kind of tripe you write?"

"Yeah, sometimes, when the inspiration's right. But I usually edit it out later." She eased back and looked me over. "I don't suppose," she said somewhat wistfully, "you could jiggle a little for me?"

"In your dreams!" We were both a little short of breath now, both struggling with the question of who'd get to do what to whom. Much as my flesh wanted to be touched, my instinct was to lash out if she tried.

"In my dreams?" There was such an odd look in her eyes that I didn't notice right away that she had raised her hands until they almost brushed the outer curve of my breasts. "In my dreams," she murmured, just barely stroking me, "you're wearing red velvet."

I hadn't thought of that dress in years. Maybe the last one I ever wore. She'd worn black satin. A college mixer, some clumsy groping in a broom closet, a few weeks of feverish euphoria…then the realization that instead of striking sparks we were more apt to knock chips off each other. Eventually, in fact, we would. I ran my tongue over my reconstructed teeth.

Terry telegraphed an attempt at a kiss, but I wasn't quite ready for that. I did let her cup my breasts and rub her thumbs over my appreciative nipples. "One-time-only offer," I said, "for old times' sake," and pulled her head downward. She nuzzled the hollow of my throat while I ran my fingers through her crisp brush cut. Then she went lower, her open mouth wet and hot on my skin, and by the time she was biting where it really mattered, her knee was working between my thighs and I rubbed against it like a cat in heat.

"Come on," I muttered, "show me what you've got!" I groped the bulge in her crotch, and then, while she unbuckled and unbuttoned and rearranged her gear for action, I kicked off my boots and pants.

She tried to clinch too fast. I let her grab my ass for a few seconds, then grabbed hers and shoved those tight leather pants back far enough that I could get a good look at what had been pressing between my legs.

"State of the art, huh?" Ten thick inches of glistening black high-tech cock, slippery even when not yet wet. I'd have been envious any other time. Hell, I was still envious.

"This one's mostly for show," she muttered. "Are you sure—" But it was too late not to be sure.

"I can handle it," I said. And I did handle it, working it with my hand, making her gasp and squirm. I manipulated it so that the tip just licked at me, then leaned into it, and for long seconds we were linked in co-ownership of the black cock, clits zinged by a current keen as electricity but far sweeter. Then the slick material skidded in my natural lube and slid along my wet folds, and I spread for it and took it in just an inch or two.

Can't hurt to see how the other half lives, I thought, and then, as Terry pressed harder, I remembered the size of what I was dealing with and realized that, yeah, it might hurt, and yeah, I might just like it that way.

She pulled back a little and thrust again, and I opened up more, and she plunged harder, building into a compelling rhythm. I gripped the safety railing behind me and tilted my hips to take her deeper inside, a hungry ache building for even more of the pounding intensity.

But I had to go after it myself. "Let me move!" I growled.

Terry, uncomprehending, resisted my efforts to swing her around. The black cock, glistening for real now, slipped out as we grappled together. "What the..." Her voice was guttural, and her eyes glittered dangerously.

We were pretty evenly matched in strength. She was a bit beefier; I was taller. She'd been working out with weights and machines; I'd been working over smart-ass punks and potbellied drunks. The tiebreaker was that I needed it more.

"You get to wear it—just shut up and let me work it!" I had her back against the railing now. I grabbed the slippery cock and held it steady just long enough to get it where I needed it. Then I swung into serious action.

For an instant she flashed a grin, and muttered, "Fair enough!" Then it was all she could do to hang on to the railing and meet my lunges. The train swayed and rattled, but I rode it, my legs automatically absorbing the shifts as I rode that black cock, train to my tunnel, bound for glory. The surging hunger got me so slippery that, in spite of its bulk and hardness, what filled me might not have been enough, except that my clit seemed to swell inward as well as outward, and my whole cunt clenched fiercely around the maddening pressure.

Terry's grunts turned into moans; she grabbed my hips and dug her fingers into my naked flesh. "Steady...damn it... steady..." she said between clenched teeth, and before I knew what was happening she forced me against the hard edge of the sink behind me.

"Hang on," I said, swinging us both around, not losing an inch this time, until my back was to the wall. I couldn't stop moving but managed to slow enough to match her rhythm and grab her leather-covered ass. The muscles there bunched as her hips bucked. I mashed my mouth into hers to catch the eruption of harsh groans, but she had to breathe, and anyway, it didn't matter how much noise she made. I felt my own eruption coming and knew there was no way in hell I could muffle it. And didn't give a damn.

I held on until Terry's gasps subsided from wrenching to merely hard. She didn't resist as I turned her again and accelerated into my own demanding beat. I saw her face through a haze, and there may have been pain on it, but she didn't flinch, just kept her hips tilted at the optimal angle for me to ram myself down onto what she offered. My clit clenched like a fist, harder and harder each time I drove it toward her. A sound like a distant train whistle seemed to come closer and closer, the reverberations penetrating into places deeper than I had even known existed.

Then it hit. My clit went off like a brass gong, and those waves smashed up against the explosion raging outward from my center. A storm of sound engulfed me.

Terry held me for the hours it seemed to take for me to suck in enough breath to see straight. Finally I slouched against the edge of the sink, letting the slippery cock emerge inch by inch. She reached past me to grab a handful of paper towels; I took them away from her and slowly, sensuously wiped my own juices from the glistening black surface. When I aimed the used towels toward the trash container, she stopped me, folded them inside a clean one, and tucked them into her pocket, avoiding my eyes. I didn't ask, just drew spirals on the steamy mirror.

Then she looked toward the door. I'd been vaguely aware at one point of Yasmin, a hand pulled free of the too hastily fastened cuffs, rubbing herself into a frenzy—apparently, by her look now, with some success. "So, princess," Terry said with the old jaunty quirk of her brow, "didn't I tell you it'd be worth it just to listen to her come? I could tape that song and make a bundle."

"You, Terry, are a prick," I said lazily, "and I mean that, of course, in the best possible sense of the word."

"I still get the shivers now and then," Terry went on, nominally speaking to Yasmin, "thinking of that alto sax wailing. The final trumpet fanfare this time, though, was better than anything I remember."

"Jeez, I hope you edit out that kind of crap," I said, turning to the sink to clean up. The mirror was so steamed I couldn't see a thing. Then I dressed, feeling more secure with my gun belt around my hips. Not that security is everything.

The rest of the trip wasn't bad. The whispers and surreptitious looks from the college kids and a few others who must have heard us were kind of a kick. Yasmin watched sleepily as Terry and I chatted about old times, old acquaintances, and the intervening years. Terry got off at Penn Station, at the last minute offering me a book with her card tucked into it. I took out the card and slipped it into my breast pocket, behind the badge.

"Moving a little stiffly, aren't we?" I said as I helped get her duffel down from the rack.

"Mmm, but the show must go on."

"I'm sure you won't disappoint your audience." I aimed an encouraging slap at that fine, muscular ass. "Go get 'em."

Yasmin made a few tentative advances between New York and D.C., but I was no longer that vulnerable, and she gave up and slept for most of the trip. The welcoming party at Union Station was headed by a tall, mature woman in a well-cut dark suit. "The princess traveled well?" she asked, with a keen, hard look at me.

"Just fine," I said, meeting her eyes frankly. "With no harm done, if you don't count a few slaps to make her keep her hands to herself."

"Excellent," she said, with the ghost of a smile. "The sultan would be happy to offer hospitality for the night, before your return trip."

"I appreciate the offer," I said truthfully, "but I have other plans. I'm catching the next train to New York. There's a literary event I don't want to miss."

Terry's schedule of readings is scrawled on the back of her card. There's a special one at midnight. I have a notion there'll be enough erotica groupies to go around. Beyond that, I wouldn't mind meeting an editor, finding out more about the writing game. I know damned well that Terry will want to use some of today's action in her fiction. I might just beat her to it.

I've got to edit out that "train to my tunnel, bound for glory" line, though. Too bad. That's sure as hell exactly how it felt.

Chosen

Renette Toliver

*B*eing a night person, I was always used to seeing the stars burn in the Louisiana sky. Still, nothing could have prepared me for this.

↕

The French Quarter has always allowed people to become lost if they so choose. It's just too easy. Around almost every street corner is a dark hole in the wall where you can listen to music or get a drink. Lately after work, I found myself doing this more often, though it seemed I would go and just be restless. At night, I'd stare out of my window overlooking the Mississippi, watching the eerie night sky, and feel this desire to walk along its dark banks. My friends thought I was crazy. It's not the brightest idea for a black woman to roam the streets of N'awlins after the sun goes down. But there I was; *searching*, I called it. For what, I don't know.

Even as a child, I often snuck out of my bedroom window, caught up in the sounds of Dixieland jazz that seemed to float in the wind. I had never been afraid to venture out in the dark alone. The demons in my dreams haunted me the most. Seemed like when it was dark you could see a different side of people—how they acted when cut loose from the ties of the real world.

Most times, I wandered around until I got to Ms. Cora's house over by the cemetery. She often let me sit on her front porch with her, while she told stories of the "old ways." A lot of people in the neighborhood didn't like her. They called her the old gypsy woman and a witch, though Ms. Cora just laughed when I asked why. Even my mama didn't like me hanging around her, but I didn't care. I'd go anyway.

Ms. Cora told us children (and anyone else who would listen) about the people of the night. She said there were those of us who were different—a special group of people who roamed the night in search for others like them. And when the hunger hit, they searched for those willing to be seduced into the dark side. It sounded like the demons I dreamed about, the demons I searched for.

Real as it seemed when I was 12, as an adult I found stories like that hard to believe—that is, until the day *she* walked into my life.

I was in one of my moods again, walking around the tattered streets of the French Quarter. I unconsciously headed toward the Night Owl, a club I had been finding myself at lately. A small jazz group played in the corner, while smoke from a machine filled the humid air. Overall, it was the perfect place to get lost in. On this particular night, though, something strange happened. *She* walked in.

She was uncanny. Tall and slender, she had almost a regal look about her. She wore all black down to her boots, and her cocoa-colored skin contrasted with her deep black hair, which was pulled back from her face. Her most striking features were her eyes, gray like a cat's and staring straight at me. Instantly a chill came over me as our eyes met and locked.

She smiled briefly, then took a table in the far corner. I couldn't help feeling her presence; the air around me grew thick with the feel of this stranger. To tear my thoughts away from her, I tried to lose myself in the music. But even with the horns blowing—a loud pulsating rhythm that vibrated through the floorboards—I still found myself distracted.

A strange feeling came over me—one I'd never experienced. I felt her eyes pierce through my soul with a heat all their own. The feeling was so intense that my nipples stiffened underneath my T-shirt, and my panties became wet with my desire. Something had definitely begun.

The music faded into the background as this sensation intensified. I felt compelled to turn around; once again she was staring straight at me. I took this as an invitation, or maybe a *summons*. Whatever it was, I decided to talk to her. I wanted to play it cool and casually make my move, but like a character in a bad movie I stumbled over my own feet, trying to get to her table.

Before I could say anything, she spoke. "I've been waiting for you."

Gathering my composure, I continued the conversation. "Oh, really? Do I know you?"

She smiled. "Don't you?"

Intrigued for the moment, I decided to play the game. "No, but I'd like to."

"Then let me introduce myself." She held out a long slender hand. "My name is Maya."

I don't remember seeing her lips form the words, and yet I distinctly heard them. As I took her hand, a bolt of electricity shot through me, as a vision of the two of us intertwined in a moment of uncontrollable passion raced before my eyes. Then the vision was gone, just as quickly as it had come. Trying to shake off the feeling, I let go of her hand. "My name is Tanya," I breathed.

I couldn't tell if the room had gotten warmer, or if my body was reacting to Maya's touch. All I knew is that I wanted, almost needed, to feel her touch again. Maya looked up at that moment, reached out, and gently stroked my hair. "You're very beautiful, Tanya."

I couldn't speak. I found myself captured by her eyes and lost in the music of her voice. The band played, and people came and went as usual, but here at this table, time stood still. Her voice again whispered in my head.

"Would you like to go for a walk?"

I nodded.

The cool night air was a welcome relief from heat of the club. My head began to clear from the fog it had been in. An old garden patch stood a block away, and the soft summer breeze blew the sweet smell of roses through the air. The moon wasn't quite full, but its presence reflected off the sides of buildings. For the most part, the streets were deserted—just a few drunks here and there trying to find their way home. Nothing unusual for Bourbon Street at 3 o'clock in the morning. Feeling more comfortable and confident, I asked Maya where she wanted to go.

"My place," she whispered.

The wind began to blow harder, and again my head started spinning. When the world around me stopped moving, the street was gone. The walls around me were made of earth. They were cold to the touch, and my body was shivering, but the room itself was warm. Candles burned silently in a corner, giving off an amber glow that softly illuminated the room.

The room was sparsely furnished with an antique four-poster bed covered in thick satin bedcovers and a matching dressing table without a mirror. I wanted to ask where we were, but when I turned around she was gone. My head was still spinning from our journey, and I sat down to gather my senses. Not only did I not know where I was, I also had no idea how I had arrived there.

As a sudden gust of cold air brushed across the back of my neck, I jumped. I turned around but saw no one.

"Maya, is that you?"

My answer—the eerie sound of silence—hung in the air. I got up and looked around, searching for a door or some other way out. There was only one large pristine window, completely covered by thick black drapes. Then I felt her hot breath against my ear.

"Tanya, I hope you weren't leaving."

I turned around expecting to see her, but like before no one was there. The candles flickered wildly, and when I turned back I was startled to find her standing in front of me. She had changed clothes and no longer wore the formfitting jeans and bodysuit she had on at the club. She now wore a long black silk gown that clung to her body like a second layer of skin. Her straightened black hair hung loosely down her back—an endless river of black water.

"You startled me."

She glided over, as if her feet, hidden under the gown, never touched the ground. She carried a tray with two metal goblets.

"I thought you might want a drink." A warm smile formed, and my uneasiness started to fade. Her gray eyes continued to stare through me as the sweet, yet unfamiliar, warm liquid flowed down my throat.

"Where are we? And how did we get here?" I questioned, more intrigued than angry. Waiting for an answer, I continued to sip from my now half-filled glass.

Her long arms stretched out in an exaggerated gesture, and speaking in distinct Creole French, she answered, "Why, Tanya, you're here at my place…just like you wanted, just like you've always wanted."

A chill ran up my spine as she repeated the last part of her sentence, and a new feeling of vulnerability washed over me, as if she were bringing some dark secret of mine to the surface. I quickly took another drink, attempting to swallow back the demons that had plagued my nightmares since childhood. *Who are you?* I thought. Feeling woozy, I sat on the edge of the bed, my body melting into the thick red satin.

"What's in this?" I asked, holding up my drink.

"Oh, that? That's an old family secret. Some have said it is an aphrodisiac. I tend to think it warms the blood."

She grabbed her silver-and-pearl-handled hairbrush from the dressing table and joined me on the bed. "May I?"

I nodded. Long fingers released my thick, shoulder-length hair, which I had carefully French-braided before going out, and I felt the weight of Maya's body against my own. The hearty scent of musk floated from her as she leaned in even closer. I inhaled deeply, caught up in her scent, her magic. The brush came down smoothly against my scalp. Her arms moved in time with my deep breathing; long strokes from top to bottom.

Up, down. Up, down. I felt her breath on the back of my neck as she moved my hair easily to the side. The brush paused for a moment. A warm hand found the side of my neck. I grew hot beneath her touch, my skin tingling. *What are you?*

"Tanya, I am the breeze that travels through the air. I am the shadow that leads to nowhere. I am the flame that heats many souls in strife, the silent watcher in the night. I call on those throughout space and time, hoping they'll join me and be forever mine."

The heat from her words burned through to my core. The shadows of the demons I had grown up believing in rose against the wall. The force of my blood rushed through my body; its pace quickened. I felt her breath closer on my neck. I wanted to give in, to surrender. To what, I had no idea.

"Maya?"

The spell was broken, the demons gone. The brush resumed its lulling pace. Up, down, up, down. I turned to face her, unsure of what I would see. Her skin, almost translucent now, glowed in the candlelight. Her gray eyes gazed deep into mine. Her face slowly started toward mine, and my heart began to pound. The moment seemed to last forever. Her eyes never left mine, and my dizziness returned. The closer she came, the less in control I felt. My body was betraying my mind.

I felt the familiar flush of desire rise to an uncontrollable level. I didn't want her to stop, but part of me hesitated. Had she captured me under some sort of spell? The familiar whisper echoed inside my head.

"I could take you that way, Tanya, but I'd rather have you come...willingly."

A flood of emotions enveloped me as her soft, sensual lips caressed mine. A vision of Maya sucking on my peaked nipples flashed before my eyes once again, weakening me. My body ached deep inside. A need I had been searching to fill all these nights was suddenly making its presence known.

Maya smiled softly, while my hands eagerly explored every part of her willing body. She left me momentarily exasperated. My breathing grew rapid and shallow, the moisture gone from my throat, only to be found much lower. She stood tall and graceful in front of me. Within seconds, the black silk garment slid to the floor, exposing her delectable curves. Full breasts and shapely hips sat atop her long legs—dancer's legs, thick and muscular. The mere sight of her clouded my mind.

"Tanya, may I have you?"

Before I could answer, I felt her weight surround me. Her tongue plunged deep into my throat, and my body succumbed to passion. Maya's movements, swift and languid, overtook me. Fluid hands reached under my shirt and released my breasts from my lace bra. I fumbled to unsnap my jeans, but before I could finish she had them in a pile with the rest of my clothes.

Skin to skin, we embraced and kissed. Each time her lips met mine, I sank deeper into a new level of submission. Maya's hands ran across my body hungrily, studying me, memorizing me, reminding me I was now her possession. Soft lips captured my breasts, sucking them until the prophecy of my earlier visions was totally fulfilled.

"May I have you?"

She bent down and kissed my thighs, starting an upward journey to heaven. My body trembled as her lips found my sex, wet and inviting. Maya continued her exploration slowly, her eyes closed, her body hot. Her tongue, long and thin, penetrated me deeply. Instantly, my walls constricted around her tongue as it moved, slow and steady. My clit, swollen and throbbing, waited eagerly for the moment Maya's tongue would embrace it.

Maya, I'm ready.

"I know, Tanya."

Firm licks attacked my clit, and my mind began to blur in the thought, the feel, the presence of her. I sensed the oncoming explosion of desire. Understanding my need, she removed her tongue and replaced it with two fingers. Her pace quickened, and our shadows began to grow against the walls.

Reality faded, and inside my head I heard the voices of thousands of souls captured by her rejoicing.

"You know, there are those of us who are different, Tanya. Some of us live and feed in the dark."

Was that old Ms. Cora's voice? Steadily Maya's fingers moved in and out of me. Somehow through the haze, I found my way to her own sex. Three fingers slipped inside easily, her wetness oozing down to my palm. It was time. My search had brought me to this place...to her. A long arm encircled my neck and pulled me close. Our lips met once again.

"Tanya, come with me." Her lips escaped mine as my orgasm approached. The roar began in my throat, heading toward the surface. Her tongue encircled my breast, preparing me, searching for the right place. As a scream of release escaped my lips, sharp teeth penetrated my breast.

I closed my eyes, caught up waves of pleasure that completely racked my body. The pain intensified the pleasure. The pleasure intensified the pain. Minutes, hours, years—nothing seemed to matter except this moment. Our hearts beat in time while Maya drank from me. Our bodies swayed. My orgasm passed from me to her in long deep draws from my breasts. Her body grew flushed, my essence freeing her from her hunger. Darkness started to come behind my closed eyelids. She then released herself, my life essence dripping down her lips in a trickle of crimson.

For moments after, my body was sensitive. I heard people's voices from the street echo above. The bedcovers beneath my flesh made me tremble in a mixture of pleasure and pain. My eyes saw faces in the shadows, and the candlelight reflected in Maya's eyes burned through my skin. The world I once believed in was now a memory.

I laid in her arms, my body recovered, waiting for sleep to

capture me. Our worlds connected; our heartbeats slowed back to their normal pace. She handed me my goblet, now refilled to the top. The familiar warm liquid burned pleasantly down my throat. My thirst seemed endless. She smiled.

"We should go. I must get you home before sunrise," she whispered.

"Will I see you again, Maya?"

"There will be a next time. I promise you that."

"You never told me what this was," I said, holding up my glass. She smiled again. "Blood."

She kissed me deeply, stifling any words I might have been able to utter. My head began to swim in a mixture of blood and lust. I closed my eyes, drugged by the magic in her kiss. Weak from our lovemaking, I drifted off to sleep in her slender arms.

When I opened my eyes again, I was in my own bed. My head was pounding as if I had drunk one too many of something. The sun was up; it seemed to be at least 80 degrees already. The clock on my nightstand read 8 A.M. I jumped up out of bed and headed to the kitchen.

On the table stood a vase with a bouquet of crimson roses. Suddenly I remembered last night. The club, the sex...Maya. I picked up the card from the vase and ran to the mirror in the hall. I pulled down the T-shirt I always wore to bed and inspected my chest. Underneath my right breast was a tiny red mark.

As I ran my finger over it, a small pulse made me shiver with pleasure. I read the card I still had clutched in my hand:

Until next time...

Maya

I ran my finger over my wound once again and smiled.

1968 Mustang
Trixi

$\mathcal{N}$ikki and Arnelle were sitting across from each other, sharing a blueberry muffin that sat like a pastry sun in the middle of a warped pink Formica sky. Stan's Cafeteria was their favorite meeting spot for three reasons: One, it sat directly between their jobs; two, it served oven-fresh muffins for a dollar; and three, it was built almost entirely out of glass, perfect for people-watching in the middle of the day.

"You need a nickname, chica. How about Mustang?" Nikki said.

"Why Mustang?" asked Arnelle.

"Because you ride like a Mustang...smooth, classy, and fast," Nikki told her through sips of steaming vending-machine black coffee. The best kind. She liked everything black, except her women and her sunglasses.

"Something about the way my skin looks against yours, you know?" she had told Arnelle on their first date several weeks before. "I don't want to go out with someone as dark as I am...I'm very visual."

And you couldn't get much lighter than Arnelle, with her

jarhead-blond hair and dangerously white skin. Said she was destined to become a dyke because her father forced her into baseball hats from birth to protect her from The Cancer. The Cancer that attached itself to almost every member on both sides of her family. Cousin Betty even lost part of her nose to it. Gramps lived with patches of circular pink scar tissue dotting his face and neck like a perverse board game.

"A primer-gray Mustang with a sagging tailpipe and strange noises when I start up on cold mornings, maybe." Arnelle leaned back with a crack to emphasize her point. She liked the sound of the crack, although it did nothing to relieve the stress in her lower back. Her doctor told her to stop lifting heavy boxes, but that was Arnelle's job as well as her form of meditation. The repetitive, mindless movements gave her peace. And the ladies just love the UPS garb.

"I just can't call you Arnelle. Ar-*nelle*. No, not possible." Nikki shook her head, feeling her braids tap the back of her neck. A matching set of dancing witches' brooms.

"So it's Mustang, is it?" Arnelle sighed at her ex-girlfriend, enjoying the flirtatious banter that continued even after they had decided that nothing else should.

"Unless you prefer Ponchita—" Nikki threatened with a chicken neck and a click of her pierced tongue.

"Don't pull your lingual shit on me. And why is it now, after we've already been on a few test rides, that you decide I need a nickname?" Arnelle asked.

"I didn't know you that well then," she smiled coyly, chewing on her coffee stirrer until it jutted over like a lone cactus in woodpecker territory.

"Mustang," Arnelle tested the sound of it. "All right, I like it." Mustang tucked in the front of her oversize bowling shirt— DALE stitched in rope cord along the shirt pocket—careful not to catch her Band-Aid on the buttons. Her finger still stung from that damn board. She'd been holding it up with her leg as she sanded down the edge when it fell and crushed her finger against the edge of her worktable. Bubbly black bruise under her nail. Thick, swollen knuckle. Goddamn thing.

Nikki tapped her mangled stirrer, leaving coffee periods on the pink tabletop. She stared hard behind Mustang, tapping tapping tapping. Mustang turned to identify the lucky lady when Nikki snapped up, reached just behind Mustang, and grabbed the elbow of a woman's black leather jacket.

"Can I ask you a question?" Nikki started right in.

"Sure," the woman answered casually.

"Which do you prefer for her...which name *evokes,* you know? Ar-nelle or Mustang?" Nikki used her most seductive south-of-the-border stare, the one where her eyes almost vibrated as she called up the deepest shade of brown she can muster. Looking up slightly with her head tipped to the right. Painted lips full, perfume louder than an Elton John outfit.

The woman, however, wasn't biting. She instead focused on Mustang, with her high natural cheekbones, broad but thin shoulders, clavicle peeking out shyly just above Dale's name. Muscular build. Rough hands.

"I like Mustang," she responded slowly.

Nikki switched off as quickly as she switched on. No sense fishing with filet mignon if they'd rather be baited with hamburger. "So do I. Thanks—" Nikki chopped it off at the knees.

But the woman didn't leave right away. She held out her hand to Mustang, who sat still, bewildered by the attentions of a woman just as much a dyke as she was but younger, more extreme. The silver locket chain necklace, the Asian dragon tattoo on her neck, the combat boots, the tattered jeans, the rag holding back her sticky tar-black hair. The various visible piercings. Mustang wondered if the one under her lower lip chipped away her tooth enamel.

"I'm Jazz."

"After the music or the hard drive?" Nikki asked, giving it one last go.

"After my father, who drank too much. He'd kick it back and say 'What's the jazz?' all night long. I don't know which came first—me or the saying. We didn't talk much." She let her hand drop away slowly from Mustang's.

"Well, thanks for taking our quiz," Nikki said, suddenly finding her nails utterly fascinating.

"No problem. Nice meeting you, Mustang."

Mustang nodded dumbly, feeling suddenly girlish and not liking it one damn bit. She squeezed her sore finger, reminding herself to toughen the fuck up. "Yeah…" she managed to get out through her finger throbbing and general humiliation. Not humiliation, really. Just a sense of being exposed. That's what women had always told her: She leaves them feeling exposed, vulnerable. They liked that, and Mustang was good at it. Now hear this: This Jazz person steps up and dismantles her throne in less than five minutes. A woman at least three years her junior, with enough attitude to paint a house. She felt her face redden.

"Mustang, I never seen you like this!" Nikki exclaimed after the woman left.

"Shut up about it. My finger hurts, that's all."

"Like an ache—"

"Nikki."

"OK, OK." She leaned back, raised a manicured eyebrow, and started chewing on her stirrer again.

↕

1968 mustang

Even though Stan's Cafeteria sat 15 feet from the entrance of Mustang's UPS building and even though it was her favorite place to eat, Mustang sidestepped it every day for two weeks, afraid she'd run into that Jazz person again. Deep down she knew the key to her being butch was not about the walk or the talk or the stalk (as it sometimes turned out); it was about the way she carried her pain. Swallowing instead of spewing. Spitting out her tears. Being the rock for others and the island for herself. Maintaining. She didn't want to feel as unguarded as she'd felt during those few quick sentences with Jazz.

"I miss Stan's," Nikki whined into the phone. "Blueberry muffins, Mustang—your favorite thing, next to the chicken bucket and football night at Old Yellers, you know? What up?"

"Nothing. Nothing." she checked the clock. "OK. Just meet me there at 12:45. I have a quick errand to run first." Mustang hung up, readjusted her back support, and headed into the warehouse to finish hauling a load. Get a little time to organize her thoughts. Prepare.

She threw on her flannel overcoat and left promptly at 12:30, wanting to arrive 15 minutes before Nikki in case that Jazz woman showed up again. Mustang felt a brittle, cold need to dominate her. She realized something had been taken from her, something she wanted returned.

And sure enough, five minutes later Jazz walked in. She looked around, took off her square, green-tinted sunglasses, and beelined for Mustang—only this time Mustang was ready. This youngster wasn't going to catch her off-guard again. No, sir.

She slouched in her chair, flayed her legs as her hands hung loosely off their armrests, and watched Jazz approach. She imagined pulling her in with the power of her clear, intense blue-eyed stare alone. Jazz was not in control here.

"Hey, Mustang," Jazz muttered with complete confidence,

brazenly meeting her cold stare with the patient heat of her hazel eyes. She flung her leather jacket over the back of a chair, turned it around, and sat down. "I was hoping you were a creature of habit," she smiled.

Mustang locked her stare, trying not to notice the dragon tattoo crawling up her neck or the Celtic band around her tight biceps. The tight wife-beater. The baggy brown Dickies with an army-green belt snaking around her boy hips.

"What can I do you for?" Mustang responded with enough boredom to stop a train.

"Lunch, then maybe dinner," Jazz answered, really meaning breakfast.

Mustang's response was undermined by the sudden appearance of Nikki in yet another black dress with yet another pair of knee-high striped socks to match her yellow Donald Duck braid clips. Nikki plunked down with her coffee.

"¡Hola! Lord, what a day. I thought office work was supposed to be less demeaning than retail. Fuck. And hi there, Jazz." Then, turning to Mustang, "Your errand?"

And again Mustang crumbled. But at least she contained the wreckage this time.

"I can only stay for a minute," Nikki continued. "My boss has turned my ass into some sort of amusement park ride. Fuck."

Mustang stopped short of leaving early too, pushing down her desire to beg off—that she was backed up at work or had to go to the bank. Jazz wasn't going to bully her out of Stan's. If anyone was leaving, it would be this little upstart.

Nikki slugged down a few Advils with her coffee, then bailed.

"So, dinner?" Jazz asked after Nikki left, her arms crossed over the back of her pink plastic chair. Mustang couldn't believe this girl's audacity.

"Won't your mother wonder where you are?"

"I'm the one wondering where she is."

Mustang flinched. "Oh, shit. I'm sorry."

"It's all good, Mustang. Doesn't really bother me anymore," Jazz said with a flash of kindness. Keeping it all in. Maintaining.

"I don't think we'll get on too well," Mustang mumbled.

"It's just dinner, no dancing." Jazz smiled.

"No." Mustang gathered up her coat.

"Tough girl like you afraid of little ol' me?"

"I'm gone," Mustang grunted. Every muscle in her body tensed up. She needed to hit the bag hard tonight. The nerve of this creature.

Mustang stomped out, hoping deep breaths and sheer will would drain the red from her face. She tried to pace herself but realized it was obvious—she was running away from some scrawny little punk named Jazz, for chrissake. Two inches shorter than her. Obviously little to do with her free time except concoct new ways to scar herself for attention. She did look like she worked out, though. Smooth sailing rope twining around bone. Sculpted, thin musculature.

"Fuck," Mustang grumbled. She did an about-face, sucked in a tankful of air, and reentered Stan's. Jazz was zipping up her jacket, her back to Mustang, who stole up behind her and hissed, "Meet me here at 8:30. I'm taking *you* out. I'll get you home when I think the date's over."

"Sure." Jazz slid the word out casually, but Mustang saw her neck tense.

Neither one turned around as Mustang walked away. She felt elated but somewhat ridiculous, as if Jazz's controlled response had blown the feeling of the maneuver. If she had turned soft or pushed her away, Mustang could have ended this whole thing and walked away feeling some sense of power.

Instead she couldn't help finding the whole scene comic—an exaggeration of the old-school butch mentality. She felt vulnerable, idiotic.

↕

Jazz walked home, her featherlight binoculars tucked inside the black lining of her jacket. She'd waited every Monday, as instructed, to catch Mustang walking into Stan's. She almost didn't watch today, but something about Mustang drew her in. The struggle, perhaps. Not their struggle, but Mustang's. Jazz's world sailed along the sharp black edge of the fringe, where butch dykes found each other and had sex like cats fighting for territory. She'd moved beyond the allure of the passive femme long ago. But Mustang was different, new to these feelings. A stone-cold virgin.

↕

"So now you're dating her, huh?" Nikki cooed into the phone.

"Nikki, shut up about it, for chrissake. Damn bitch," Mustang swore, as she tried to pop open her beer can without injuring her finger or dropping the phone. Her back hurt. She had a headache. And this fucking can.

"That's just what I think. Now, I have a right to ex-*press* myself, you know?"

"Always—"

"So where are you taking her?" Nikki pried.

"I dunno…" She bumped the fridge door shut with her hip and dropped into the couch, beer foaming and head pounding. "Maybe we'll go for a beer at Margaret's—"

"Ugh! That place is so beat-down, Mustang. Come on, go

somewhere befitting your new name. Someplace edgy." Nikki popped her gum.

"Someplace edgy?" Mustang sat back, waiting for an end-less stream of overexplanation to drift through the phone.

"Yeah, chica. Ed-gy. Where the lesbians don't all drive trucks and refuse to wax. There must be five clubs near you, and yet you fly back to where you're safe. Margaret's. No more of that, please. Let's see where you can go to impress her...because she is hot, you know? Someplace exciting."

"Mustangs are reliable and cool, not hot and exciting."

"Only if they haven't gotten a new paint job in for-*ever*! You've been moaning to me since I met you that you're un-sat-is-fied. Something's not right. You feel in a rut, right? Isn't that what you said? When did you say that—hold on, I have it writ-ten down. I actually wrote that down in my journal because it made such an impression on me, you know? You said...hold on—" and she dropped the phone.

Mustang heard the cat scream under Nikki's foot as she frantically searched the place.

"Here," Nikki panted. "You said, and I quote, 'I feel in a rut, like I want to be more but don't know what I'm doing.' A direct quote, ma'am." Nikki popped her gum proudly.

"All of this is some way to get me to move my plans to someplace hipper?"

"Yes. You need to go to Fire on Central near that tranny place. Grab some coffee at Stan's first, then walk over. It's only 10 blocks away. That'll stall things. Give you time to get there around 9:30 or 10. When it gets up and going!"

Mustang clanged her empty beer on the coffee table, the same one her father had given her when she left home 10 years ago. She looked over at her flannel coat: the one she'd bought in college. Her boots had been resoled three times. She gave each of her successive goldfish the same name: Titanic the first, the second, and the third. Rut.

"OK. I'll do it. I have to go now." Mustang's iron sides shook anxiously.

"Fabulous! What are you going to wear?"

"For fuck's sake, Nikki," and she hung up. What was she going to wear? What she always…

What was she going to wear? Shit…

↕

Jazz didn't have that problem; only two of her shirts were clean, and one belonged to an ex-girlfriend. Bad luck. So she threw on her orange T-shirt with the red sleeves, tucked it into her black jeans held up by her army belt, slipped on her boots, and gargled. She'd have brushed except she ran out that morning. She'd have flossed except…she never flossed.

At her living room window Jazz popped open her binoculars and spied down to Stan's glass front. No sign of Mustang. She'd been told Mustang always showed up early to get the upper hand on her ladies. If she wanted to grab her, she had to move fast. That was the deal: "You just have to grab her and show her who's boss. Then I'll pay you," the message said. Jazz had first tossed it off as some freak fuckin' with queer-escort ads, but something about it was intriguing. The instructions were simple: Come to Stan's on Monday at 12:30 and wait to be summoned.

Jazz had been running her ad for three months now, partly as a way to earn extra cash and partly as a means to interesting queer encounters: "Young tough girl willing to show other tough girls the new way to sexual freedom. Outcalls only." Mustang had proved to be her most interesting meeting, especially since Mustang hadn't requested it herself.

8:15 P.M. *I should just drag her into the alley when she shows up,* Jazz thought. *Oh, I don't know, maybe I'll wait. The deal was I had to pin her, but no specific time frame was set up. I've waited over two fucking weeks for her just to show for lunch again, what's another couple of hours?*

Truth was, Jazz enjoyed the wait, the squirm. In her world dykes circled each other and played ego games, but they all knew the end result. Here, Mustang had no choice but to play. And better yet, she seemed unclear about what ending she wanted even if she did win. You can't really play unless you want to win what everyone agrees is the prize.

Jazz picked up her binoculars again. There was Mustang— 10 minutes early, as usual. She looked good.

↕

Inside Stan's, Mustang grabbed a cup of black coffee, resisting the urge to snag a pinch of Red Man like her big brothers had showed her. She sat back, examining her reflection nonchalantly in the window. She admired the new tight black turtleneck Nikki had bought her for Christmas, her usual hiking boots, and her favorite Levi's. One thing at a time.

Jazz watched her, smiling from above. She plotted. Planned on having a little fun with this one. Fucking tough girl, my ass, she laughed. She called down to Stan's and had Mustang paged. Told her to meet her at the coffee shop around the corner, since Stan's closed at 9 and she was running late.

The pompadoured cashier put down his copy of *American Psycho* and delivered the message to Mustang. She thanked him through gritted teeth. Mustang hated tardiness; it undermined her. She should not be made to wait.

But wait she did. It was almost 9 by the time Jazz pushed open the green wooden door of Beans. Mustang had her coat on, ready to bail.

"Going somewhere?" Jazz's eyes sparkled under the flashing Christmas lights twinkling in syncopation around the edges of the scalloped ceiling.

"Home. I don't wait on dates," Mustang said, pushing in her chair.

"I'm sorry. Wait, wait—" Jazz ran behind Mustang. "Stay, please. I'm sorry. I couldn't decide what to wear."

"Liar."

Jazz shrugged. Mustang smiled back. "All right, I'll stay."

"Good." Jazz zipped her jacket. "Where are you taking me?"

"Fire."

"Cool." Jazz wondered if Mustang had ever been there or whether she was trying to impress. She looked nice in her turtleneck, showing off a body Jazz hadn't thought she had. Firm breasts, wide shoulders, flat stomach. Her skin as white and soft as a Swiss toddler's.

"We're padding it?" Jazz asked.

Padding it? Oh. "Do you live nearby?"

"Right over there," Jazz said, pointing to the brownstone in front of them.

"And you were still half an hour late?"

"I'm sorry." Jazz smiled.

"Listen, is this some sort of game for you? Topping the top or something?"

"Relax, Mustang. It's not about that—"

"I think it is. I really like to get to know people, and I can't know you with this butch facade you wear like armor."

"Facade? This is just who I am—" Jazz sputtered.

"Yes, as long as you're in control."

"You're projecting."

"Yes," Mustang smiled, finally feeling the tension break, "I guess I am."

Jazz laughed. "Ding! Ding! End of round 1. Come on, let's go."

They stepped into Fire after a 10-minute walk dotted with talk about the WNBA and Dinah Shore—the circuit party, not the tournament. Jazz had never been there, afraid of power-suit dykes with manicures. Mustang told her it wasn't that bad—she'd met Nikki there, after all.

"Opposites attract," Mustang said.

"But alikes endure," Jazz countered.

Fire breathed with the pulsing moves of about 75 women and maybe half a dozen men. The crowd ranged between 21 and 35 years old, with a few fake ID-ers downing cosmopolitans on the dance floor and a few mamas poking limes into their Coronas along the wall: DIE, KITTY, DIE! T-shirts, snowboard pants, caps, piercings, pink yellow green red hair, vinyl, hair spray, tattoos, sweatbands, long-john shirts, Dickies.

Mustang didn't feel out of place, just nervous—the way she always felt around new crowds, new people. Bordering on anxiety. She ordered a vodka gimlet. Jazz ordered a Jack and Coke.

The bartender nodded. "Hey, Jazz. Anything new?"

"Yeah, this is Mustang. Mustang, this is Julie."

"Hey, Mustang," Julie nodded, before being called away to fix more drinks for a laughing group of skater chicks who'd just moved up beside Jazz.

"Jazz!" one of the skaters cried, reaching out to give her a hug.

"Well, hi, Crystal. What are you doing?" Jazz laughed.

"Did you hear they're training dogs to sniff out X in airports? Just X—nothin' else. No good, Jazz. Fuckin' no good." Her friends pulled her away.

"Feisty," Mustang said above the pounding music.

"That's the word."

Mustang was surprised to find herself looking at Jazz and wondering if she herself hadn't been game-playing her entire adult life. Maybe she was so desperate to find some type of rules to guide her in the maze of homosexual dating that she took on the "male" role, the most comfortable spot for her. But in doing so, perhaps she ruled out the possibility of letting different types of women into her life. As if she subdivided her gender, then forced it into the same narrow roles played out by housewives and businessmen throughout the decades. Maybe it would be comforting to date someone similar. Someone who understood.

Jazz watched Mustang from the corner of her eye and mistook her mental wanderings for detachment. "If you don't like this place, there's this groovy dive I know a few blocks away. Quieter. You can smoke inside."

"What? Oh, no, I'm good. I like this place. And I don't smoke."

"No? Good. I only smoke when my dates do. It's the closet codependent in me."

Jazz wanted to know more about her. Mustang wasn't afraid or shallow or unwilling to change—all the things Jazz had assumed by her reaction the first time they met. Of course, Jazz knew she'd turned on the control stare pretty strong. She knew Nikki was the woman who'd ordered her services, and Jazz had wanted to strut her abilities for the client, even if that meant emasculating Mustang. In an odd way, Mustang calmed Jazz. She wasn't into the typical butch attitude—the smoking and leering and inflexibility. Mustang watched everyone with interest, not judgment.

"Wanna dance?" Mustang asked.

"I usually don't."

"Good, that makes us even. I usually don't wear turtle-necks or go to Fire or tell people what it is I usually don't do." Mustang walked to the edge of the dance floor, where a small space sat open in the vibrating lights and sound. Jazz reluctant-ly followed after downing the rest of her drink. The bartender watched in amazement as Jazz took to the floor.

"Do you usually kiss on the first date?" Jazz asked, trying to bring attention away from her awkward dance moves.

"I usually start kissing during the first date…"

"And finish?"

"The next morning."

"Me too." Jazz admired the way Mustang danced—under-stated and stylish, another surprise. She didn't know it, but Mustang was also surprising herself. She was usually more of a watcher than a dancer but had decided to break out of a few molds tonight.

"But tonight's different." Mustang met Jazz's heated stare.

"I agree, Mustang. I agree."

Mustang danced in close to Jazz and kissed her firmly, assertively. Jazz was taken by surprise but recovered quickly. She kissed her back passionately, feeling Mustang deep in the spaces inside her.

"First and last for tonight," Mustang told Jazz as they separated.

"What about tomorrow night?"

"Maybe two kisses…" Then Mustang grabbed Jazz's hand and pulled her up to the balcony. "I want to smoke. OK, some-times I smoke—but only when I drink. Old habits die hard."

They hung out casually at the edge of the balcony, shar-ing a cigarette Mustang bummed on the way up the stairs. Jazz put her arm around Mustang as they watched the danc-ing below. Rather than recoil and try to one-up her date,

Mustang moved closer and allowed herself to feel comfortable. Jazz felt light-headed.

"Let's go."

"I have some beer at home..." Jazz started.

"Hmm..." Mustang looked over, knowing full well, despite her earlier remarks, that the night wouldn't be ending for at least another day or two. But she didn't want to repeat her typical four-step dance: meeting, wooing, fucking, leaving. "Just like the Texas two-step, because you always end up where you start," she'd told Nikki.

Mustang wanted this one to last a while. Something about the way Jazz smelled, like soap and cinnamon; something about the connection she felt, as if things didn't need to be talked about. Mustang wondered how Jazz's skin felt, if it was as soft as her lips, as firm as her arms, and as hot as the intensity in her eyes.

"We can talk," Jazz said.

"Don't use that old line on me. I don't want to talk, and neither do you. Let's go."

Jazz stepped back in shock, then allowed Mustang to guide her to the exit.

When they stepped into Jazz's messy studio 10 minutes later, Jazz frantically yanked up dirty laundry, thinking how odd it was that she cared. Usually she felt her place added to her bad-girl image, but now it just felt unkempt.

"I think I have a cat in here somewhere," she mumbled.

Jazz popped open a couple of beers and dumped the rest of her Chee-tos into a clean salad bowl. *Cheese breath?* she thought. *No. That's no good.* She rooted through her cabinets, then remembered a bag of baby carrots left to die in the vegetable bin. Only three days old. Perfect.

"Here, nourishment," she said, plunking down the carrots and beer.

Mustang grinned, then pulled Jazz to her. She walked back-ward into the living room wall, letting Jazz push her hands up and back against its brick face. Jazz pushed her hips into Mustang's, moving slowly as if finding the middle point of two swirling cur-rents. She kissed her softly, pausing to look into her eyes.

"This is peculiar," Mustang drawled, looking at her pinned hands.

"Good?"

"Very."

Jazz released Mustang's hands but left her own pressed against the brick wall on either side of Mustang's head. Mustang moved her rough hands over Jazz's breasts. She watched Jazz intently, circling each hard nipple through her T-shirt. Mustang stopped with her fingertips on both nipples and gently twisted. Jazz moaned.

"I like it rough," she said.

"Go on." Mustang smiled sarcastically.

She watched Jazz's eyes wince then close as she pinched and twisted her nipples, feeling herself get wetter with each turn, each groan. Jazz opened her eyes, their fire burning into Mustang.

They kissed again, Jazz still bracing against the brick. Mustang released her nipples. She felt Jazz flinch as the blood flowed back into them, causing an echo of pain. She pulled Jazz's T-shirt from her belt and worked her hands up her smooth, hard sides. She looked down at Jazz's belly, now fully exposed under her low-slung Dickies. Hairless, ripped, tanned.

"Surfer?"

"Snowboarder."

Jazz leaned in and sucked on Mustang's lower lip, feeling her warm hands sliding closer to her sensitive nipples. Wanting to feel her mouth there. Wanting to feel the heat inside her. Wanting Mustang to feel her also.

Mustang felt Jazz's piercing on her own lip. *That's going to be amazing,* she thought, anticipating the rest of the night. She wanted Jazz to go down on her. Usually she was content to give pleasure, but tonight she felt like being torn into.

"What are you thinkin'?" Mustang asked.

"I'm wondering how wet you are."

Mustang spread her legs apart and undid the button on her jeans. She took Jazz's hand from the brick wall and guided it down. Jazz kissed her, punching her tongue deeper into Mustang's sweet mouth as she pushed her hand into the heat. Mustang leaned back, kissing Jazz hard in return. Mustang bit on Jazz's lip and pulled her hips closer.

Jazz pushed her middle finger into Mustang's wet opening, turning it in teasing circles until Mustang grabbed her wrist. "I want to feel your hand. Go deeper."

Jazz sucked on Mustang's neck, smelling traces of her cologne. Drakkar. She dipped her tongue in and around her ear, nibbling on her earlobe while her finger pushed in and out of Mustang's wetness.

"I need more," Mustang said, no longer caring how "bottom" she sounded. Mustang wanted to be taken.

Jazz led her to the recliner, threw off an old newspaper, and sat her down.

"Take off your pants," Jazz commanded.

"No—you do it."

Jazz grinned. She knelt before Mustang and gingerly pulled off her pants. They both wore boxers.

"At least mine are plaid," Jazz laughed.

Mustang took off her turtleneck to reveal a perfectly white body dotted with tiny brown freckles and high, pink nipples.

She had a light-blond hairline leading to where Jazz plunged her hand again, this time putting more force behind it. Probing deeper with fucking motions, hitting the small space tucked up inside. The soft, spongy spot. The spot that made Mustang clench and suck in her breath.

"Yeah…"

"I need to taste you," Jazz whispered.

"No…"

"I want to push my tongue inside you. I want to make you come."

Jazz kissed Mustang's belly. Mustang tried to stop her by grabbing her hair, but it was too short, nothing to grab onto. Jazz smiled and dipped her tongue into Mustang's short blond hairs, finding the hard place. She rammed her fingers in deeper, three bunched together, and sucked on her clit, feeling Mustang on her lips and chin.

Just before Mustang was about to explode, Jazz put her index finger inside and circled around her G spot. She pulled her tongue back and applied the gentlest pressure. Barely a touch. Mustang tightened up to feel more; she raised her hips and tried forcing Jazz's mouth onto her. But Jazz was too strong. She held her ground with feathery touches until Mustang started breathing fast and letting out small, completely unself-conscious moans.

"Oh…fuck…Oh, my God…Jazz…God…oh…"

Then she came in three waves, each with their own style. The first felt fast and hard; the second was slower, starting in the middle of the first; and the third was less intense but deeper. The third one came…from inside. Jazz felt her open up.

"How far have you gone with this?"

This? "Ah…this far," Mustang said, a red blanket covering her pale chest and neck. Her eyes clearing. Her cunt still throbbing.

"I want to feel you come before you do—"

trixi

"What?"

"Let me fist you."

"Oh, God, no." Mustang started to move back, but Jazz held her shoulder down.

"Relax. Trust me. You know I know what I'm doing. And if I know me, then I know you, and I know you want this now."

Mustang's mind reeled…yes, she did want that. She wanted as much as she could get.

Jazz brought her fingers to a point and pushed inside Mustang, trying not to concentrate on how hot she, herself, felt. Focus on Mustang. She grabbed her by the throat and pushed her back, applying gentle pressure to hold her still. Their eyes locked.

Jazz slid inside slowly, spreading the way. Mustang released. She shut her eyes, and Jazz let go of her throat. She pulled back slightly to ball her hand up, still keeping it inside. Jazz tucked her thumb under her fingers, put her left hand under Mustang's ass, and slowly slowly slowly pushed in. Powerful but soft pressure.

Mustang opened her eyes and breathed heavily. Concentrating. Was this too much? Could this happen? The pain was intense, but it felt so good. So strong.

Then Jazz felt the door open, and she fell into Mustang. Into a place where one small movement of her fist could send Mustang into spasms of repeat orgasms. She felt the tender spots all around her hand, then touched the upper wall with a light repeat thrust until Mustang started moaning loudly. She was losing control.

Her moans increased to cries, wild tantric cries. Mustang managed to keep her hips still, grabbing onto Jazz's shoulder for support. Bruising her.

"You're all I feel," she moaned.

106

Jazz increased her fuck pressure as Mustang's entire body tensed. Her face reddened, and she screamed out with the waves that took over her body. Jazz felt her tighten around her fist, deep in a flood of liquid heat.

"Relax again, honey," Jazz told her.

Mustang took a deep breath while Jazz shifted her hand out gently. Her body jolted at the last step, right as her fist dropped out. Jazz kissed her softly.

"Lord," Mustang sighed.

They lay there kissing tenderly for a few minutes until Mustang regained her senses. "We're not done, girl," she said as she struggled up and grabbed her jeans. "You can't play the Solo Top with me."

"Good," Jazz smiled.

They grabbed their beers and sauntered over a few feet to the futon. Mustang felt dizzy but didn't say anything. Jazz felt overwhelmed by desire but didn't have to say anything.

↕

Nikki met Jazz at Beans the following Monday, check in hand.

"*Hola,* Jazz! Did you complete your mission? Mustang won't tell—she's quite cavalier, you know." Nikki applied some cherry lip gloss, using the back of a spoon as a mirror.

"Keep your money," Jazz said in a low voice.

"No success? Was Mustang too macho for you?"

"Yeah, that's it." Jazz grinned. She flipped her chair back around, tugged on her jacket, and left to join Mustang back at her place…but first she decided to stop by Stan's and pick up a few blueberry muffins.

Bridal Party

Anne Seale

Debs and Kirsten are getting married this afternoon, and they've asked my lover, Selah, to be maid of honor. She's been in the bathroom for 40 minutes trying to get her hair to fluff up around a floral headpiece. Every so often I hear her cuss.

I'm dressed and standing in the kitchen eating a bologna sandwich. Selah has ordered me not to sit down because it would make creases in my tuxedo trousers that were designed for a man with no butt. (He didn't have 44D breasts either.)

I'm not in the wedding, but Selah insisted I rent a tux. She said it would look funny, her in a fancy long gown and me in my chinos. I protested, but she wore me down.

Debs and Selah were once lovers. They parted several years ago and have been best friends ever since, something I've never been able to pull off. Selah, therefore, has been very involved in the nuptial plans, which is good because if she sticks with me, she'll never have a wedding of her own. I don't make commitments.

Selah runs into the kitchen, turns her back, and says to zip her up before I leave to pick up Kirsten. I've been assigned the task of driving Kirsten to the church to keep Debs from seeing her in her gown before the ceremony. Debs, in turn, is coming to pick up Selah a little later, and they are stopping on the way for ice cream and half-and-half for the reception coffee.

As I pull on the zipper, it keeps catching in the lacy fabric. Finally I give a great tug, and it closes, but a two-inch length of purple thread now hangs from one of the snags. I try to break it off, but it won't break. To distract Selah, I say "Hey, your hair looks great!" as I fumble in the tight tux pocket for my key-ring jackknife. She grunts and heads back to the bathroom, the thread trailing in her wake. I decide to let it go (she's stressed enough).

Since the Saturday traffic is light, I'm a little early getting to Kirsten's mother's suburban home. Kirsten isn't ready, so I have to sit and chat with her mom like a high school kid picking up a date for the prom. She offers me coffee, but I say no. All I need is a brown stain on my starched white shelf.

Just when I'm wondering what time it's getting to be, Kirsten floats down the stairs. I catch my breath. She's gorgeous in a cloud of net over pure white satin. Her red hair curls around a halo of tiny flowers and ribbons. I've always liked red hair. For a moment, I wish I were that high school kid.

Kirsten's mother rushes to gather her train, and after a great deal of arranging we get her settled on the bench seat of my S-10. I can't see the rearview mirror on the passenger side for all the skirt.

"Don't be late, Mama," Kirsten tells her.

"Don't you worry, honey, I'll be there in that front pew when you walk down the aisle." She kisses Kirsten through the open window. "And Nana will be there with me, and Aunt Bern and Uncle Jack."

It makes me wonder who from my family would come if I

were to marry Selah—or anyone, goddess forbid. My cousin
Jimmy might show up—I've had suspicions about him for years.

"Nervous?" I ask Kirsten as I back out the driveway.

"A little," she says. "I hate being the center of attention."

"What I meant is, aren't you nervous about promising to
stay with someone the rest of your life? Through sickness and
poverty and all that? I'd be petrified."

"You're right," she says softly. "It's a big step to take."

I mentally kick myself. What am I doing, frightening the
poor woman with my paranoid feelings about commitment? I
change the subject. "Hey, that Debs! Ain't she a great gal?"

"She's wonderful. How long have you known her, Tammy?"

"As long as I've known Selah, about eight years, I guess.
They were already broke up by then."

"Oh."

We ride in silence for a few miles; then Kirsten says, "Do
you by any chance know why they broke up, Selah and Debs?"

"No, I don't. Why?"

"Oh, no reason."

After a couple more blocks, she says, "Was Debs faithful
to Selah, do you know, when they were together?"

We're in the city now, stopped at a red light. I look at her.
"Of course she was. Selah never told me she wasn't, at least.
What's this all about, Kirsten? Do you think Debs is running
around on you?"

"No, no," she says, patting my arm with a white-gloved
hand. "She's just gone a lot, that's all. Like she says, she's a very
busy woman. But I never really thought...till lately..." She
laughs a self-conscious little laugh. "Oh, it's nothing, Tammy.
Forget it. Wedding-day jitters."

I can't stop looking at her. I've seen Kirsten a lot in the
months she and Debs have been going together, and I've always

considered her nice-looking. Today, however, seeing her in that, well, virginal wedding gown, I just want to lean over and...

A car behind me honks its brains out, and I see the light has turned green. I cross the intersection, pull into the church lot, and park next to Debs's Honda. After delivering Kirsten to something called a "Bride's Room" off the church lobby and suppressing the urge to kiss her goodbye, I go off in search of Selah.

It's still 45 minutes until the ceremony, but a few people are already seated in the pews when I peek in. A woman from our euchre club spies me and runs over, and I have to listen to a description of her wedding—she calls it a "union"—many years ago. She provides me with detailed descriptions of her gown, her attendants' gowns, and all the flower arrangements. When I ask about her spouse, it turns out the union didn't last much longer than the flowers. I excuse myself and take the stairs to the basement, where the reception is going to be. Maybe Selah is helping set up.

No one is in sight, but there are lots of folding tables covered with pink plastic, one of which holds a four-tiered wedding cake with a nauseatingly heterosexual bride and groom standing stiffly on top. Jeez! I look around to make sure I'm alone, then carefully lift them off, placing the gardenia from my lapel over the bare spot. Much better!

Now, what to do with Mr. and Mrs. Hetero? There's no wastebasket in sight, so I cross to a swinging door marked KITCHEN. As I raise my hand to push it open, I hear a low husky voice from inside that I recognize as Debs's. The voice is saying, "Oh, baby, I want you so much." I freeze.

Kirsten was right—Debs is messing around with another woman! Since Kirsten shared her suspicions with me, I feel I owe it to her to find out for sure. It may save her from making a big mistake today. I crack the door and peek in.

There's a woman standing between Debs and me who is wearing a dress, a long purple dress. I can't see her head because of protruding cupboards, but I'd know that zipper anywhere. There are snags in the lace alongside of it, right where I snagged them, and the two-inch purple thread is still hanging.

Debs's left hand reaches around and begins pulling the zipper down. It doesn't catch even once. I watch transfixed as the dress opens and falls to the floor. The hand pushes the bra strap off the right shoulder, then moves over and does the same to the left. I can't help but wonder what the other hand is doing. Debs's mouth enters my vision as it kisses its way down the side of the neck and in the general direction of what must be Selah's nipples.

I draw back, let the door close, and tiptoe back through the room and up the stairs, ditching the cake-top couple on the landing. When I reach the top, I lean against the wall, feeling dizzy. What was it Kirsten had told me? "I never really thought...till lately...." I try to think if Selah's patterns have changed recently. Has she been spending more time with Debs than usual? Well, yes, but they've been working on wedding preparations...haven't they? Oh, what a fool I've been!

I have to tell Kirsten. But how can I tell her that it's my own Selah that Debs has been messing around with? How mortifying! But if I don't tell her, she'll go ahead and marry the dirty two-timer. I find the Bride's Room again and, after hesitating a long time, knock.

"Who is it?" It's Kristen's voice.

"It's Tammy. Can I come in?"

After a moment a latch turns, and the door opens. After I enter, Kirsten quickly shuts and locks it again. "Tammy, thank goodness. Where's Selah? She was supposed to meet me here a long time ago."

bridal party

"Selah? She's...uh ...downstairs."

"Downstairs? What's she doing there? She's supposed to be here with me."

"Kirsten, honey, why don't you sit down?" I steer her to a gold brocade sofa and sit beside her, taking her white-gloved hand in mine. She looks so scared and vulnerable, I can hardly say it. "I'm afraid you were right, Kirsten; Debs does have someone else. I...I saw them."

Kirsten turns white. "You saw them? Debs and another woman? Who is it?"

When push comes to shove, I can't do it. "Her back was to me," I say. It's not a lie.

Kirsten bursts into sobs. "I knew it! I knew Debs had someone else. How could I ever have believed her? Oh, Tammy, you're so lucky to have a good woman like Selah. So lucky."

"Lucky," I say, picturing in my mind what's happening down in the church kitchen right about now. I see Debs and Selah writhing all over the purple dress, Debs's hands still very busy.

Kirsten rants on. "How could Debs do this to me? I thought we were happy together. I thought she loved me. And all the time she was running around with this...this hussy. She doesn't want me. Nobody wants me!"

I wipe a drip from her chin with my thumb. "Anybody who doesn't want you is brain-dead."

She takes my hand and presses the palm to her mouth. I feel her lips move against it as she says, "Do you want me, Tammy?"

She raises her face to mine and stops an inch away from my lips, staring into my eyes, daring me to close the gap. Her brazen manner starkly contrasts with the implied innocence of the gown. Her cheeks are flushed, and arrested tears sparkle in her eyes.

Without thinking, I meet the dare—I lower my lips and

use them to open hers. Our tongues meet and communicate as we shift until I am flat on the cushions. The wedding dress whispers as her body moves on mine.

I don't realize she has opened my fly until I feel a hand slip in and begin softly stroking. The seams on the fingers of the glove add a nubby dimension to the caress. My hands move to her breasts and squeeze them through the silky bodice. Her nipples stiffen against my palms. Everything I own stiffens in response.

Kirsten's lips suddenly abandon mine, leaving me gasping. She pushes herself up and unhooks my suspenders and everything else that's in her way. I feel a wetness on my exposed middle as she eases down, tracing my nakedness with her tongue until she finally gets where she wants to be. A medley of soft curls, ribbons, and silky veil plays on my thighs as she moves her head in concert with the tongue.

White-gloved hands shoot up, aiming for my breasts. I waylay the hands and pull the gloves off, crushing them against my nose and breathing through them. They smell hot and earthy. The now-bare fingers expertly unbutton my shirt and push under the cups of my bra, quickly scaling the heights and celebrating the summits.

My lower body begins moving, gliding against satin, and I find myself groaning. In case anyone is near, I stuff the gloves into my mouth and bite down, but my delighted tongue begins moving against their roughness, and instead of being muffled my groans increase in volume.

The mouth that has been working me begins to move in for the kill. "Not yet," I mumble around the fingers of the gloves, wanting the excruciatingly blissful anticipation to last forever. I am trying to pull away when the giant breakers hit. Tsunami! Kirsten's tongue keeps moving until the last tiny wave has ebbed.

She emerges grinning from the deeps, halo askew. "My turn," she says.

I tear the gloves from my mouth and fling them across the room. Pushing Kirsten back, I prop her against the sofa's arm, displacing the voluminous skirts until I find damp lacy panties. I don't remove them right away but use them to tease. I run my finger along the elastic, blow on the dampness, pull the crotch aside for a quick touch now and then, letting it snap back.

Kirsten arches her back, thrusting her mound up. "Tammy, please," she whispers.

I'm as ready as she is. Pulling the panties down, I dive into her slippery eelness. As I thrust with my tongue, Kirsten leans over, pulls up the back of my shirt, and rakes her nails across my back. I move my hand down to my own wetness and pace myself to explode when she does. Her scream is loud enough to be heard on the next block.

Wondering how long until someone comes to the door, I don the tux in one eighth the time it took me this morning while Kirsten slips on the panties, smooths her skirts, and retrieves the gloves. "Tammy," she says, "you won't tell Debs, will you?"

I freeze in the middle of tying my tie. "You aren't still going to marry her, are you?"

"I don't know. I need to talk with her."

I can't believe it. "What was all this about, then?" I indicate the sofa, the scene of the crime.

"Guess I was…vulnerable."

"Vulnerable." I echo. "Yeah, guess I was vulnerable too." I unlock the door and leave, passing without a word the dozen or so who are gathered in the hall searching for the source of a scream.

I drive home, wondering where I'll go after I change and pack. As I cross the living room, Selah calls from the kitchen, "Is that you, Tammy?"

I look in and stare. She's wearing jeans and a T-shirt and is mixing something that looks like it's going to be meatloaf. "How'd you get home so fast?" I say.

"What do you mean? I never left home. Didn't Debs tell you what happened?"

"I didn't see Debs. Well, I saw her, but...where's the purple dress?"

"I took it off and threw it at her. Told her to let her paramour stand up for her—I wasn't going to have any part in that charade of a wedding!" She gives the meatloaf a good kneading.

"She told you she was having an affair?"

"Yes, she did, when she came to pick me up. There was a woman waiting for us in the car, and I asked who she was. 'That's my new girlfriend,' Debs told me. 'Your what?' I said. 'Just a little something on the side,' she said. Then she had the nerve to tell me, 'You should know better than anybody that one woman at a time isn't enough for me.'" Selah wipes at an angry tear, smearing ketchup on her cheek. "It brought back all the hurt and humiliation I felt when we were together and I found out she was cheating."

"Debs cheated on you? You never told me."

"I was ashamed. I blamed the breakup on myself. Debs said it was my fault, that I was a cold woman."

"Well, you're not!" I say indignantly.

Selah washes and dries her hands and cheek and crosses to me, putting her arms around me. "Thank you, Tammy," she whispers. "I needed that."

"Wait a minute, you took your dress off in front of Debs?" I say jealously, in spite of what I just bared to Kirsten.

"Right in this room! I threw it at her, like I said. She grabbed it and left."

"What a jerk!" I say.

Selah backs up and gives me a serious look. "You'd never do that to me, would you, Tammy? Cheat on me?"

"Absolutely not!" I say. "I promise to be true from this day forward."

She hugs me again, then says, "My goodness, honey, you look sexy in that tux! Wanna get married?"

"If we do, will you wear white?"

She's surprised at my answer. "Well, sure, if you like."

"Anytime, then."

She backs up and stares, not knowing whether to take me seriously. Finally, she goes back to her meatloaf. "We'll talk about it," she says. "So did Debs and Kirsten get married or not?"

"I have no idea. I didn't want to be there without you," I tell her and go to take off the tux, hoping Kirsten's fingernails had not drawn blood.

SEAL Team Bravo

Thomas S. Roche

*I*nsertion was accomplished at 0500. Witgenstein, elected leader by her comrades, led the crawl under cover of half-darkness as dawn cracked an egg above the stinking morass of the Florida swamp. The Mud Bath, everyone called the swamp in question—and as for the sergeant, everybody called her Witty.

At age 29 Monica Witgenstein, Master Sergeant, U.S. Marines, held a black belt in judo; she could field-strip an M-16 faster than anyone in the Western hemisphere and shoot the fruit out of Carmen Miranda's hat at 1,500 yards. Witty was the oldest among them save Eve Singer, the 30-year-old Navy lieutenant who had a hopeless crush on her.

Singer found it beautiful, the way Witty moved in the darkness, swathed in the stink of the swamp, testing each step ahead for enemy booby traps, all focus and fire as she slid through the gloom, raising a silent hand to wave on her compatriots behind her.

There was Singer herself, former Olympic swimmer and second in command; Missy Tompkins, Demolitions; Antonia Bresler, satellite uplink expert; Liz Garcia, who had busted the record for the obstacle course by a full three seconds; and pool shark Jane Palovitch, who took endless shit being called "hell of a bitch," even though she was the most easygoing (as long as she wasn't playing pool).

They were SEAL Team Bravo of the first all-female Navy SEAL class: the Pentagon's solution to rising public pressure when the fruit salad realized that the frat boys they'd signed up to protect the sanctity of this country's borders and interests didn't want to share their toys with icky girls. Singer, Witgenstein, and the others had been picked from hundreds at the tops of their respective callings.

SEAL Team Commander Witgenstein paused in a crouch at the edge of the fetid river. There in the middle of the sluggish green water was a rusted-out old Caddy, a bright yellow beach ball duct-taped to its roof. The Caddy was about 1,500 yards downriver, inaccessible from the shore because the cover of swamp grass and cypress petered out a hundred yards down. Walking on the exposed shore would be asking to get taken out by a sniper. Retrieval of the beach ball (ostensibly a nuclear warhead from a crashed B-2) would have to be achieved by water. While they were all expert swimmers, there was only one former Olympian among them: Singer.

Witty chewed on a smokeless cheroot, the kind you order from a catalog for psycho survivalists who don't want ATF helicopters to spot them hiding in the hills with their stockpiles of AK-47s and kilos of Mother Nature. Witty took the cheroot out of her mouth, spat on the ground, and pressed the throat-mike against her jugular. Singer eyed the way she held that mike against her taut flesh. Damn, that throat was kissable.

"Target has been spotted," muttered Witgenstein. "Stay alert for enemy snipers. Retrieving by covert river assault. Singer, it's your show now."

"Aye, aye, Commander," said Singer, blood pumping as she slipped off her pack and unslung her air rifle. Taking the extra dagger from her belt and putting it between her teeth, she crawled forward, belly against the ground. Singer slithered into the water like a sea snake, disappearing under the murky, slime-covered surface as the dawn sunlight lit it up. Witty chewed on her cigar, watching the trail of little ripples as Singer broke the surface every hundred feet.

"Almost there..." Witty muttered, her pulse pounding. Singer came up close to the edge of the little island, right where the Caddy stuck into the swamp. Waterproof binocs held against her eyes, she scanned the area for enemy personnel—snipers, patrol boats—and, finding none, crawled onto the trunk of the Cadillac.

"Come on...come on, Singer..." Witty growled low in her throat, watching through her own binoculars as the lieutenant crawled from the trunk of the Cadillac onto the roof. Singer took the dagger from between her teeth and was about to sever the single strand of duct tape when Witgenstein snarled, "Jesus! Jesus!" into the throat mike. "Singer, you've got—" But by then it was too late. Floating soundlessly up on the trunk of the Caddy was the enemy, in the form of Master Chief Lazarus, that smug son of a bitch—and he already had Singer's hair gripped in his hand, her head pulled back, an eight-inch commando knife at her throat while Singer's dagger dropped harmlessly into the river. Lazarus was so close to Singer that the rumble of his voice transmitted through Witty's mike—almost unintelligible but there nonetheless—a smug "fuck you" to all of them.

Sounded like "Afternoon, Lieutenant."

It was an impossible shot; the effective range of the air rifles was 1,200 yards, maximum. But Witty wasn't thinking about that—she wasn't thinking at all. She was nothing but well-oiled training and razor-sharp precision as she raised the paint gun to her shoulder and sighted the Master Chief's head.

↕

"You should have stayed in Washington," growled Lazarus, his breath hot on Singer's neck. "Making coffee for generals who haven't seen combat and never will. Not trying to play Army with the big boys."

"Yes, Master Chief," said Singer calmly, her body twisted at an impossible angle. She felt the switchblade next to her ankle and wondered if there was some way she could get her hand down to take it out before Lazarus cut her throat.

"You looking for this?" asked Lazarus, casually reaching down with one of his long arms and plucking the switchblade from Singer's boot. Then there was the explosion, the splash of red spraying Singer as she grabbed Lazarus's wrist and twisted, bringing her hand down on his elbow and hearing him scream as she plucked the little switchblade out of his hand. She said quickly, "Yes, Master Chief, actually I was looking for that. Thanks," and then kicked him in the balls as hard as she could, businesslike and no-nonsense, taking only small satisfaction from the obscene choking sound he made as he disappeared into the filthy water.

As the paint pellets from the Master Chief's buddies exploded all around her, 30 of them hitting the Caddy at once, Singer quickly slit the duct tape holding the beach ball to the roof of the car. She grabbed the ball and dove into the river, ignoring the Master Chief's gurgling sounds as he sought desperately for a handhold on the Caddy. Singer crushed the bubbling beach ball to her chest as she swam underwater, hearing the muffled chirps of the paint pellets leaving red and green and yellow trails through the frothing water as she headed for rendezvous with SEAL Team Bravo.

Fifteen hundred yards away, Witty put another pellet in the Master Chief's forehead—impressing even herself—when he tried to crawl out of the water. She chewed on her cigar and chuckled to herself.

"That's my girl," said Witty as Singer rose from the swamp, slime-covered and dusted with red that might have been the Master Chief's blood—in a perfect world, that is.

↕

It happened later, much later, after Witty and Singer had spent an hour in the admiral's office being fitted for new assholes. The admiral wanted to talk to Witty alone for a minute or two, but then he ordered Singer into his office so the two women could sit side by side while he waved that cigar at them threateningly and yelled about the way they "went overboard, the worst thing you can do in the Navy!"

Hey, how many times could the pompous bastard expect Singer to apologize for kicking Master Chief Lazarus harder than was necessary for training purposes, or Witty to say she was sorry she had blown him away a second time while he was trying to climb out of the water? "Truth be told, sir, I didn't really expect to hit him a second time...I just figured I'd squeeze off a shot, you know, scare him a little, but I surprised even myself."

Which was not the right thing to say under the circumstances. Singer and Witgenstein had placed government property—that is to say, the Master Chief—under risk greater than was necessary to complete the exercise, and the admiral was having none of it.

Jesus, thought Singer, *it's not like the guy's really hurt—sure, broken forearm, OK, broken in two places, and a sprained ankle, but for Chrissake, SEAL trainees take those kind of lumps all the time during training exercises!*

Both Singer and Witty felt somewhat vindicated when the admiral stood for a long time staring at them, puffing on his cigar and shaking his head. Then the corners of his mouth twisted upward in a grotesque display, and finally he couldn't suppress the laughter any longer.

"You two killing machines are dismissed," he growled through his chortling. "Try not to whack anyone before reveille—is that understood?"

"Yes, sir!" they both barked.

"Your team's already scrubbed down—they're headed for chow. You bad-asses can eat too." The admiral's nostrils flared distastefully. "But for God's sake, shower first, will you? You smell like the Mud Bath."

"Yes, sir! Thank you, sir!" they said in unison, and hauled their slime-covered asses out of the admiral's office, leaving trails of rancid swamp water behind them.

↕

After it happened Singer couldn't say for sure why she did it. She'd been thinking about it since the first day of SEAL training, even though they could get washed out in a second for what they'd done.

But after seeing Witty—Monica—that morning, moving like a well-oiled machine, leading the tightest-operating SEAL team that ever graced the swamps of Florida's Camp Washington, nothing could stop the flood of love and respect she felt for her team commander.

Then again, maybe it was just the sight of Witty, covered in slime, stripping off her fatigues, her ropy muscles flexing under that smooth white skin. Singer had watched Witty undress dozens of times, of course, but she'd never *really* watched her. She couldn't have gotten away with really watching—someone might notice, and then there'd be hell to pay.

But this time, with all the rest of the team off getting chow, there was nothing to stop the way Singer's eyes roved over Witty's taut-muscled body as she stripped down to her mud-soaked skivvies and stood there in the bunk room, looking back at Singer.

"What the hell do you think you're staring at, Lieutenant?" snapped Witty, and Singer would have turned aside and mumbled an excuse if it weren't for the cocky way Witty stood with one filthy, naked foot up on Singer's bunk, close to her pillow, her toned thigh close to Singer's face, so close Singer could smell the sharp musk even over the rank swamp odor. Singer was sitting on her bunk, naked except for her sports bra and underpants, her bare thighs smeared with drying mud. Witty didn't need a sports bra—she just wore the tank top, which, before Singer could answer, Witty wriggled out of, pulling it over her head to reveal the firm apples of her pert little tits, with their hard, mauve, grape-sized nipples.

Singer would probably have looked away even *then,* if Witty hadn't taken that filthy tank top, redolent with swamp mud and the smell of Witty's sweat—and draped it over Singer's head, pulling the fabric down into her face.

Was it the cheekiness of the gesture, or the way Witty's scent worked its magic in her body that made Singer's pussy go hot and molten? Singer felt herself getting wet fast as she took a deep breath, inhaling as much of Monica Witgenstein as she could.

That's when Singer knew she was going to make a pass at her SEAL team commander come hell or high water. Nothing could stop the torrent of hunger that was building inside her—hunger for this soldier who was doing everything but ordering her to use that mouth of hers the way it was meant to be used.

Something held Singer back, though; some sense of duty, or the knowledge that what they were about to do was, in military terms, a shit magnet. But it all became academic the instant Witty bent over her and she felt the sergeant's hot, violently hungry mouth against hers, felt Witty's tongue pressing through the thin white membrane of the discarded tank top. To do that, Witty had to bend over pretty far—the sergeant was four inches taller—and with her one combat-booted foot up on Singer's bunk, the bare flesh of her thigh rubbed against Singer's side, even brushing her left tit through the soaked cotton of her bra. Singer didn't know how her hands so easily found purchase around the slender meat of Witty's upper body, her moist palms rubbing those small, dark nipples and finding them firm with arousal. They just sort of ended up there as she fell into Witty's demanding kiss, into the rush of need that welled inside her. But it felt deliciously right to be touching Witty's breasts like that, to feel them small and tight and hard in her hand. Such an intimate gesture between comrades—so natural.

Singer could taste the salt and smell the tang of Witty's body, so unfamiliar and tantalizing; she could even taste the rank slime of the Florida swamps, so familiar and unappetizing. Witty pressed her body against Singer's, their tongues thrusting against each other until the moment Witty bit Singer's lower lip—not enough to break the skin, but enough to make the battle-hardened lieutenant gasp with pain. Then Witty pulled back, running one hand up her sweat-and-slime-streaked body till it cupped one tiny breast, pinching as her other hand gripped Singer's hair.

Singer felt the tightness of Witty's muscles, knew a wrestling match between the two of them would be a dangerous battle indeed. But wrestling wasn't what either had in mind.

Witty jerked her head toward the showers. "My guess is that we got about 15 minutes of semiprivacy before those ladies get done with their chow. I'll be in the showers. Heating up."

Then Witty turned on her heel and marched to the showers, her walk the pace of a professional soldier. The grace with which she deftly hooked her panties with her thumbs and hopped out of them without breaking stride only heightened the pure militarism of those precise movements. As Witty disappeared, naked, through the door to the white-tiled latrine, Singer noticed for probably the thousandth time what a goddamn fine ass that soldier had. A pulse of anticipation and a throb of hunger shot through her as she realized that this time was different: This time she was going to *get* some of that ass.

Singer stood, noting the wet butt-print she left on her bunk—*Ten demerits right there, Jesus Christ*—and automatically smoothed it. She marveled yet again at how foul and filthy she felt. She didn't think a shower with Sgt. Monica Witgenstein was going to help one goddamn bit, but at the moment that didn't seem like a problem.

Singer stripped out of her skivvies in nothing flat.

↕

When Singer entered the showers, Witty had all eight nozzles blasting the white tiles at top volume. Singer weaved in and out of the scalding-hot sprays as she approached Witty, who looked like a fucking Grecian goddess in all that steam. She was lathered up, her short hair foamed with white and her back dribbling suds. Witty turned as Singer approached. Her front was soaped, the outline of her body shrouded as if by a faint white exoskeleton. Clouds of steam boiled and rolled with her every movement.

"What's with all the water?" asked Singer.

Witty fixed her with a pointed stare, harder than any the Master Chief had ever given them. "We're gonna need all the noise we can get, recruit, to cover the noises you're going to make."

Singer stepped into the spray, moved closer, and stared into Witty's hard eyes, saw the upward curve of her lips as their naked bodies pressed together, sliding easily against each other.

"Monica—" Singer began, but Witty stopped her with a single straight finger across her lips.

"Call me Sergeant," said Witgenstein. "It's more military that way."

And with that, the single straight finger became a hand, prying apart Singer's lips, and their lips met, hungry, devouring as Witty slammed Singer against the white tiles. With a surge of energy Witty brought her knee up between Singer's legs, and Singer felt a shudder go through her body as the hard ridge of Witty's kneecap pressed into her swollen clit. A moan escaped Singer's lips when Witty pulled back for an instant, and Witty chuckled. "I can't hear you," she singsonged softly, and kissed Singer hard again, working her knee around in a grinding circle, up and down, until each steady thrust almost lifted Singer off her feet. The hot water scalded Singer's skin, making it sting, but the pain lessened as the pleasure of Witty's thrusts brought her closer.

Now the water just felt good, damn good—as hot as hot

could be without hurting, without *really* hurting, and Singer was groaning as Witty kissed her one last time and then growled "Hang on" and disappeared—down on her knees, coaxing Singer's thighs apart and pushing her back to lean harder on the white-tiled wall, as Witty's mouth molded to the contour of Singer's pussy. That tongue was pushing its way in—this time not demanding, but asking to be let in, gentle but firm, and with a shiver Singer admitted it, her swelling pussy lips parting for Witty's mouth as the sergeant drank from Singer's gushing cunt, gulping the water that ran in beads and rivulets down Singer's belly and into her shaved crotch, letting it mingle with the ripe taste of Singer's juice, flowing faster and hotter than all eight nozzles combined. Then Witty was on her clit, suckling and licking, nursing like a baby seeking the only nourishment she had ever known, until Singer was almost screaming at the intuitive dance of Witty's tongue tip on her clit. But there was only a minute of that blind, raw bliss—Singer gasping and hovering on the edge of her climax—before she felt a finger slide into her, the nail clipped close with military precision, finger curving up to tease Singer's throbbing G spot as it stroked its way into her pussy.

"You like that?" groaned Witty hungrily, her tongue only leaving Singer's clit for an instant, not even pausing for the answer before her mouth molded again to Singer's cunt, tongue working the lieutenant's clit.

The answer from Singer was a rapturous "Oh, yeah...oh, fuck yeah" as Witty's middle finger stroked its way in and out of her pussy, and Witty let a second finger join it, bringing another moaning, squirming assent from Singer as Witty gave her the come-hither motion to beat all—and Singer could hardly say no, how could she? This was the orgasm she'd been wanting for weeks, ever since she first saw Witty standing rigid at attention that first day of SEAL training—this orgasm: twisting, writhing, and moaning on Witty's mouth, on her fingers, feeling Witty inside her, feeling Witty's tongue on her clit. And so she came hither, hard, harder than she'd ever come before, her thigh muscles spasming, her knees threatening to give out as she convulsed and moaned, her pussy contracting tight around Witty's thrusting fingers. And as she finished her hot, hard come, her body still tingling with the power and her brain feeling like the top of her head had just come off, Singer saw her whole fucking career flash before her eyes, her "operational experience" gone down the shitter because of how bad she wanted to get her pussy eaten by this sergeant from Oklahoma, and goddamn it, like it or not, she didn't give a shit. She didn't care one goddamn bit, because tomorrow morning she was going to fall out at reveille and go do her fucking job, and if that wasn't good enough for the U.S. Navy, then fuck 'em—at least she'd come hard on Monica Witgenstein's hungry tongue, and that would do nicely, thanks.

Then Witty was up, pressing naked against Singer, steadying her against the white wall as she kissed her, one more time, then twice, then a third time, their tongues mingling as the Navy orchestra began to play outside—that is, as they heard the sounds of women complaining ("They gonna make us do it again? All 'cause of that fuckin' hot shot..."), their voices carrying as they straggled past the fogged-over window, just inches from the place their team commander was having the cunt juices licked from her face by an eager, bright-eyed Lieutenant Singer.

"Tit for tat, Sergeant," said Singer as their bodies separated, and she gracefully grabbed a white cake and began to soap herself. "You saved my ass today, I'll save your ass tomorrow."

Witty was whirling around the shower room killing six nozzles—all but an adjacent pair. She took the soap out of Singer's hand and began to lather herself. "You'll have the chance, Lieutenant," said Witty. "We're back in the Mud Bath tomorrow morning."

For an instant Singer just stared. "You shitting me?"

Witty shook her head. "Admiral's orders. Reveille at 0300."

Outside the shower, the bunk room was filling with the rest of their class. Singer took a long, deep breath of hot steam as she imagined hauling her ass out of bed at that obscene hour. Then she thought about doing it with Monica Witgenstein, imagined the sight of Witty in action, imagined doing tomorrow what they'd done today: Functioning as a team, the best team in the service, for another of the most grueling days anyone on earth had ever experienced. And she thought about the few minutes she and Witty might be able to steal from the Navy at the end of that day—when, tired and miserable, Singer could prove to this cocky Marine that she could do as good as she'd just been done. That's what made reveille at 0300 sound like the invitation to a friggin' party.

Singer grinned and shrugged. "Oh-three? They're letting us sleep in, eh, Commander?"

And when Witty scowled and flipped her off, Singer grumbled, "Don't tempt me, Sarge, not with the ladies at home."

Witty smirked and turned off the water.

subway ride 4 play

Rosalind Christine Lloyd

It was a Friday, approximately 5:45 P.M., and I was about to be held captive on the New York City IRT #2 train. By the time I would board the train at Chambers Street after work, dreams of a seat would be considered delusional even by your less-seasoned strap-hanger. With strangers of every persuasion imaginable pushing, shoving, cramming, breathing on me, and, God forbid, touching me, it is the absolute worst part of every day. The experience is a horrific assault on the senses. The sights: homeless, hopeless, and hungry people (whom I can't help even though I want to) inhabiting the system; dirt and pollution everywhere, cigarette butts, candy wrappers, remnants of fast food cartons, discarded newspapers, filth; the visual abuse of the ugliness of an architecturally uninspired transportation system. The smells: body odor, sweat, urine, halitosis, vomit, gas, trash, loud perfumes and aftershaves. The sounds: the loud roar and screeching of aging equipment; boisterous, angry, and often violent arguments; a potpourri of languages and accents attempting to out-talk everyone else against an already annoying background of noise pollution. Strange cumbersome bodies monopolizing space, sharp-edged briefcases, smelly underarms, spiked heels threatening toes, all in war for the very minimal amount of elbow room. And the perverts: the ones who consider the tightness of the crammed subway cars as more than suitable carnivals to soothe their carnal cravings for flesh; their infractions can destroy the illusion of innocence any day.

On this particular evening, I stood in my usual spot about midway down the platform for the perfect position so that when the train came into the station, the door of the sixth car would open right in front of me. When I'd arrive at my stop I would be directly in front of my exit for an easy escape. A ritual I am a bit embarrassed to admit to, but a necessary behavior.

It was a hellish week at work. Logging in unwanted hours of overtime, I looked to the upcoming weekend as dead time to relax and unwind. The subway platform was somewhat festive. This is usually the case on Fridays. Couples looking forward to dates; yuppies slinging weekend bags over their shoulders; white- and blue-collar workers rushing to their favorite hot spots to tie one or more on; teenagers and coeds jubilant about parties. All I could think about was going home, showering the week off my tired body, and diving into a good book. Luckily, within two minutes a dull red train in all its urban glory came barreling into the station symbolizing my departure from 9-to-5 hell to deliver me to my safe haven uptown.

As usual, the subway car was jammed with bodies, but I managed to squeeze in and arrange myself in an excellent position close to the door at the opposite end of the car, where the doors would not open for about four express stops. This spot would allow a minimal amount of contact with people coming into the train. I would make the five stops to 110th Street with a minimal crush-factor effortlessly—quite a coup for a Friday.

After the exchange of outgoing and incoming bodies at

Chambers Street was complete, the doors closed. At this point, I tend to shut down, closing my eyes, lulling myself into this fake sense of serenity, blocking out the negativity that can permeate New York City air. On this day, however, I was compelled to open my eyes due to some unpredictable mystic vibration inside the train. Through the crowd, halfway to the other end of the car, I could see the thickest, poutiest lips and the largest, most magnificent eyes—eyes blacker than a moonless night. The owner of those lips and eyes had skin the color of warm toasty waffles and bushy hair sprinkled with natural twists and spirals the color of raspberry preserves. The subtlety of the woman's beauty was resounding as certain men stole opportunities to leer at her, fighting over one another to give her their seats. Her reaction to them was, in a word, oblivion. I couldn't take my eyes off her and strained for a better look. She was styling a small vintage leather jacket, the color of a fine cognac. It seemed tailored to fit her tiny, statuesque frame. A cream-colored turtleneck stretched across her tiny bosom, while overly confident nipples, fat and edible, poked out without shame. Obviously she wasn't wearing underwear (well, at least not a bra, as far as I could tell). Yes, I managed to see all of this through the crowd. I'll never forget those brown plaid boot-cut slacks, so tight I could almost feel the outline of the soft W between her legs.

I stared at her as the men did, only harder.

The train left Chambers Street, picking up speed as it entered the tunnel. She started to fidget, preparing to get off at the next stop. Clearing a path was no small feat as the train was crammed, wall to wall, shoulder to shoulder, but the crowd parted for her as if she were royalty. Without even looking at me, she squeezed past me before maneuvering her back directly to me. She was so close I could smell her shampoo and conditioner, which saturated her kinky hair—something sweet and nutty. The heat of her back was flammable, threatening to torch me. I couldn't believe how easy it was for me to become aroused by this absolutely beautiful stranger. As I enjoyed her warmth and her smell, the train careened wildly through the tunnel. The car started to buck and jolt from the high speeds, hurling Ms. Honey into me. Her back and legs flung against me violently, but it was her bottom, now pinned against me, that sent powerful impulses to my brain (not to mention other body parts). It seemed she decided for us both that it was a good idea for her ass to remain where it was, crushed right against my pussy.

I was near the door and I couldn't move. A large woman with far too many bags wedged her thick shoulder deep into the small of my back, while the beautiful stranger held herself against me, persistently pressing her hot ass deep into my hard clit. The train bolted to a stop.

Fourteenth Street station: The car barely thinned out. There were more than enough people on the train to camouflage what was happening. My stranger was still pressing against me as I tried to appear unaware of her immediate proximity. Had the train been near empty, I felt she would have done exactly the same thing she was doing at that very moment. When the doors closed and the train moved on, she began to move against me very slowly, rotating provocatively.

Riding a perfect stranger on the subway was completely unexpected and quite enticing, but my clit needed more as it rubbed the backside of this wondrous beauty. My nipples were so hard they hurt, and I knew I needed to do something to partake in the lusty moment she had initiated. With my right hand tightly gripping the strap above, I steadied myself against her. The leather backpack I wore gave me balance. I eased my left hand near my thighs closer to her, where a swirling circle of clit-numbing heat lay just under her ass. She moved against my hand, and as she rubbed, I slid my finger slowly along the fabric of her slacks, down the crack of her ass and between her legs. Suddenly she stopped moving, almost as if she were holding something in. Slowly I began to stroke her, moving my finger in and out of the space between the voluptuous cheeks of that phenomenal ass swathed in those plaid slacks until she moved with me. At this point I felt pairs of eyes lightly brushing over us, but I knew I couldn't stop—the embarrassment too weak, the will too strong.

My finger moved like a pencil in a sharpener as if it had a mind of its own. My fingers curled into a fist as I began to gently apply pressure underneath her. Each of us took deep breaths. I was loose and liquid; my thighs felt as if they were melting. She started to move round and round against my fist as I sunk myself into her as far as I could go with her fully clothed. My eyes darted nervously to confirm that no one was looking. I didn't want to be noticed. But weekend anxiety levels filled the car like bad air; these commuters didn't give a damn about anything but getting to their next destination. It got so intense, I thought she'd burn my fist off as I continued to bury it deep into her inferno.

The doors opened abruptly. We had come into Penn Station, and it seemed there was some interruption in service on a train in front of ours. In a variety of verbal and nonverbal ways, those with a view of the platform expressed their displeasure with the sea of commuters anxious to board. Some exhaled, others spewed profanity, some even attempted to block doors. My stranger craned her lovely caramel neck, straining for a better look out the window to view the platform. The temptation to kiss her neck, to taste the caramel, to wrap my tongue around her slick loveliness, was stretching my case. With my fist fitting snugly between her hot thighs, she squeezed around me as if it were meant to be. I started to sweat. My heart beat strangely and irregularly. The unruly crowd on the platform, pissed off and armed with bad attitudes, did not allow the departing passengers a clear path out of the train. Those entering tumbled in like crazed, testosterone-driven football players prepared to get on the already-filled train at all costs. I could have sworn the train sighed as the incoming bodies joined ours and formed an ugly sculpture of human flesh. I felt mangled and manipulated, when suddenly I realized my stranger was now facing me. She didn't dare meet my gaze, but turned her eyes away. A subtle hint of her scent lingered in the air. I blushed. We ignored the other bodies crammed against us: bodies contorted in strange angles, some holding onto the ceiling to steady themselves. A commuter mosh pit.

She was perfectly still at first. Then the train picked up speed, accelerating through the dark, cavernous tunnels deep in the belly of the city, the cars rocking wildly, gripping themselves against the silvery, slippery tracks, fueled by the energy of the dangerous third rail. We allowed our bodies to absorb, merge, dissolve, and exchange the very essence of our now frontal collective body heat and hungry, aimless desire. Breasts were hot, pressing together, nipples stinging; our heavily breathing stomachs danced, the expanse of womanly hips on such a slender body laid flat against mine. Then thighs, hers, started a slow roll against me. Catching her breath, I rolled my bigger, more muscular thighs deeper. Pushing, swirling gently, we slowly humped each other with as much subtlety as we could stand. The train's rocking added to the feminine rhythm we so courageously developed in this public place. Thighs rolled slowly then quickly against each other, sometimes in synchronicity, sometimes deliberately out of sync, her gaze as far away from me and from us as possible. Her hips rose to meet mine, and I thought I was going crazy. When I felt the grip of her tiny hand with its long painted nails on my waist, I could wait no longer. The train was moving so fast; bodies swayed everywhere around us with lights inside each of the cars blinking on again off again. Slipping my hand between us, nervously I unzipped her slacks and eased my finger inside. A moan escaped from her cranberry lips, but it was swallowed in the sound of the train. I dug deeper in my search and discovered she had skipped the underwear entirely—just as I suspected. Instantly I felt the soft heat of her downy bush. Her scent was even stronger now, so strong it made my mouth water. I felt her raise her hips toward me, spreading her legs so I could get my finger in. With an abrupt rock of the car, my finger became submerged in a curly womb of hot wet heat. Her entrance was hot and slippery. She wiggled her hips with a slow but intense rhythm while my middle finger worked itself deeper between her soft-smooth-slick-silky lips. Her grip was so tight around my waist it pinched. As the train shook wildly, she moved toward me while I jammed my finger in her as hard and as far as I could. She was melting around my finger like chocolate on a hot summer day as her very soul started to tremble in the palm of my hand in a pelvic dance, not a belly dance—my anonymous Nubian princess.

As 72nd Street approached, she pushed her large leather bag in between us (to hide her now open plaid slacks) and pushed through the crowd, almost running as she neared the doors. She stepped out. She did not look back. All I could do was catch my breath in an attempt to convince myself this had not been a dream. To confirm what had happened, I took a seat and raised my left hand to caress my face. Instantly, I inhaled the banks of the Nile River after a torrential downpour.

Falling Away
Linnea Due

Glorious light flashes through the darkness and then runs off fast as a yellow dog, as if the sun carries too many burdens in this weary age to climb up over the hill and howl away the night. Over and over the sun struggles into the sky, then sinks away behind a brow of gloom, until I begin to lose heart that I'll ever again bask in her warmth or glimpse dappled light twinkling through skeins of pale-green leaves. Then I comprehend that in my extremity I have taken the sun's measure when I should have looked to myself: It is I lingering cold in the gloom, tumbling fast down that darkened hill, unable to crest the summit. I strive for a reason, think of none, and open my eyes. Then snap them shut, trying not to shout. Too many are doing that for me to add to the clamor: Opening my eyes has unstopped my ears, and I don't like what I hear.

I reach a hand to my head. Nor do I like what I touch. As I finger the crusted, matted hair, I recollect Lucas walking ahead through a hellish field the likes of which no body should have to see, the trees half shot up, twisted branches on top of dead men, dead men on top of dead horses. Drifting across it, a snowfall of letters. Letters written in handwriting so beautiful or cramped or angular or near-illiterate primer printing. Photos of wives and children and mothers and fathers on top of the horses and men and trees. Men lie there reading still; reading the words of a loved one as they wait to die. I see myself skirting a cairn of stones someone has erected, but after that, there is nothing in this broken head for me to find. No shot, no cannon, no yelling horde of half-starved men, no explanation for this dried blood and stabbing pain.

Where is Lucas? My one real friend here, a baker. Imagine, a man who combines simple ingredients to create the miracle of sustenance is reduced to subtracting lives as if he were a banker toting up a debit sheet. For Lucas is a very good shot, and he has saved me on more than one occasion. He would say I had saved him, but he is a better shot than he is a liar.

The sun is warm on my face and it wakens a powerful thirst. So powerful I forget the pain that almost made me faint. I open my eyes and see naught but leaves swimming through a blue sea inverted over my head. The clouds are puffy as cotton and I hope they don't come down to be sullied by us, the grand destroyers. A cloud is a sacred event, like bread, though it takes a bigger man than Lucas to bake a cloud. I have to remember to tell him. I want to close my eyes but I don't. Too much darkness can't do me good. I have to swing my head to retch and this time I can't help but yell.

Comes then an angel. Who speaks. Pats my brow. Wipes my mouth. This time the darkness gallops at me, and good or bad, I must succumb. All I can see in the brief moment between the light and the shadow are worried eyes and a mouth too tight for the wearer. I have a powerful thirst. I say as much. And then I fall away.

↕

I hope to tell him that he will be gone from here as quickly as I can get him on his feet. I've seen the panic that comes into their eyes when they wake up to see the surgeon and hear the screams. But he faints before I can make him understand. At least I have put him where he can see the sun when he awakes again.

His friend came twice already. I wonder if he knows. In this hospital no one knows but me. Perhaps this man is a friend for life, and so he can be trusted. I wish I knew this as well as the other, for then I could talk to him.

I must keep the surgeon away. This is not hard because there are so many who are critical, and he is in the area of the lightly wounded, reserved for those who will not need a surgeon's saw. Ira, the only other here, spends time behind the curtain with the dying. He tries to make them comfortable, give them water, talk to them if they are conscious. He has promised so many that he will find parents, sweethearts, brothers. I asked him once what he will do when the war is over, and he said he will take a year to travel, to fulfill what pledges he can. I envy him. His life seems simple and good.

I linger by the side of this young soldier with the head wound until duty forces me onward. There are just the three of us, and the surgeon is half-drunk, his apron covered with blood, his wild eyes as red as the cloth. A line of men awaits his horrific carpentry. Ira comes out from behind the curtain to administer whiskey, to the men, not the doctor. The surgeon administers that to himself.

↕

When I come to again, the pain is less, probably because the light is fading in the sky. A man with a slight limp hobbles

by, carrying an oil lamp. Men scream as much as they did earlier. Perhaps it never ends; perhaps they just keep screaming.
I wonder if I dreamed the nurse. There has been no alarm,
so I have passed undiscovered. The uniform is my savior. No
one looks close; people see only what they expect. It is my
shield and my sword; if it kills me it does not matter because I
was dead before I donned it.

It still stuns me that Robert was killed in the first few minutes of battle. We heard so quickly, from the man who returned
home because his brain was addled. Mother said we could not
believe him, but I saw he told the truth and I left.

I am Robert's younger brother. None saw reason to doubt.
I have come to avenge his death. Their weary eyes filled with
resignation, and one said revenge was solace only for the weak.
It pained me to test their patience, but I knew they would
ignore me if they thought I was hotheaded.

It has been both harder and easier than I thought. My
courage, apart from fighting boredom, is rarely tested. We do
nothing for long stretches but play cards and write letters.
Lucas has no one to write either. His fiancée died soon after he
enlisted, struck down by sickness. It seems to me that the war
has brought contagion to all of us. So many have cramps, so
many spend their time hunkered over a hole. Sometimes I think
it is the hardtack, sometimes the salt pork. Once Lucas found
some flour and made frybread. That plugged us for a spell, but
then the cramps returned.

I have not dreamed the nurse. Here she is, wiping my
brow, giving me water. My thirst is less, and I realize she has
been by my side before. Her hand under my neck is familiar,
my head a weight she has lifted already. Her fingers part my
hair and she explores gently. She asks how old I am. I sub-
tract four years from my age. She is grave and tells me to go

home. I do not tell her I am avenging my brother.

Her eyes are crystalline, shiny and brown, with great depth and reflection; I can see the flutter of the wick and under that a caring that is at once marvelous and puzzling. When she takes my hand, I nearly rip it away, then realize that will never do. I tell myself I am sorely tested.

Your friend Lucas was here three times. I told him you can go soon.

I make her say it again for I can hardly believe it. Lucas is alive; I shall leave with four limbs and a functioning brain. Her hand feels so warm in mine. I wish I could stay and look into her eyes at the dancing pins of light.

I ask why she is here.

She wanted to better her station, she says. I wonder what she did before. A teacher. Yes, she seems a teacher. But how is her station bettered? I do not ask, for that would be impolite.

My brother wanted me to get married, she says.

I know about that, though not from Robert.

Her parents are dead, she explains. They left her a small inheritance, but her brother guards the capital, says it should not be spent except as an investment in the future. He believes she should work when she is young, while she can meet people. He is unhappy because he has introduced her to several men and she has spurned them. They do not interest her. Teaching also does not interest her. She would like to go west, but perhaps she is a dreamer. She is talking too much.

Her apologies are sweet. Her eyes waltz with the light as she talks about the west, her brows rise with excitement as high as Lucas's dough. I would love to bring her there, but my uniform can only take me so far. My savior and my prison, I cannot abandon it nor can I leave as long as I wear it. My uniform has become my religion; I am like a missionary venturing into danger, protected only by my cross and my faith. Yet this religion is my own invention, one of necessity only I can understand.

She strokes my hand. As I cross a boundary of comprehension, I understand clearly that this territory is the most dangerous of all.

↕

Three days have passed, and we have not talked since that afternoon when I felt him pull away. I am certain it had not to do with my foolish prattling. Perhaps he realized that I might know and feared exposure. Or perhaps he feared that I did not know.

There are men here with grievous injuries who still have not seen the surgeon. I feel so for them. Jed—that is the name he told me—has taken over the task of cleaning wounds and fetching water. He doles out coffee for them, even the Rebels, who weep when they smell the brew they have not smelled for months. Jed's friend Lucas has come several times to help, and so have others from his unit. They seem so tight-knit that I feel lonely and bereft. I even wish for my sober brother, with his scowls and dark brow.

A man came today and sang "Home Sweet Home." Tears rolled down gray cheeks, leaving clean lines through mud and half-grown stubble. I blinked my own away. So many here are but boys, and they expect me to be the pillow on which they can rest their weary souls. Some even address me as "mother," though I am hardly older than they.

Yet this idyll, if it could be called such, when lightning splits the sky and men lie crying in their filth, must end. We are following the march and will move up closer to the front in our ambulance. Ira has elected to stay here, while the surgeon and I leave tomorrow. By the time the sun is high in the sky I will be in another place, with these wounded left behind, and the cannon booming and the guns blazing. As for Jed, he shall return to his unit. I will miss him, though we have barely talked since that first day.

I sense him watching me as we work. I am fond of him but cannot go close. If my mother were alive, I would tell her it is like hunting a rabbit. When you go near, the rabbit disappears down a burrow, but each time you look from the side of your eye, he is staring at you, nose quivering.

If Lucas and the rest know, I have seen no sign. But what effrontery, to essay such a hoax! I have stayed awake these past two nights, aghast at the boldness of it. I have heard of this, and more that I shall not speak of here, but never thought that I, Anne Gilchrist, would ever see such with my own eyes.

And heart. For it would be untrue to pretend that Jed has not touched me. I question my own fascination—am I captivated by the ploy itself or its actor? If I saw "Jed" in another circumstance, would I give him a second glance? Since he is so shy of me, I fear I shall grow no wiser. Perhaps that is best for both of us. When one hunts a rabbit, one ends up with dinner; I have no wish to make Jed my supper simply to satisfy a curiosity about myself.

Yet to my startlement, my real hope—that I should have more time with him—is granted. The surgeon and his kit must ride ahead on his fast horse, while Ira shall stay here at the base hospital. Someone must drive the wagon with me and the supplies, and who better than Jed, well enough to fetch water and change dressings? I saw the shadow cross his face when he was chosen, and I cringed inside. He sees me as danger, and perhaps I am. With his life at risk, I care not about my motives but know them for the pale, ghostly wraiths they are, undeserving of the light of day.

↕

The boys come to see me before we drive off at dawn. Payne and Lucas and John, each so dear. John unlettered and rough but valiant, Payne a gambler, wants to cheat and never be cheated; he taught the sutlers a lesson when they tried to overcharge us for some tobacco at the last camp. Lucas, of course, loyal and proud. He never says about Robert, whether they were friends, whether he saw Robert die. I think not. Surely he would say.

As we share coffee in our tins, I think that for these, my brothers, glory is a birthright. Even Lucas, who just wants to bake bread, who never thought he'd have to defend the Union, who says let the Rebels go, what do they bring us but shame and strife, even he answered the call to arms. They are prepared to sacrifice their mortal souls to keep a united America. For me, everything I do is muddied, like a river the horses have tromped through. Am I escaping my destiny, making big of myself? Am I a criminal (and I'm sure many would think such)? Yet why cannot I sacrifice for my country? Of the lot of us, I have the strongest views—and express them, to the annoyance of some, like German Karl, who joined for the bounty and lets us know it every hour of every day. He says some men are born to slave and it's folly to pretend other.

I know about what is prevented to me, just as freedom is prevented from the black man. I cannot achieve glory because of my birth, I am not allowed the grand gesture. Whatever gesture I can make is to family, and then it is only expected and far from grand. This is a bitter draught I have not been able to choke down. It is why I am dead even as I draw breath, my uniform a magic shroud that lets me walk among the living so long as I wear it. These thoughts carry their own danger, though less to me than to my fellows. Twice I have put Lucas in jeopardy when he has followed me into the center of the fight. This is why I have agreed to drive the nurse in the wagon; Lucas will survive the coming battles better without me, for in truth I *am* hotheaded. Playing the fool when I first arrived was easy, as I am a bit of one.

The nurse comes to say hello to us around our campfire, and the boys tease and trial me, asking when is the wedding. The words bring tears to my eyes so unexpected I scrub at my face and scold John for kicking up the damned dust. Would that I could marry her! It is a cry from my still-beating heart that does not know my brain has already surrendered. It is a cry from deep under this coat of blue, a cry I have concealed from my own consciousness yet truer than any I have ever uttered, even that with which I greeted this world. Once I felt her hand on my brow and saw into her eyes, I wanted not to leave her side. I am aware of how her eyes follow me, and how mine own are on her as she tends to the wounded in her long cape and bonnet. We seem bound by yarn intent on being knitted even as I try to break the needles. For I know this sweater is unholy and, in being made, shall unmake us. It must be unraveled. I cannot let her partake of my folly.

↕

He swears at the horses, but I know it is for show. Four horses, a light load, it should go quickly. But the roads are messy from these days of rain, with the sky dark and threatening. War turns men nomads; everywhere troops are moving, so the mud is churned up to the axles, and the horses must tug and slide and tug some more. Our slipping has tossed me against his shoulder again and again, until finally I move close as if for a rock to lean on, and he allows it. I wish this ride to go on forever.

And as we travel across this drenched, scarred landscape, all gray and black-green and brown, my spirit becomes strangely animated, as if I could dance atop the sodden grass. I feel in the center of a grand paradox: It is only by being carried away by this flood of events that we are allowed to be ourselves. Jed's body tells a different story than his soul has embarked upon; were he to follow his body he'd leave the greater part of him behind. My situation is less apparent, but no more consonant. My brother's intentions for me are identical to my own in almost every way, yet he would banish me were he to learn the truth. We legislate each other without knowing the depths of the souls we judge, and thus pass rulings that make lives mockeries. Only when lives become less important than grand events can those lives be lived true, and perhaps that tells the tale, that we should always look to the grand and let the truth seek its own.

A mile from our destination a man gallops up to say we are wanted nine miles to our south. Jed questions him closely; who told him so, was he sent to find us or just a nurse, why should we believe him when the sounds of battle are so clear ahead? But he answers well and soundly, even stating my name, and Jed is forced to believe him. We must continue driving into the worsening weather. This time when Jed curses, he means it.

And he is to curse more. Barely a mile down the road, we are rocked by thunder, and the horses spook till Jed must stop and go steady them. He comes back soaken wet from the road, his old boots clumped with the red clay that characterizes this Virginia countryside. Another mile gone we are deep in a wood, and the road forks. Our guide had said nothing of this, and the sky is slate. Jed takes the right, for it seems to head toward the direction we want. But shortly it begins to flag, and we end up at a large mansion, deserted except for an elderly colored man with shock-white hair who wants to know our business. None here, Jed tells him shortly, and explains what we are about. The man knows where the fighting is, he says; tells us Jeb Stuart has been taking the long way around McClellan's forces, and that battles are being waged along the railroad. There's a shortcut, he says, around mile four.

So we take off again, back the way we came. This time we go left, with Jed gnawing at the problem like a dog at a bone: Shall we take the short way and maybe run aground, or go on the road like we were ordered to? It's getting dark when we come to the track off to the right, and Jed hesitates. The horses are nervy again, and I think he just wants to end this ride. He takes the cut, partly, he says, so we'll be in more open territory, which will calm the horses.

↕

The old man knows his business. Once I get the lay of this valley, I see we can cut a mile or more off our route. What he couldn't have known is that Stuart's damned raiders blew the bridge across what they call Chester Creek. Some boys throw rocks at us till I threaten to scatter their brains 'cross the road, and they tell us Stuart's men stopped hardly an hour earlier and busted up the bridge. They say two days past we could drive the creek in such a fine carriage (ha!), but now the water's high and unruly, and the horses high as the creek. I'm in trouble for sure, taking this track when I should have stayed on the main road. Fine one I am, here to be the walking dead for however much time I can glean in this uniform—and now I'll probably get shot for disobeying orders.

We're barely on our way back when the skies break free with a bang that shies the horses again. I get down and lead them into a copse off to the side of the track. In this deluge we'd just mire ourselves and never get out. Best to let it blow past us before we continue. After I picket and grain the horses and tuck them back into the trees, I head to the driver's seat, but Anne Gilchrist just shouts out the back of the wagon. Says if I intend to sit out there in the pouring rain she'll have to as well, and she'll get out the hind end and walk around in the mud to do it too. I tell her it isn't right for a man to be in back of a wagon with a woman he isn't married to, and she asks me if I do everything by the rule book or just what I find convenient? While I'm puzzling on that, she starts to climb out over the back and so I must run and stop her, and finally haul myself in. Once there, she starts to clucking over how wet I am and wants me to take off my jacket. "No, ma'am," I tell her, and she can see I won't bend.

It's dark in the back of the wagon, shelves on either side blocking out what light might filter through the canvas. The shelves are stacked with medical necessaries for the battle up ahead, necessaries that men are probably dying in need of. I curse myself again, for listening to the old man, even for listening to the rider. If we'd just gone on the way we were going, at least we'd be where someone needed us! I wonder about Lucas and John and Payne, marching to another battle. We've made headway this week. I pray that the Rebels will see reason, and we can all go home. Not that I shall. I won't talk of that. Not to Anne Gilchrist, though she seems to want to tell me everything, of her brother and his wife and her parents and mostly of her escape, she calls it, to the war. She says that my escape is just as profound, and then she looks at me, expectant. I'm still as a stone. This is treacherous footing inside this wagon, and I must be a sure-stepper to keep us safe.

↕

I convince him to take off his jacket only after he starts shivering uncontrollably. I tell him that as a nurse, I can't allow him to sicken himself just for modesty's sake. I even get his muddy boots and pants off, saying he'll dirty the stretcher. His legs are hairy and well-muscled; he's a hard worker, with smooth, bulging muscles. Yet I can't believe they don't know, don't see a smoother behind, a shapelier buttock. Perhaps they turn away in their tents, do their best in crowded circumstance to give as much privacy as they're able. Or perhaps the uniform is such a blinder no one looks beyond it.

And he so fits that uniform. I've never seen handsomer, with chiseled chin and heavy eyebrows, fine cheekbones and delicate lips. He's a solace for lonely eyes like mine. I could stare and stare, yet when I do he begins to stammer and won't meet my gaze. I would give years of my life for an honest conversation.

I give him burlap to scrub away the wet, and in time he stops shivering. He insists on sitting near the back flap to guard me from the cold. And it *is* cold, with the wet beginning to seep through and the wind buffeting the wagon back and forth on its axles till I fear it will fall. When I start to tremble, Jed loses sight of his own trouble and comes forward quick to rub warmth into my hands and shoulders, even holding me close to stifle my shakes. Just then a clap of thunder like a bellow from the Almighty startles us, and I cling to him as if I were a monkey cleaved to a broad tree trunk. He comforts me as the wagon rocks, our own wet cradle. He worries about the horses, saying he should by rights go out into the storm, and it is then that I catch his chin and kiss him. I just do it before I've thought it out, like a branch will suddenly trip you, and there you are on the ground before you know it.

So there we are on the ground, and this time the thunder strikes him. We stare at each other, and then he kisses me. I've never known such sweetness. I knew not such sweetness existed in the whole wide world. Is this what my brother wanted for me? If so, I've been cruel to him, for his intentions could not have been better. It was only his target that was wrong.

↕

How could her mouth open a universe? Kissing her is like falling into a liquid that seems to flow everywhere at once—into the realm of the angels, through the crust of the earth, into my body that I now grasp is connected by strong cords to the sky and the earth and the deep beneath the earth. I have wandered blind for life, glimpsing this only when I swam in the river with the fish at my side, when I came up for air and startled the frogs. This kiss does the same, throws me into the river where I swim and can breathe the liquid and rejoice.

And there is Robert at my side, swimming too, his head thrown back to let it all slide down his throat, his long dark hair trailing behind in the fluid, all bubbles and light. Did he feel this in his flesh? Surely this is a wondrous gift, a marvelous boon that must only be visited rarely. He looks exultant. Do I feel this because I am about to die? Then I wonder how I know.

I begin to pull away though I can bare stand it, for I figure if Anne Gilchrist is swimming, she is afloat not only with a dead man but in a lake of lies. She grasps my wrist to hold me and puts her hand under my shirt to show me she has known all along. She says she has heard of such things, has heard it whispered. I tell her decent folks aren't described by whispers, and she says back sharp that I have made my neighbors and kin Saint Peter on Judgment Day. It's true it hurts me that Ma and Pa are so mightily disappointed in me, and not just 'cause I'm better at plowing than sewing. They don't like my book learning, and they think I work too hard.

When I tell Anne Gilchrist this, I conjecture that working too hard must be the devil's doing. She chuckles and admits she was afraid I had no sense of humor. "I thought," she says, "it would be my cross to bear." I stammer and stutter, for I can't believe she means what I hear, but I do manage to say this is the first time I ever felt so fine with a woman—a real one, that is. She commences laughing and can't stop for so long, my face flames up. When she finally gets calm of herself, she says, "My brother had such high hopes when he sent me off, and here I've succeeded in finding the one man in the Union Army I *can't* marry."

I suppose that's a knee-slapper, but I can't find the fun of it. She traces a finger down my cheek and says that separation of church and state should apply to marriage. The church says they marry soul to soul, but the state wants to pass laws on the bodies too. I snort and tell her no minister would marry us, much less the state. And how can I be two people at once? She says she feels only one and that is me. Then she kisses me again, and every inch of her flesh against mine is salvation. I am unbuttoning her dress with shaking fingers, and she is helping. She keeps kissing me as we go, and it is all I can do not to leap on her, but I know that is wrong from Robert, who is counseling me to go slow and not startle her with rough behavior. I become smooth as a fine-gaited horse; even my hands steady down. But when I see her breasts fall from that bodice I gasp, and she smiles at me, proud as she ought to be. Cream they are, soft as a kitten's belly, and they fit my palms like they were born to rest there. Looking down, she says she never saw such a perfect match: my hands, her breasts. I say she's fresh and she gets all saucy and asks do I want to see the rest of her. Well, I don't deny it, so she struggles out of the underthings she has on, with my helping at the tugging parts, and I never thought I would see a sight so beautiful on this earth. I tell Robert this can't be happening, and he says to keep my head.

A head is nothing to lose, not with Anne Gilchrist, because she has plenty to say even now. Between the words she makes sounds, and when she begins to breathe like a winded horse, with that whistle of a good race run, I can't hold off any longer. I sink somewhere beyond but more myself than I have ever been, and I know how to find where she is swimming and soon she is twisting against my chest and biting my collar bone, and her whistle joins the wind's wail until they sound near the same.

Then she wants to kiss me and we do, and we spoon with each other until we start up again, and I think in the middle of it that I am saved. The rain pounds on the canvas and starts to drip in on the bandages and the stretchers and our foreheads, as if the sky is crying tears of happiness and gratitude and grief. We cover each other with my big cape from this Brothers' War, and it is then that we sleep, with me blessed to have this night, to have swum with Anne Gilchrist on this last eve of my life.

↕

I tried to talk with him near dawn. I told him we could go away after the war, even during it after his enlistment was over. He wouldn't hear talk of the future, said his uniform was his protection. There are other uniforms, I told him gently. There are other ways to gently weave a fiction. But he shook his head and touched me so tender and said only that he wished he could leave me what he had. And he did give me a coin, said I had to carry it with me. We left barely a quarter hour later, with him driving hell-bent for leather. He was sure we were needed, and we were.

I hardly saw him after we got to the battleground near Fair Oaks. He helped establish a surgery and found a couple walking wounded to staff it. We worked until we were wavery on our feet all the following day through the night to the next day when Jed went off to fight, having found his friend John and learning that Payne had been struck and that Lucas was missing.

The base hospital was overrun two days later by Rebel forces, and the wounded taken prisoner. Most shall surely die. Ira is gone; no one knows whether he stayed and fought for the hospital or whether he surrendered. The surgeon did perform miracles, I'm told, on another section of the front.

When I heard a ball had cut Jed down near Gaines Mill I was not surprised. I had seen it in his eyes. I kept on nursing through the whole long war, though my heart shriveled in my breast. When I returned, my brother said he thought I would find a man in the first months, and I told him I had. After that he treated me better. I put Jed's coin on a chain and I keep it close at my throat.

I wondered if Lucas had survived, but then I heard from a friend who visited Jed's hometown that a baker had come to the home of Jed's parents and told them how their daughter, who had disgraced the family by running away to be a nurse, had saved so many Union men that she was called the Angel of Mercy. He said she nursed 18 hours or more, day upon day, until no man could complain about being overworked. My friend says that after the baker left, Jed's father looked so much lighter and bragged on what a worker his daughter was, how she could outdo most men with her plowing and shearing and woodsmanship. A crack shot, the baker had said as well, but all agreed that she hadn't had a chance to practice that skill in the nursing profession. And the baker told them his daughter had a friend name of Anne Gilchrist who might be calling on them one day.

I might, I suppose. But first I go west. I tried my own speech to Jed's parents and it felt like treason to call him Sarah. Lucas is a baker indeed—he can make pride rise in unleavened bread. I have no such talent, only the love to carry on.

Blood and Silver

Patrick Califia

Once upon a time (and still), there was a young woman who was very tired of being treated like a little girl. Her name was Sylvia Rufina. Like most female persons in her predicament, the only available avenue of rebellion was for her to pretend to obey the commandments of others while protecting a secret world within which she was both empress and impresario. Having frequently been told, "Go out and play," more and more, that was what she did. Her family lived in a small farmhouse, which felt smaller still because of the vast wilderness that surrounded it. She was at home in this untamed and complex landscape, if only because there was nothing false or sentimental about it.

One of the games she played was "holding still." This was a game learned under confusing and painful circumstances at home. But hidden within a stand of birches or scrub oak, she was not molested. Instead, if she learned to let her thoughts turn green and her breath slow to the pace of sap, she became privy to an endless variety of fascinating events: how beavers felled trees, how mice raised their children, the way a fox twitched its nose when it spotted a vole.

One day, when she was studying the spots on a fawn that dozed in a copse just a few dozen yards from where she held her breath, the wolf appeared. He (for there was no mistaking the meaning of his big face, thick shoulders, and long legs, even if she had not espied his genitals) was an amazing silver color, with dark black at the root of his stippled fur. His teeth were as white as the moon, and his eyes were an intelligent and fearless brown. They studied each other for long minutes, wolf and woman, until he lost interest in her silence and relaxed limbs, and went away.

The next time he came, he walked right up to her and put his nose up, making it clear that he expected a greeting of some sort. So she carefully, slowly, bonelessly lowered her body and allowed him to examine her face and breasts. His breath was very hot, perhaps because it was autumn, and the day was chilly. His fur smelled of earth and the snow that was to come, and the air he expelled was slightly rank, an aroma she finally identified as blood.

Satisfied with her obeisance, he went away again, tail wagging a little, as if he were pleased with himself. This was the only undignified thing she had seen him do, but it did not make her think less of him. She appreciated the fact that the wolf did not caper, bow down, yelp, or slaver on her, in the slavish and inconsiderate way of dogs. The wolf was no whore for man's approval. He fed himself.

She did not see the wolf again for nearly a week. But when he returned, he brought the others: two males and three females, one of them his mate. This female was nearly as large as her spouse, and as dark as he was metallic, the eclipse to his moon. Some instinct told Sylvia Rufina that she must greet them on all fours and then roll over upon her back. This seemed to excite everyone no end. She was nosed a good deal, fairly hard, licked three or four times, and nipped once. The surprisingly painful little bite came from the leader of the pack, who was letting her know it was time to get up and come away with them. It was later in the day than she usually stayed out-of-doors, and as she fled lights came on in the little house, dimming the prettier lights that bloomed in the deep black sky.

Racing with the wolves was like a dream, or perhaps it was normal life that was a dream, for the long run with the wolf pack was a flight through vivid sensations that made everything that had happened to her indoors seem drained of color and meaning. She never questioned her ability to keep up with them, any more than she questioned the new shape she seemed to wear. Her legs were tireless, running was a joy. Even hunger was a song in her belly. And when the group cut off and cornered a deer, she knew her place in the attack as if she had read and memorized a part in a play.

After they ate, most of them slept, yawning from the effort it took to digest that much raw red meat. Unaccustomed to so much exercise and the rich diet, she slept also.

And woke up miles from home, alone, in harsh daylight. Every muscle in her body hurt, and her clothing was ripped, her hair full of twigs, leaves, and burrs. Her shoes were gone and her stockings a ruin. Somehow, she made her way home, hobbling painfully, trying to think of a story that would excuse her absence without triggering a proscription against hikes in the mountains.

There was no need for an alibi. Her family had already decided what must have happened to her. She had followed a butterfly, or a blue jay, or a white hart, and gotten lost in the woods. When she crossed the threshold and heard inklings of this story, she saw that each of her family members had picked a role, just as the wolves had memorized their dance of death with one another. And she gave herself up, too exhausted to fight back, letting them exclaim over and handle and hurt her with their stupidity and melodrama. Though a part of her sputtered indignantly, silently: Lost! In the woods! Where I've roamed for three-and-twenty years? I'm more likely to get lost on my way to the privy!

Unfortunately, when she had gone missing, they had called upon the Hunter and asked him to search for her. He was someone she avoided. His barn was covered with the nailed-up, tanning hides of animals and thatched with the antlers of deer he had slain. Sylvia Rufina thought it grotesque. Her father had taught her to recognize certain signals of an unhealthy interest. After having finally grown old enough to no longer be doted upon by her incestuous sire, she could not tolerate a stranger whose appetites felt revoltingly familiar. When the Hunter lit his pipe, waved his hand, and put a stop to the whining voices so glad of their opportunity to rein her in, she gaped at him, hoping against her own judgment that he would have something sensible to say.

He had brought something that would solve the problem. No need to restrict the young woman's love of nature, her little hobbies. No doubt it gave her much pleasure to add new leaves and ferns to her collection. (In fact, she did not have such a collection; but she was aware that many proper young ladies did, and so she bit her tongue, thinking it would make a good excuse for future rambling.) The Hunter shook out a red garment and handed it to her.

It was a scarlet sueded leather cloak with a hood, heavy enough to keep her warm well into winter. The lining was a slippery fabric that made her slightly sick to touch. He had kept hold of the garment as he handed it to her, so their hands touched when she took it from him, and her eyes involuntarily met his. The predatory desire she saw there made her bow her head, as if in modesty, but in fact to hide her rage. Even during a killing strike, the wolves knew nothing as shameful and destructive as the Hunter's desire. She knew, then, that he had bought this red hooded cloak for her some time ago, and had often sat studying it, dreaming of how she would look laid down upon it. If she wore it in the forest, she would be visible for miles. It would be easy for a hunter, this Hunter, to target and track her then.

She was poked and prodded and prompted to say thank you, but would not. Instead she feigned sleep, or a faint. And so she was borne up to bed, feeling the Hunter's hard-done-by scowl following her supine body up the stairs like an oft-refused man on his wedding night.

It was weeks before she was deemed well enough to let out of the house. The red cloak hung in her closet in the meantime, its shout of color reducing all her other clothes to drab rags. It would snow soon, and she did not think she would survive being stranded behind the pack, in human form, to find her way home in a winter storm. But she must encounter them again, if only to prove to herself that the entire adventure had not been a fevered dream.

Her chance finally came. A neighbor whom nobody liked much, a widowed old woman with much knowledge about the right way to do everything, was in bed with a broken leg. This was Granny Gosling. As a little girl, Sylvia Rufina had gone to Granny Gosling with her secret troubles, mistaking gray hair and myopia for signs of kindness and wisdom. Her hope to be rescued or at least comforted was scalded out of existence when the old woman called her many of the same names she had heard in a deeper voice, with a mustache and tongue scouring her ear and her long flannel nightgown bunched up painfully in her armpits. The child's hot sense of betrayal was quickly replaced with stoicism. We can bear the things that cannot be altered, and now she knew better than to struggle against the inevitable.

Other neighbors, a prosperous married couple with a bumper crop of daughters overripe for the harvest of marriage, were hosting a dance with an orchestra. People were to come early to an afternoon supper, dance in the evening, and spend the night. Mother and father had their own marketing of nubile damsels to attend to, but their house stood closer to Granny Gosling's than anyone else's. They were expected to go and lend a hand. What a relief it was to everyone when Sylvia Rufina said quietly at breakfast that she thought it might do her soul a great deal of good to visit the sick and unfortunate that day. She was young. There would be other cotillions.

As the other women in the household bustled around curling their hair and pressing the ruffles on their dresses, she made up a basket of victuals. She picked things she herself was especially fond of because she knew anything she brought would be found unpalatable by the injured granny. She helped everyone into their frocks, found missing evening bags and hair ribbons, sewed a buckle on a patent leather shoe, and kissed her mother and her sisters as they went off, consciences relieved, to the dance. Her father, realizing no embrace would be offered, avoided the opportunity to receive one. As soon as their carriage disappeared around a bend in the road, she set off in the red cloak, and kept the hateful thing on until she had gone over a rise and down the other side, and was out of her family's sight.

Then she took off the cloak, bundled it up as small as she could, and put it inside a hollow tree, heartily hoping that birds and squirrels would find it, rip it to shreds, and use it to make their winter nests. At the foot of this tree she sat, snug in the nut-brown cloak she had worn underneath the Hunter's gift, and ate every single thing she had packed into the basket. By the time she finished her feast, it was nearly dark. Cheerful beyond measure to be free at last from human society, she went rambling in quest of her soul mates, the four-footed brothers and sisters of the wind.

Faster and faster she went, as her need for them became more desperate, and the world streamed by in a blur of gaudy fall colors. The cold air cut her lungs like a knife, and she found herself pressing the little scar the wolf had left on her collarbone, using that pang to keep herself moving forward. The sun plunged below the hills, and she ran on four legs now, chasing hints among the delicious odors that flooded her nose and mouth. At last she found a place where they had been, a trail that led to their present whereabouts, and the reunion was a glad occasion. There was a happy but orderly circle of obeisances and blessings—smelling, licking, and tail-wagging—and favorite sticks and bones were tossed into the air and tugged back and forth.

Then they hunted, and all was right with the world. She was happy to be the least among them, the anchor of their hierarchy. Despite her status as a novice, she knew a thing or two that could be of value to the pack. The crotchety neighbor would never be in pain again, nor have occasion to complain about the disrespect of young folk or the indecency of current ladies' fashions.

But this time, forewarned that dawn would put an end to her four-footed guise, the young woman took precautions. While everyone else turned in the direction of the den, where they could doze, meat-drunk, she bid them farewell with heartbroken nudges of her nose and retraced her footsteps back to the hollow tree. There, she slept a little, until dawn forced her to put on the hateful red cloak again and return home. She was lucky this time, and arrived well before her hungover, overfed, and overheated relations.

She thought perhaps, with what she now knew, she could endure the rest of her life. She would have two lives, one within this cottage, and the other in the rest of the world. Knowing herself to be dangerous, she could perhaps tolerate infantilization. And so she made herself agreeable to her mother and her sisters, helped them divest themselves of their ballroom finery, and put out a cold lunch for them. She herself was not hungry. The smell of cooked meat made her nauseous.

She had not planned to go out again that night. She knew that if her excursions became too frequent, she would risk being discovered missing from her bed. But when the moon came up, it was as if a fever possessed her. She could not stay indoors. She pined for the soothing sensation of earth beneath clawed toes, the gallop after game, the sweet reassuring smell of her pack mates as they acknowledged her place among them. And so she slipped out, knowing it was unwise. The only concession she made to human notions of decorum was to take the hated red cloak with her.

And that was how he found her, in the full moon, catching her just before she took off the red leather garment. "Quite the little woodsman, aren't you?" he drawled, toying with his knife.

Sylvia Rufina would not answer him.

"Cat got your tongue? Or is it perhaps a wolf that has it, I wonder? Damn your cold looks. I have something that will melt your ice, you arrogant and unnatural bitch." He took her by the wrist and forced her, struggling, to go with him along the path that led to his house. She could have slipped his grasp if she had taken her wolf form, but something told her she must keep her human wits to deal with what he had to show her.

There was something new nailed up to his barn, a huge pelt that shone in the full moonlight like a well-polished curse. It was the skin of her master, the lord of her nighttime world, the blessed creature whose nip had transformed her into something that could not be contained by human expectations. The Hunter was sneering and gloating, telling her about the murder, how easy she had made it for him to find their den, and he was promising to return and take another wolf's life for every night that she withheld her favors.

His lewd fantasies about her wolfish activities showed, she thought, considerable ignorance of both wolves and women. The wolves were lusty only once a year. The king and queen of the pack would mate; no others. The big silver male had loved her, but there was nothing sexual in his passion. He had been drawn by her misery, and decided out of his animal generosity to set her wild heart free. And her desire had been for the wilderness, for running as hard and fast and long as she could, for thirst slaked in a cold mountain stream and hunger appeased nose-down in the hot red mess of another, weaker creature's belly. She craved autonomy, not the sweaty invasion of her offended and violated womanhood. But the Hunter slurred on with his coarse fancies of bestial orgies, concluding, "After all this time I pined for you, and thought you were above me. Too refined, and delicate, and sensitive to notice my mean self. Now I find you're just another bitch in heat. How dare you refuse me?"

"Refuse you?" she cried, finding her voice at last. "Why, all you had to do was ask me. It never occurred to me that such a clever and handsome man would take an interest in someone as inexperienced and plain as me. I am only a simple girl, a farmer's daughter, but you are a man of the world." Where this nonsense came from she did not know, but he lifted his hands from his belt to wrap his arms around her, and that was when she yanked his knife from his belt and buried it to the hilt in the middle of his back.

He died astonished, dribbling blood. She thought it was a small enough penance for the many lives he had taken in his manly pride and hatred of the feral. She took back the knife, planning to keep it, and let him fall.

By his heels, she dragged him back into his own house. Then she took the hide of her beloved down from the wall, shivering as she did so. It fell into her arms like a lover, and she wept to catch traces of his scent, which lingered still upon his lifeless fur like a memory of pine trees and sagebrush, rabbit-fear and the froth from the muzzle of a red-tailed deer, the perfume of snow shaken off a raven's back. It was easy to saddle the Hunter's horse, take food and money from his house, and then set fire to what remained. The horse did not like her mounting up with a wolf's skin clasped to her bosom, but with knees and heels she made it mind, and turned its nose to the city.

Since a human male had taken what was dearest to her, she determined, the rest of the Hunter's kind now owed her reparations. She would no longer suffer under a mother's dictates about propriety and virtue. She would no longer keep silence and let a man, too sure of his strength, back her into a corner. The wolves had taught her much about wildness, about hunters and prey, power and pursuit. One human or a thousand, she hated them all equally, so she would go where they clustered together, in fear of the forest, and take them for all they were worth.

In the city, the Hunter's coins obtained lodging in a once-fashionable quarter of town. Down the street, she had the red cloak made into a whip with an obscene handle, cuffs, and a close-fitting hood. For herself, she had tall red boots and a corset fashioned. The next day, she placed an advertisement for riding lessons in the daily newspaper. Soon, a man rang her bell to see if she had anything to teach him. He wore a gray suit instead of the Hunter's doeskin and bear fur, but he had the same aura of barely controlled fury. He was wealthy, but his privilege had not set him free. It had instead deepened his resentment of anything he did not own, and made him a harsh master over the things that he did possess.

Since he despised the animal within himself, she forced him to manifest it: stripped of anything but his own hide, on all fours, forbidden to utter anything other than a wordless howl. He could not be trusted to govern himself, beast that he was, so she fettered him. And because he believed the animal was inferior to the man, made to be used violently, she beat him the way a drunkard who has lost at cards will beat his own dog. He forgot her injunction against speech when it became clear how the "riding lesson" was to proceed, but she had no mercy. Like most men, he thought of women as cows or brood mares, so if he wanted to experience servitude and degradation, he would have to experience sexual violation as well as bondage and the lash. Bent over a chair, wrists lashed to ankles, he bellowed like a gored bull when the wooden handle of the whip took his male maidenhead.

In the end, he proved her judgement of his character was correct—he knelt, swore his allegiance to her, and tried to lick her, like a servile mutt who wants a table scrap. She took his money and kicked him out with a warning to avoid attempts to sully her in the future. He went away happy, his anger temporarily at bay, his soul a little lighter for the silver that he discarded in a bowl on the foyer table.

Soon Sylvia Rufina's sitting room was occupied by a series
of men who arrived full of lust and shame and left poorer but
wiser about their own natures. But their pain was no balm for
the wounds the Red Mistress, as she came to be called, carried
in her psyche. Her self-styled slaves might prate about worship
and call her a goddess, but the only thing they worshiped was
their own pleasure. She knew, even as she crushed their balls,
that they remained the real masters of the world.

Her consolations were private: the occasional meal of raw
meat and her nightly slumber beneath a blanket of silver fur.
For one whole year, she tolerated the overcrowding, bad smells,
and disgusting scorched food of the city. Her fame spread, and
gossip about her imperious beauty and cruelty brought her paying customers from as far away as other countries. The notion
that one could buy a little freedom, pay for only a limited
amount of wildness, bored and amused the Red Mistress. But
she kept her thoughts to herself, and kept her money in an iron-
bound chest. She lived like a monk, but the tools of her trade
were not cheap, and she chafed to see how long it took for her
hoard of wealth to simply cover the bottom of the box, then
inch toward its lid.

When spring came, at first it simply made the city stink
even worse than usual, as thawing snow deposited a season's
worth of offal upon the streets. There was a tree near Sylvia
Rufina's house, and she was painfully reminded of how beautiful and busy the forest would seem now, with sap rising and
pushing new green leaves into the warming air. Her own blood
seemed to have heated as well, and it grew more difficult to
curb her temper with the pretense of submission that fed her
treasure chest. An inhuman strength would come upon her
without warning. More than one of her slaves left with the
unwanted mark of her teeth upon their aging bodies, and

thought perhaps they should consider visiting a riding mistress who did not take her craft quite so seriously.

The full moon of April caught her unawares, standing naked by her bedroom window, and before she willed it she was herself again, four-footed and calm. After so many months of despicable hard work and monkish living, she was unable to deny herself the pleasure of keeping this form for just a little while. The wolf was fearless and went out the front door as if she owned it. Prowling packs of stray dogs were just one of the many hazards on this city's nighttime streets. Few pedestrians would be bold enough to confront a canid of her size and apparent ferocity. When she heard the sound of a conflict she went toward it, unfettered by a woman's timidity, ruled by the wolf's confident assumption that wherever there is battle there may be victuals.

Down a street more racked by poverty than the one on which the Red Mistress plied her trade, outside a tenement, a man in a moth-eaten overcoat and a shabby top hat held a woman by the upper arms and shook her like a rattle. She was being handled so roughly that her hair had begun to come down from where it was pinned on top of her head, so her face and chest were surrounded by a blond cloud. She wore a low-cut black dress that left her arms indecently bare, and it was slit up the back to display her calves and even a glimpse of her thighs. "Damn you!" the man screamed. "Where's my money?"

The wolf did not like his grating, hysterical voice, and her appetite was piqued by the fat tips of the man's fingers, which protruded from his ruined gloves, white as veal sausages. He smelled like gin and mothballs, like something that ought never to have lived. When he let go of one of the woman's arms so he could take out a pocket handkerchief and mop his brow, the wolf came out of the shadows and greeted him with a barely audible warning and a peek at the teeth for which her kind were named. He was astonished and frightened. The same pocket that had held his handkerchief also contained a straight razor, but before he could fumble it out the wolf landed in the center of his chest and planted him on his back in the mud. A yellow silk cravat, darned and stained, outlined his throat, and was no obstacle.

The wolf disdained to devour him. He was more tender than the querulous granny, but dissolute living had contaminated his flesh. She did not want to digest his sickness. Licking her muzzle clean, she was surprised to see the disheveled woman, waiting calmly downwind, her bosom and face marked by the pimp's assault. "Thank you," the woman said softly. She knew her savior was no domesticated pet who had slipped its leash. Her life had been very hard, but she would not have lived at all if she had not been able to see what was actually in front of her and work with the truth.

Human speech made the wolf uneasy. She did not want to be reminded of her other form, her other life. She brushed past the woman, eager to sample the evening air and determine if this city held a park where she could ramble.

"Wild thing," said the woman, "let me come with you," and ardent footsteps pattered in the wake of the wolf's silent tread. The wolf could have left her behind in a second, but perversely chose not to do so.

They came to the outskirts of a wealthy man's estate. His mansion was in the center of a tract of land that was huge by the city's standards, and stocked with game birds and deer. A tall wrought-iron fence surrounded this land, and the golden one made herself useful, discovering a place where the rivets holding several spears of iron in place had rusted through. She bent three of them upward so the two of them could squeeze beneath the metal barrier. The scent of crushed vegetation and freshly disturbed earth made the wolf delirious with joy.

Through the park they chased each other, faster and faster, until the girl's shoddy shoes were worn paper-thin and had to be discarded. The game of tag got rougher and rougher until the wolf forgot it was not tumbling about with one of its own and nipped the girl on her forearm. The triangular wound bled enough to be visible even by moonlight, scarlet and silver. Then they were two of a kind, one with fur tinged auburn, another with underfur of gold, and what would be more delicious than a hunt for a brace of hares? One hid while the other flushed out their quarry.

Knowing the potentially deadly sleep that would attack after feeding, Sylvia Rufina urged her new changeling to keep moving, back to the fence and under it. The two of them approached her house from the rear, entering through the garden. The golden one was loath to go back, did not want to take up human ways again. But Sylvia Rufina herded her relentlessly, forced her up the stairs and into the chamber where they both became mud-spattered women howling with laughter.

"You are a strange dream," the child of the streets murmured as the Red Mistress drew her to the bed.

"No dream, except a dream of freedom," Sylvia Rufina replied, and pinned her prey to the sheets just as she had taken down the hapless male bawd. The wolf-strength was still vibrant within her, and she ravished the girl with her mouth and hand, her kisses flavored with the heart's blood of the feast they had shared. Goldie was no stranger to the comfort of another woman's caresses, but this was no melancholy, gentle solace. This was the pain of hope and need. She struggled against this new knowledge, but the Red Mistress was relentless, and showed her so much happiness and pleasure that she knew her life was ruined and changed forever.

The bruised girl could not remember how many times she had relied on the stupor that disarms a man who has emptied his loins. No matter how bitterly they complained about the price she demanded for her attentions, there was always 10 times that amount or more in their purses. But instead of falling into a snoring deaf-and-blind state, she felt as awake as she had during the change, when a wolf's keen senses had supplanted her poor blunted human perceptions. The hunger to be tongued, bitten, kissed, and fucked by Sylvia Rufina had not been appeased; it drove her toward the small perfect breasts and well-muscled thighs of her assailant and initiator.

Goldie did not rest until she had claimed a place for herself in the core of her lover's being. It was the first time in her life that Sylvia Rufina had known anything but humiliation and disgust from another human being's touch. Her capacity to take pleasure was shocking, and yet nothing in the world seemed more natural than seizing this cherub by her gold locks and demanding another kiss, on one mouth and then upon and within the other. They fell asleep on top of the covers, with nothing but a shared mantle of sweat to keep them warm. But that was sufficient.

Dawn brought a less forgiving mood. The Red Mistress was angry that someone had breached her solitude. She had not planned to share her secret with another living soul, and now she had not only revealed her alter ego but had made herself a shapeshifting sister.

Goldie would not take money. She would not be sent away. And so the Red Mistress put her suitor to the severest of tests. Rather than imprisoning her with irons or cordage, Sylvia Rufina bade the blond postulant to pick up her skirts, assume a vulnerable position bent well over, and keep it until she was ordered to rise. With birch, tawse, and cane, she meted out the harshest treatment possible, unwilling to believe the golden one's fealty until it was written in welts upon her body. The severest blows were accepted without a murmur, with no response other than silent weeping. When her rage was vented, Sylvia Rufina made the girl kiss the scarlet proof of her ambition that lingered upon the cane. And the two of them wept together, until they were empty of grief and could feel only the quiet reassurance of the other's presence.

That night, the refugee from the streets, who had been put to sleep upon the floor, crept into the bed and under the wolf hide which covered the Red Mistress, and made love to her so slowly and carefully that she did not fully awaken until her moment of ultimate pleasure. It was clear that they would never sleep apart again as long as either one of them should live.

They became mates, a pack of two, hunter and prey with each other, paired predators with the customers who were prepared to pay extra. With the comfort and challenge of each other's company, the work was much less onerous. The Red Mistress's income doubled, and by the time another year had gone by she had enough money to proceed with her plan.

On a day in the autumn, a month or so before the fall of snow was certain, she locked up her house for the last time, leaving everything behind except the trunk of coins and gems, the maid, and warm clothing for their journey. They went off in a coach, with a large silver fur thrown across their knees, headed toward the mountains, and no one in the city ever saw them again. On the way out of the city, they stopped to take a few things with them: a raven that had been chained to a post in front of an inn; a bear that was dancing, muzzled, for a gypsy fiddler; a caged pair of otters that were about to be sold to a furrier.

They had purchased wild and mountainous country, land no sane person would ever have a use for, too steep and rocky to farm, and so it was very cheap. There was plenty of money left to mark the boundaries of their territory, warning hunters away. There was a cabin, suitable for primitive living, and a stable that had already been stocked with a season's worth of feed for the horses. Once safe upon their own precincts, they let the raven loose in the shade of an oak tree, freed the old bear from his cumbersome and painful muzzle in a patch of blackberries, and turned the otters out into the nearest minnow-purling stream.

And that night, amid the trees, with a benevolent round-faced moon to keep their secrets, Sylvia Rufina took the form she had longed for during two impossible years of bondage to human society. The golden-haired girl she loved set her wild (and wise) self free as well. Then they were off to meet the ambassadors of their own kind.

They lived ever after more happily than you, or me.

I've told you this story for a reason. If your woman has gone missing, and you go walking in dark places to try to find her, you may find Sylvia and Goldie instead. If they ask you a question, be sure to tell them the truth. And do not make the mistake of assuming that the wolf is more dangerous than the woman.

Ain't Nothin' But a She/He Thang

Jackie Strano

*2*t was my eighth day in a row of working, but I was getting overtime plus time and a half since it was a holiday, so I wasn't complaining too much. To make it more appealing for me, I got assigned the best gig for the whole night: backstage. Not only did I get to be up close to all the girlies hanging out 'cause they would have to go through me and talk to me—you know, that was my job—but I also got the best gig of backstage: dressing room duty. That meant I'd stand and guard the entrance to where the stars would be before and after the show. Check this out, though: The very best part of it all—and why I wasn't complaining for real—was that in the house would be none other than Salt 'n Pepa, as in fly, for real, honest-to-goodness, hottie and luscious babes getting dressed and undressed and walking past me all sweatin' and pumpin'. Nope, no complaining here.

I was hoping they'd turn out to be nice and talk to me and ask me for a favor or two, 'cause that's how you get to talk to the backstage folks without messing with their minds as they get worked up for a show. I dated a gal a ways back who sang back-up and danced in some Vegas shows, and she told me how the moments before you go onstage are sacred and how she would be still and say a prayer to herself before she walked out to the stage. She told me how there's nothing in the world like walking onstage to a crowded room that's clapping and screaming for you, the lights blinding you, the sounds of the band starting up. All those sounds and lights swirling and echoing in your head along with your heartbeat that's busting to get outta your chest—whew—makes me tired just thinking about it. Anyway, so I know how to stand back and just be there in a way that says I'm ready, willing, and able to take care of business.

I brought my *Very Necessary* CD along to listen to with my player and phones while I was on break the day before the show. It's one of my favorite CDs, you know, the one with "Shoop," "Break of Dawn," and "Sexy Noises Turn Me On." I *love* how these girls sing about sex.

I rose early the morning of the show to get ready the right way. I took my time shining my boots, buffed 'em to a sheen until I saw my reflection in the steel toe. I ironed my pants to a crisp line. Wore the ones that hang a little low on my waist so I could wear my favorite belt with thick leather pieces interwoven and interlocked all the way around like a cop's belt—but more crocheted and '70s-looking, with silver studs running along the length. I snapped on my favorite buckle, the one with the skull and crossbones and the words no mercy above it.

I'd probably have gotten written up if my supervisor had seen it, 'cause it was definitely not standard issue, but neither was getting assigned shifts without having a proper weekend, so I thought between the union rules and the belt buckle I would have the upper hand.

I put on my best and whitest muscle tee, the one that fits me nice and tight and shows off my arms and chest. I tucked it into my boxer briefs for an added streamline under my work shirt. Slapped my hands together with my favorite cologne, padded the sides of my neck and under my arms to spread the scent. I worked some pomade into my hair after I'd brushed and flossed my teeth twice.

I was looking good and fierce and ready to watch any babe's back door.

Last but not least was my gun. My Beretta 9-millimeter semiautomatic pistol. Matte black. I'd cleaned it the night before while watching TV. Sometimes I get into my zone that way, slow mode, just blissing out smoking a bowl, not thinking about nothing, just spacing out while I take it apart and put it back together. Some guys I know get off on shooting theirs at the indoor range down near the airport. I do that for practice, but I just like to take it apart and look at all the pieces knowing that without bullets it's just some metal scraps in a little pile. I feel like I can relax when I take the holster off my belt, but like some phantom weight it's always there on my side making me walk upright and uptight. I like my gun when I'm working. It makes me more equal to all the other guys, and everybody looks me in the eye when I'm wearing it.

Some chick I dated once told me I was power-tripping with my gun and that with it I was like all the other pigs. I was like, *Yeah, babe, whatever.* I didn't need a gun to make me feel powerful. Of course, she loved the power-tripping when she crashed at my house once and somebody tried to climb through my back window while we were sleeping. When he heard me cock the shotgun I keep under the bed, you've never seen a motherfucker run so fast. After that she learned some kind of judo, and now she owns a Glock 9-millimeter and shoots it on the weekends at Jackson Arms, the place down by the airport I was talking about. Then she tells me one night while we were fucking that she wants me to make her suck the barrel off like it's my dick. I was smiling...looking down at her calling her a hungry little power-tripping whore while she sucked my big thick shiny black gun.

She came without even touching herself. She rubbed her cunt all over my boot while she moaned, and drool came out of the corner of her mouth, running down the barrel, getting it as slick and wet as my boot was getting from the juice that was flowing out of her.

She liked power—a lot.

Anyway, so I finished dressing that morning, putting on my deodorant, buttoning up my shirt, doing up my tie, clipping on my tie pin, putting on my rings and my neck chain. I was listening to "Break of Dawn" on my Walkman as I checked myself in the door mirror to make sure it was all put together. I was feeling good: "Keep-keep it on till the break of dawn / Boom boom bam slam keep-keep it on."

My close-cropped hair was styled and smelling good. I love taking my time getting ready like I'm going on a date. My grandfather took forever getting ready every morning before he opened his bar each day. I'd sit on the edge of the bathtub listening to him sing in Italian while he brushed on his shaving cream and rubbed in his hair oil. I was always entertained just sitting there while he talked to me from the mirror about his philosophy of life. He'd be scrubbing his fingernails with his nailbrush while he told me stuff like: "Men are animals. Women are the true grace of God. Men are just pigs waiting to learn how to live right" or "Make sure you take a shower every day, and beware of someone with a Bible in their hand." But my favorite was when he talked about the war and his boxing days back in Italy while he plucked his nose hairs. "You gotta work hard to get what you want, or it isn't yours to have," he'd say in his thick accent. He was a man's man but a total gentleman. I modeled myself after him.

And he always prided himself on his appearance and his manners. Even though he had hands that could rip a man's head off, he never once raised a hand to my grandmother. He never used his force to get his way; he never had to—he was respected. She wanted her diamond ring and her Cadillac and her piece of the American pie after coming here with nothing, and he worked his ass off every day to get it for her.

I ain't got a woman I'm working for right now, but one day I'll find her, and she's going to be a sweet, nasty girl who likes country music and Sunday drives. I got enough money in the bank right now for a down payment on a house, a small one maybe, but still my own house with a yard, room enough for a couple of kids to run around in. Ain't too much to dream about, now is it?

So at work that night I was daydreaming while keeping my eyes on everybody and making sure people are where they're supposed to be and nobody's acting stupid. I got a little nervous before the girls, Cheryl James and Sandra Denton, showed up backstage for their sound check. I'd already met Dee Dee Roper, you know, Spinderella. She showed up earlier to check in with the engineers. She was real nice but all business, of course. I walked alongside her with my flashlight beaming ahead to make sure she didn't trip on any wires. She thanked me and went her way. That was cool. I laid low and didn't say much, just smiled. You know, I didn't want to trip up her concentration with any small talk that she would have to get stuck in. It was a special show for them all, a benefit show that was going to be on TV, and this was the first big gig for them in a long time. The civic auditorium ain't too shabby, if you know what I'm saying. TLC has taken over the charts now for hip-hop girl acts, but, hey, *these* ladies are the queens of all that. Salt 'n Pepa started it all; they are grown-up women. They've had babies. They got hips and all that.

So I was standing there at the door at attention, with my hands about crotch level, one over the other, when the Ms. Hella Fine Salt and Ms. Super Fox Pepa walked up with bags on their shoulders, wearing sunglasses. They were surrounded by their people, who were all talking fast. Some were on cell phones, and they were all official and tense-looking. They all had their passes around their necks like they should have. I greeted them formally and stepped to the side to open the door to their dressing room. Cheryl (Salt) smiled and said thank you. Sandra (Pepa) tilted her head down and lowered her sunglasses to look at me. She made a little *hmph* sound, but I took notice that it was done kinda slyly and not dissy at all. She had her hair done red and long. The rest of the group didn't even notice me, even though I was holding the door for them as they went in. I closed the door behind them, but it was opened a minute later by the guy with the cell phone stuck to his ear.

"Hey, you—you wanna get the refreshments that are supposed to be here?"

"Sorry, sir, that's not my department. I can call someone for you."

He heard my voice, and though it's pretty deep for a woman, it was now obvious that I wasn't a man. I was hating that my job predetermined that I call him "sir." I saw that familiar mixed look of disdain for me and the "ha, ha, I was born with a penis and you weren't" look wash over his face as he puffed his chest a little and said, "Yeah, call someone and let them know they fucked up—and do it quick; the girls are hungry."

I stared back with my best "you Viagra-eating, two-inch dick, balding, rude bastard, you know your wife wants me to

fuck her" look and said, "No problem. You tell 'em Jake is taking care of it."

"Jake?"

"That's right."

"Well, that's great, Jake. I'm in charge around here, and I
get paid a lot to be asshole number 1."

Maybe it was because my back hurt from standing too
many days in a row; maybe it was because I was wishing that
more men were like my grandfather; maybe I was just sick and
fucking tired of being talked down to day after day because I
was a woman, because I was a butch dyke, because I was a
security guard in the middle of a city that has been overrun by
rich little snots working for the Internet. Maybe it was just
because I wanted to be at the bar nursing a cold one, checking
out the girlies and not here taking shit from a short little toad
with an attitude. Whatever the reason, I heard the words come
out of my mouth before I could stop myself...

"Well, then, you must make an awful lot of money, 'cause
you're really good at it."

I couldn't back down now. He opened his eyes wide for a
second, then threw his head back and laughed real hard. He
clapped his hands as he roared with laughter.

"Oh, Jake, you're a funny guy! Yes, sir, you got balls! Oh,
man, that was good! Yeah, you get on the walkie-talkie and tell
hospitality to get their butts down here, and I'll tell the girls
Jake is taking care of it...yes, I will."

He reached into the breast pocket of his sport coat, took
out a business card, and handed it to me.

"I sure as shit make a helluva lot of money, Jake, and if you
ever want to stop fucking around and do some security on the
road, let me know. The pay is better and the pussy is free."

I didn't move. My shoulders relaxed a little when he started laughing, but I didn't reach for the card. He put it in my hand anyway and turned, still laughing, to go back into the room. I heard the muffled sounds of his voice through the door, knowing he was giving an instant replay to the crowd inside. I radioed to services to get someone down there to fix their little predicament while sighing to myself that this just sucked and I didn't need this shit. I put the business card in my breast pocket and snapped it shut, thinking this was going to be a very long night.

The door opened again, and the noisy group all busted out of the room laughing. This time they all looked at me and then at each other while stifling more laughs. I couldn't tell if they were laughing at me or at me just having helped their boss call himself an asshole. At any rate, I was glad they were leaving.

"Remember what I said, Jake...travel, good pay."

"Yeah, and bargain-price pussy. Thanks, I'll keep in touch."

He roared with laughter again and slapped me on the back as he walked away. It'd be a sad day in hell with my brain falling outta my ears before I'd be calling him to get close to some fine tail. Gimme a break. Like I would ever want his sloppy seconds of some deer-in-the-headlights chickie-girl who had dreams of being on MTV and thought she had to go through him to get there. Besides, I get women wanting me to take them home who he could only dream of touching while he whacks off in front of a computer screen. Then I started thinking about how the women I thought were so fierce were working with this guy, like he was their manager and how the hell could they put up with this schmuck? Kinda made my daydream go sour.

Just then the door ripped open again, and Cheryl was right up in my face.

"Jake, want a glass of champagne?"

"Sure."

Without hesitation I walked into their room and took the glass of bubbly she offered me.

"Thanks. Cheers."

"Sorry about Gary—but you moded him. The record company sent him. He doesn't work for us…and thanks for taking care of business."

"No problem. My pleasure."

While Cheryl went back to the mirror to put on more makeup, Sandra came over and turned around in front of me. "Jake, help me lace up my corset, will you, honey?"

Out of the corner of my eye, I caught the two of them giving each other a look, and I knew I was in. *I'm going to be their toy for a little while,* I thought. *I'm going to be their boy.* They'd learn that I liked to be called "Daddy" sometimes and that I didn't care if I got fired or thrown in prison, that I was going to fuck like my life depended on it if I got the chance. I was packing a dick because it felt good, because it completed the uniform, because it was necessary, because it made me feel like a sommatime man.

"Yes, ma'am," I said, putting my champagne down. I took the corset loops on each side and started working them, making sure the corset was stacking her tits right and pulling her waist in properly, just like an ex-girlfriend once showed me. She backed up close to me and pressed her ass slightly into my crotch, pushing her ass into my hard dick underneath my pants.

"Oh, are you feeling good, baby?"

"Yes, ma'am. Your ass is turning me on."

Moaning with gratitude, she moved her fine round ass into me as Cheryl came over and sidled up behind me, touching my ass, running her hands up my back and my arms while nibbling my neck.

"Mmm, you feel good. You work out?"

"Yeah."

"You like black girls, Jake?"

"I like horny girls."

"You're pretty fly for a white guy."

Cheryl reached around to the front of my pants to unzip my fly, then rubbed my dick with her whole hand through my briefs. She worked my dick out of the hole in my underwear and stroked it. Moaning, I leaned my head back into her. Then Sandra turned around and slowly fell to her knees. Looking up at me so sweetly and sassy, she took my dick in one hand, one hand with long painted fingernails and diamond rings on it, and said, "You gonna be my vanilla daddy, baby?"

"If you'll be my sweet chocolate babygirl."

Smiling, Sandra kissed the tip of my dick. I rested back on my heels and thrust my pelvis forward as she licked her lips, her glossy full lips, and took the head of my dick in her mouth like a Popsicle with a fat head. She worked it and sucked it and took it in her mouth deeper, more hungry like. She was looking so fine. I was looking down at her mouth on my dick, her tits, her eyes gazing up at me all sweetly then closing like she was getting all high from sucking me off.

"Oh, shit, girl, you're gonna make me come in your mouth. You are so fucking sexy."

Cheryl turned to kiss me fiercely and deeply while she pulled my shirt out of my pants and got her hands on my bare skin, reaching down to touch my bare ass, which was tight from pumping into her band member's mouth. Her mouth tasted so good—like lipstick and champagne, and her. She inserted one of her fingers into my mouth, and I sucked on it with the same rhythm my dick was getting sucked. She took her finger all wet with my saliva and got in down to the crack of my ass. I knew what was gonna happen, and I wanted it, so I pushed my ass slightly against her finger, letting her know to go for it. She worked her finger down to my asshole, rubbing and pushing against it with steady pressure until I was pushing harder. I was ready to explode with orgasm against the back of my dick, through it and down this babe's throat, all the way to her pussy. She was whimpering like she was too horny while she had her hands on my waist. One hand on my gun, I held her head with my hands, pushing her face down on me. I wanted to fuck her pussy like I was fucking her mouth....full and hard and relentless. My belt buckle cast a spark of light as it reflected in the mirror. Sandra looked at it with my dick still in her mouth, then turned to me and smiled. In that second we had an understanding beyond explanation. I wanted to be fucking her on the counter, spread open for me while I pounded her, wanted to make her tits shake while she screamed my name.

"You want my finger in your ass, baby?" Cheryl breathed in my ear.

"Yeah, come on, fuck my ass. Fuck my ass while I fuck her mouth."

I took her finger all the way in my ass in one motion as I jerked back on it and thrust my dick deeper, gyrating with orgasm as all three of us stayed in rhythm with each other. I felt a bite on the back of my neck, I felt my asshole pulse around her finger, I felt my pussy and dick become one as my voice shouted from my chest a couple of "fuck, yeah"s and other poetic statements until the moment subsided and things came into focus again. Cheryl pulled her finger out slowly as I was still shuddering from waves of orgasm induced by Sandra's tongue slowly and playfully licking the tip of my dick.

"Mmm, you smell good, Jake."

Cheryl's voice played softly in my ear, her lips touching my skin, sending shivers down my spine.

"Thanks."

"You got a regular girl?"

"No one special."

Just then we heard a knock at the door. I hustled my dick back into my pants and tucked in my shirt. Sandra stood up and, like she was reading my mind, walked over and stood by the counter.

The door swung open to reveal Dee Dee. But she wasn't so businesslike anymore.

"You guys having a little party without me?"

"We got ourselves a little freak daddy who likes to play."

"For real?"

Before I knew it, I was in the middle of a full-on fuckfest. These girls knew how to party, and if this was how they got ready for a show, I wasn't about to complain. So I traded off fucking pussy and ass and mouth with my dick, then showed them why lesbian hands have a fan club.

I fucked Cheryl with one, two, three dyke fingers until I knew she wanted my whole fist to fill her up, making every spot the right spot. She came, screaming, right there on the couch until I thought she was going to break every bone in my hand.

At one point Dee Dee was sitting on my lap, her back to me, with my dick in her ass. I reached around to give her clit and pussy some attention until I worked my fingers inside her. I felt my big cock pumping her ass through the walls of her pussy.

"Are you my little bitch hole, baby?"

"Yes, Daddy."

"Does this tight little pussy belong to me?"

"Ooh, yes, Daddy. My pussy worships your cock. I can feel it getting bigger inside me."

I fucked and fucked her, until she started crying, leaning back into me, begging me not to stop.

"I'm gonna come in your ass, girl."

With her ass and pussy so full of me, she beat me to it and came hard, sweat dripping off both of us. The other girls started fighting over who was going to get fucked next. But I noticed the time and knew they needed to get ready for the show. I pulled a joint out of my gun holster and lit it up, took a long, deep toke, then passed it on. They told me which hotel they were staying at and gave me orders to be there when I got off my shift later that night. When I asked them if they always shared a dressing room, they just laughed.

Mrs. Sullivan Takes Off

Ilsa Jule

*B*lindy brought the wheeled carry-on bag to a dramatic halt at the bar. She collapsed the handle inside it and let out a loud protracted sigh meant to get attention. She sat right next to the young woman who was the only other patron in the airport lounge.

Blindy wasn't sure why, but today she needed to get a lot of attention in public. She had argued with the male flight attendant over the ice cubes he'd served with her complimentary can of ginger ale. She knew she was being preposterous when she told him, after inspecting the ice, that it wasn't cold enough. He rolled his eyes and said, "The ice is frozen. I believe that meets FAA regulations."

Blindy acted as if she hadn't heard him and said, "While this ice may be as cold as water gets when it assumes a solid state, ice can become much colder."

The more she frustrated the attendant and her fellow passengers, the more glee she derived from making a spectacle of herself. This was how bored she had become lately. Where she used to take pleasure in distancing herself from others, she now took pleasure in watching herself annoy them. She continued her informed diatribe. "Ice at the polar caps," she explained, "where the annual mean temperature is minus 18 degrees Fahrenheit, is obviously far colder than the ice I have been served." She looked to the two passengers seated beside her, noted their spirits sinking, inhaled to signify that she was not quite done, and concluded her monologue by stating, "Glacial ice, while not only extremely cold, often turns a lovely hue of blue." She then exhaled.

The attendant seized the opportunity to interject and quipped, "We ran out of both glacial and polar-cap ice on the last flight. You'll have to rough it like the rest of us." He then directed his attention to the woman who occupied the middle seat.

Instead of taking offense at the barb, Blindy regarded it as the small reward due for her inspired commentary on ice. In her head she began to quickly draft a letter of complaint to the airlines, wherein she would forgo any mention of her remarks on glacial ice; rather she would complain that her polite request for clean ice after she had been served dirty ice was met with a rude refusal.

She inspected the top of the can of ginger ale she had been handed and noted that except for a few small particles of dust, it looked clean. She opened it, and with a flourish she pushed the cup with the low-grade ice to the side, then drank straight from the can.

As the two passengers who sat next to her continued to exchange looks, she turned back to *People* magazine, a guilty pleasure reserved for in-flight reading, and pretended to read. In fact, she couldn't concentrate. Her mind wandered aimlessly. She was beginning to sense that her recent languor was indicative of something greater than boredom.

Now seated at the bar, Blindy realized that the young

woman had noticed the bumping of the carry-on bag as it was brought to a stop but had not become agitated. Blindy felt unsatisfied by her nonreaction.

The bartender, a weary Irish man with a '50s-style haircut, now gone completely white, took a last drag off his cigarette, stubbed it out, and walked toward Blindy.

"A champagne cocktail," she said as he came to a stop in front of her.

She'd never had a champagne cocktail, but she liked the name. It sounded annoying. Would she annoy the bartender with this request? He shrugged as if to say, *Suit yourself,* and began mixing the drink.

For a moment Blindy wondered if bartenders went home to their wives and smelled like a bar in the same way that a cook smells like a kitchen. Could a bartender smell of anything more than smoke, emptied ashtrays, and stale beer?

Blindy's thoughts turned to Sandy, the female chef she had dated for several years in San Francisco. Sandy often came home with the smell of long hours spent in an active kitchen lingering on her hair and clothing. It had not been a pleasant smell. What was impressed upon Blindy's memory even more than the smell was the condition of Sandy's hands and forearms. They were chronicles of bumps into hot pans and nicks to the flesh from knives. According to Sandy, both dull and sharpened knives were hazards in their own ways. Sandy's arms and hands never quite healed; while bruises and burns faded, fresh ones appeared daily. Her skin was mottled by her vocation. Sandy didn't care about the branding of her flesh; she pleased herself and the eaters with a continuously evolving menu. Blindy also recalled that Sandy had been a bit of a grump.

After the breakup, Sandy went on to open a successful bistro in the wine country of Northern California, and Blindy made a habit over the years of flipping through food magazines in hopes of finding mention of her. Sometimes she was rewarded with small articles. Sandy appeared in the black-and-white photos that accompanied the stories, a little older and somewhat heavier, in the way one expects a middle-aged and successful chef to fill out. Blindy's past association with Sandy pleased her.

"I fucked you," she'd say softly to the photo in the magazine. "You fucked me. You fucked me and cooked for me. Why didn't it work out?"

Blindy turned her thoughts back to the woman seated beside her. The woman had flawless white skin, and her dark-brown hair pulled back into a ponytail highlighted the soft angular features of her face. A small forehead, high cheekbones, a thin narrow nose, a thin mouth, and a fine jaw and chin. Blindy felt she was appraising the woman as one might a purebred dog or horse.

This woman wasn't pretty, but she was very attractive. Her looks, a combination of conventional attributes, were imbued with a sense of the unknown as attractive, not scary.

The woman looked straight ahead at the bottles of alcohol that rested in rows along the mirrored wall. As the bartender placed a napkin and the champagne cocktail in front of Blindy, the woman turned to look. Blindy couldn't catch the woman's eye, which frustrated her. *Not until I have annoyed you will I feel satisfied*, she thought.

Blindy let out another protracted sigh and kicked her high heels off her feet onto the floor so that one of them rolled under the woman's chair. She massaged her feet through her knee-high stockings and groaned slightly. The woman finally turned. Blindy rubbed her toes, made eye contact, and said, "Bunions."

The woman formed her mouth into a meager smile, and

Blindy ruled this response: not good enough. *You are bothered, but not completely. You will not go home and complain of your dealings with me to a lover or friend. My work here is not done.*

Blindy picked up the shoe that was nearest to her with her toes and then said, "Excuse me," and nodded in the direction of the other shoe.

The woman leaned over, picked up the shoe, and handed it to her.

As the woman gave her the shoe, Blindy thrust the question, "Where you coming from?" at her.

The woman hesitated in answering, but Blindy persisted, "Or is it going to?"

Blindy smiled a warm broad smile. Something about using honey versus vinegar to attract flashed through her mind. She felt herself pulling more of a spider-and-fly routine. *You will be caught by me*, thought Blindy.

"I like dick," the woman said icily and tossed her head so that the ponytail moved back and forth.

The corners of the smile shifted, and now Blindy's lips were drawn into a thin even line. A surge of adrenaline coursed through her veins. In her mind she railed against the woman: *I haven't attended dyke marches, gay pride parades, Take Back the Night vigils, and volunteered at a rape crisis center to have you, Miss Prissy Straight Girl, throw your sexuality in my face.*

Blindy offered, "I have one in my bag," and nodded to the carry-on at her feet. "If you're not too busy, I'd be more than happy to show you how it's really done."

In fact, she did not have a dildo in her bag. She had stopped traveling with one after catching the questioning looks of the guard examining the X ray of her luggage as it was scanned at the security checkpoint. Blindy left her dick at home unless she traveled with baggage to be checked.

She took a large drink from the cocktail and concluded that it was too sweet. Now she longed for a double bourbon, straight up, both for the taste and to reverse the impression that she was a sissy. Blindy would show this chick who was boss.

The woman snickered, turned toward Blindy, and stood up to leave. Blindy couldn't say whether she meant to block the woman from departing or not, but her leg moved behind the woman, and as she attempted to back out she met with Blindy's knee. Blindy smiled, placed her hand gently on the woman's arm, applied pressure, and said, "Why don't you take a seat?"

The woman would have had to make an awkward climb in the opposite direction to get out. She knew she was trapped, so she sat down again, her cheeks flushed slightly pink.

Blindy snapped her fingers to get the bartender's attention. He looked up from the newspaper or racing form he was reading. "Another round." Blindy waved her fingers over the two glasses.

The woman sat facing forward, her eyes shining with anger. Blindy looked at her in profile until the bartender placed fresh napkins and drinks in front of each woman.

Blindy took a sip of the cocktail. "Drink up," she said, and lifted her glass.

The woman turned and said, her voice cracking, "I know all about you. You're trying to recruit me."

Blindy smiled at this charge. She matched the woman's piercing gaze but said nothing.

"I'm married to a man," the woman said, and waved her left hand at Blindy.

Unlike a vampire who recoils at the specter of the cross, Blindy did not shy from the wedding band. Instead she took the woman's hand and held it so that their palms met. The engagement ring, a large diamond in an attractive setting, was worn beside a wedding band that was tasteful in its simplicity.

Something had passed between them while their palms were in contact. Blindy let the woman's hand slip to the bar. "Platinum?" she asked.

The woman nodded.

"Drink up, sweetie. I am going to fuck you," Blindy boasted and took a long drink of champagne. The sugar in the drink was giving her a buzz. She had forgotten all about her boredom.

The woman looked at Blindy and smiled. "You seem awfully sure of yourself."

Blindy nodded and wondered if she really wanted to go through all the trouble of fucking this woman.

"What's your name, Miss I-Like-Dick?"

The woman took a sip of her drink, then stated matter-of-factly, "Mrs. John Sullivan."

Blindy leaned in close to the woman so that both of their faces seemed quite large and said "Blindy," extending her hand.

The woman took Blindy's hand, and Blindy held it instead of shaking. Mrs. Sullivan shook her hand free of the grasp.

Blindy liked the feel of the smooth, warm, dry skin and the small bones in the fingers of Mrs. Sullivan's hand.

They looked at each other. Blindy noted that the woman had velvety blue eyes. Mrs. Sullivan broke her reverie with the question, "What makes an anonymous fuck between women any better than one between a man and a woman?"

Blindy was taken aback by this.

After a pause, in a playful tone, she said, "I give up. What makes anonymous sex between women better than between a man and a woman?"

Blindy's urge to annoy was being assuaged. Blindy looked at Mrs. Sullivan's small breasts underneath the gray sweater she was wearing. She asked herself: *Have I been too well behaved?*

Do I need an hour with this woman to change all that? Could hand-holding be enough? When can I declare a victory? Do I want war or will a few battles appease me? Will a kiss? The feel of this woman's tongue in my mouth?

As the list of questions in Blindy's head increased, Mrs. Sullivan interrupted her thoughts. "Pride," she stated.

Blindy flinched at this. Could Mrs. Sullivan be right?

Blindy looked at her fingers as she traced small circles in the condensation on her glass and replied, "Maybe."

"You want to crush my pride," stated Mrs. Sullivan, and Blindy saw tears well up in the woman's eyes.

"I don't want to crush your pride. I want to keep mine in one piece."

Mrs. Sullivan, in an angered tone, said loudly, "And what? Your rubber dick inside me, that keeps your pride intact?"

Blindy looked at the bartender. If he heard the question, he acted disinterested.

"Shhh. Don't get all excited," Blindy said. She felt a small headache coming on from the champagne. She snapped her fingers to get the bartender's attention. "A glass of ice water," she said.

When he placed it in front of her she asked him, "Don't you have some tunes? This place is a crypt."

"CD player's broke," he answered, and headed back to his newspaper.

The women sat in silence for a few minutes. The roar of jet engines broke in at intervals. Blindy wondered about Mrs. Sullivan. Were there tiny particles of Mr. Sullivan sprinkled about her? Something from a kiss, a caress, a fuck? Where was Mr. Sullivan? What kind of a fool was he? His wife was not the kind of woman to be left unattended in an airport bar.

Mrs. Sullivan looked at Blindy, and Blindy noticed an

unmistakable "Yes" being conveyed to her. Her heartbeat quickened and her mind flew into gear. They needed a plan, and they needed it within the next two minutes.

They heard a jumble of voices approach the lounge. Shortly a group of people, male and female, in matching uniforms entered the lounge. They were a flight crew. Someone yelled, "First round is on me." Then the bartender was addressed by his first name, Henry, and the somber mood of the lounge was disrupted by the commotion.

Blindy looked at Mrs. Sullivan and said, "Let's get out of here," and tucked a $50 bill under Mrs. Sullivan's glass. Blindy gently took the woman's elbow, releasing it once Mrs. Sullivan had taken a few steps toward the door. As they stood next to each other, Blindy noticed they were of equal height, but Mrs. Sullivan was slender, with a boyish figure. Blindy was voluptuous. Mrs. Sullivan wore a short-sleeved charcoal-gray wool sweater, dark gray slacks that zipped up the side, and black heels.

Blindy picked up Mrs. Sullivan's bag from the bar and, handing it to her, said, "You're traveling light. Did you lose your luggage?"

She didn't answer the question, and as they exited the lounge Blindy noticed a dark mood come over Mrs. Sullivan. Blindy grew concerned. Her own mood was equally erratic. She still wanted to fuck this woman, she had said as much, and the boredom that she had tended to so carefully for so long was interrupted, but what to do about this situation?

As they left the terminal on the street level, the last light of day faded from the sky, and Mrs. Sullivan's silence spoke of impending misfortune. Blindy wasn't sure she wanted to be let in on the details, but trained as she was in crisis intervention she knew Mrs. Sullivan should not be left alone. When the Marriott shuttle bus pulled up, without thinking about it,

Blindy guided Mrs. Sullivan on board. Upon arriving at the hotel, Blindy led Mrs. Sullivan to a seat in the lobby and secured a room with two double beds for the night.

Once in the room, Blindy cracked open the bar. "Were you drinking gin or vodka?"

Mrs. Sullivan mumbled, "Vodka."

Blindy mixed a weak vodka tonic and opened a Heineken for herself.

She placed the drink on the table beside Mrs. Sullivan, then she began to undress, carefully removing her skirt and blouse. She sat at the edge of one of the beds in her bra and slip. As she rolled off the stockings she felt a little self-conscious in her underwear. She also felt, and she couldn't say why, happy. Here she was, sitting in a hotel room with a gorgeous and disturbed woman. Only hours before she had been mulling the possibilities to quell the dullness of another Sunday night. She had come up with the thoroughly unoriginal: clean the kitchen and rent a video.

"He left me," said Mrs. Sullivan.

"Did he?" asked Blindy.

Their eyes met. "Yes, he did."

Blindy thought, *You have beautiful fucking eyes,* then asked, "When?" and took another sip of beer.

"Last year."

"Hmm," said Blindy, and wondered, *Is this just sinking in?*

"I'm coming from my sister's wedding."

"And?"

"And I haven't told anyone."

"And?"

"I feel awful about lying to everyone."

Blindy stood up and stretched. Her mood now switched tracks, and she thought, *What the fuck do I care if you've been left?* "Well, I'm going to take a nice hot bath. Are you hungry? I want some room service."

Mrs. Sullivan continued to brood while Blindy walked to the phone and placed an order for a burger and a small salad.

Once in the tub, Blindy heard the sounds of the TV. As she relaxed in the bubble bath she heard a knock on the door and called out, "Will you sign for that?" Blindy heard the sound of the tray being placed on the table in the other room. She hoped that Mrs. Sullivan gave the guy a good tip. She couldn't stand meager tipping.

After a moment or two Mrs. Sullivan peered her head around the door and asked, "Enjoying yourself?"

"Quite," replied Blindy swishing some of the bubbles.

"Good," replied Mrs. Sullivan, and then she hurled the plate with the burger on it at Blindy. Blindy raised her arms to protect herself. The plate rebounded off Blindy's forearm and landed with a crash on the floor. Blindy was unhurt and not shaken. She had once protected a woman at the shelter from an ax-wielding former boyfriend. It took a lot to get her worked up.

The burger had fallen on the bath mat. Blindy fished the soggy bun out of the bubbles. She reached over, took a bite of the burger, decided it was still edible, and rested it on the edge of the tub.

The lettuce, tomato, and slice of onion lay on the floor.

Blindy stepped out of the bath and stood on the bath mat, in no hurry to dry herself. She watched as trails of bubbles slowly slid down her breasts and stomach. Then she rested her palms against the edge of the sink counter and examined her body in the wall mirror. The water dripped from her long, dark pubic hair onto the mat. A rare feeling of admiration filled her. For a second or two she didn't feel middle-aged. As of late she liked that she was older and wasn't even bothered by the slight bulge around her waist and the way flesh had gathered at her hips in recent years. Blindy stooped to pick up the pieces of the plate and marveled that it had been broken neatly in two. She placed the halves back together, producing the illusion that the plate was whole.

She dried herself off and wrapped a towel around her body. Her breasts swayed as she went into the main room in search of ketchup. At that moment she didn't care if she looked desirable or not.

Blindy swallowed hard as she entered the room. Mrs. Sullivan was lying on the bed naked, her white skin in stark contrast to the unattractive dark brown bedspread.

Blindy took a few bites of the burger and turned off the television as she passed it. She stood at the bedside and looked at Mrs. Sullivan lying rigidly on the bedcovers.

"Well, aren't you going to fuck me?" asked Mrs. Sullivan defiantly.

Blindy looked at Mrs. Sullivan's body and licked some grease off her fingers. Was this woman's body an ideal? Yes. She felt her hands begin to speak to her. *Touch her,* they said. *What are you waiting for?* they asked.

"You're not such a big tough dyke after all?" taunted Mrs. Sullivan.

"Who, me?" replied Blindy, and gestured to the curves of her body beneath the white towel. Her breasts sagged under their weight and age. "I never said I was a dyke."

Mrs. Sullivan's bone-white skin gleamed, and Blindy eyed the small breasts with large, dark nipples. Her eyes traveled past the detailed outline of her ribs, past her taut stomach, and rested on the pubic area. Mrs. Sullivan's lips were visible since she shaved all the hair down there.

"You look taller when you're lying down," said Blindy, and Mrs. Sullivan laughed.

"How old are you?" asked Blindy.

"Twenty-seven. Why?"

Blindy picked up the edge of the bedspread and covered Mrs. Sullivan. She then seated herself and finished eating the burger.

"Why did you ask me how old I was?" the woman asked.

"Just curious."

Blindy had a strict no fucking-anyone-under-the-age-of-30 policy. Of course she had come up with that policy when she had turned 30. But that was 18 long years ago. She wondered if 27-year-old women always had such nice bodies. It had been more than a year since her last lover, and while there were many reasons to fuck Mrs. Sullivan (namely that she was completely hot and lying there naked, waiting), there seemed to be more reasons for not fucking her, none of which she cared to contemplate at this moment.

Blindy swallowed the last bite of the burger. She then grabbed a fresh beer and sat at the foot of the bed where Mrs. Sullivan was wrapped up like a burrito. She pressed the cool glass of the bottle to her temple. The headache from the champagne had subsided. She placed her hand on top of Mrs. Sullivan's foot. She'd had a pedicure recently, and the nails were painted a dark blue. The skin on top of the foot was smooth like flour.

Blindy looked up from the small ankle and met Mrs. Sullivan's gaze. Her previous trepidation was replaced with a craving. The roles had switched. Blindy knew she would not be able to resist being wanted.

Blindy's hands, which had found their way under the fold of the cover, moved slowly up Mrs. Sullivan's smooth leg. When her hand reached the top of her thigh, her fingertips edged along the border of the fine stubble. Her fingers pleaded, do it, slide up inside her. Go on. Do it.

She ignored their urgings and continued to move her hand up along the flat stomach. Blindy's towel had fallen open, and when her hand reached the woman's neck she pulled the cover back and pressed into Mrs. Sullivan, her arm resting under the woman's breasts.

Mrs. Sullivan rolled onto her side, pressing her coccyx into Blindy's pubic bone. Blindy thought, *The beast with two backs, indeed.*

"What now, Mrs. Sullivan?" Blindy's lips gently pressed to the nape of the woman's neck.

"Fuck me."

Blindy felt her clit swell, and pressed the dense covering of her pubic hair into Mrs. Sullivan's ass. She pulled back and let her fingers, which required no historical knowledge or instruction, do what they longed to do.

She pressed her index and middle finger into Mrs. Sullivan's pussy, the heel of her palm pressed against her anus. With this Mrs. Sullivan pressed herself deeper into Blindy's embrace. Mrs. Sullivan was either a quick study, or Blindy was one of several who'd attempted to recruit the elusive Mrs. Sullivan. A woman of no experience with other women never seizes fingers in this way and doesn't know which parts of herself to give to a woman.

With her fingers inside Mrs. Sullivan, Blindy felt the desire in both women increase 10-fold, or maybe it was a hundred times. She knew this wasn't the time to work on a math problem, but it was clear that Mrs. Sullivan was a whole lot closer to giving in than Blindy had hoped for.

Blindy thought, *Did you get this wet for Mr. Sullivan?*

Mrs. Sullivan pressed against Blindy vigorously. The contractions against Blindy's fingers were strong.

"Your pussy is…buttery," said Blindy.

"I want your whole arm inside me," the woman implored.

Blindy laughed at this request. She pressed her remaining fingers inside Mrs. Sullivan's overwet pussy and noticed the more fingers she pushed inside Mrs. Sullivan, the bigger she got.

Blindy removed her fingers, and Mrs. Sullivan asked, "Where are you going?" "Nowhere," replied Blindy as she rolled Mrs. Sullivan onto her back. Blindy got on her hands and knees so that she was crouched over Mrs. Sullivan, and they looked into each other's faces for a minute or so.

Blindy pressed four fingers into Mrs. Sullivan and thought, *Perhaps my arm will fit inside you.* Slowly she curled her fingers around her thumb, and then with a decisive push her fist was inside. Mrs. Sullivan, who had been sucking on Blindy's forearm, gasped and then closed her jaws into the flesh. Blindy winced and Mrs. Sullivan bent her leg and Blindy rocked her clit against the small kneecap and came in a short bright burst.

Blindy slowly uncurled and withdrew her fist, pleased she still had it. The air in the room felt cool on her hand up to the wrist. She wrapped her hand in the sheet.

"What was that?" Mrs. Sullivan asked after a moment.

"I don't know," replied Blindy, and thought, *Straight women can be such a chore.*

"Hmm," said Mrs. Sullivan.

Even though the rough texture of the bedspread was unpleasant against her skin, Blindy covered herself and Mrs. Sullivan with it. She lay there waiting for the horror of what had happened to make its way into her thoughts and feelings. The "Oh, my God! What have I done?" failed to materialize. She half enjoyed Mrs. Sullivan lying by her side. Blindy thought it felt nice and perhaps it was nice.

As she lay there, her fingers twitched for more while the

rest of her reposed happily in that doped-up way the body feels after sex.

Mrs. Sullivan spoke. "He said I didn't love him anymore."

Blindy pulled Mrs. Sullivan closer to her, thinking, *What's not to love?* and said, "That sounds like projection."

Mrs. Sullivan said nothing but tugged Blindy's arm, which held her fast, indicating not to let go.

In an effort to comfort Mrs. Sullivan, Blindy said, "It's hard enough to know what's in one's own heart. Could he really know what was, or in this case was not, contained in yours?"

"That's the thing of it: He was right," said Mrs. Sullivan, "Not that I had stopped loving him, but I was no longer *in love* with him."

"Was he still in love with you?" asked Blindy.

"Oh, I don't know. Maybe I don't care."

"Then why are you upset?"

"Because my sister is really in love with her husband, and seeing the joy in her face made me sad. She was beaming, and I thought, *She can't be serious.* And I felt jealous because I don't have that."

Another straight woman swindled, Blindy thought, but said, "Maybe she isn't as happy as you think. Maybe she was grinning out of a state of nervous exhaustion."

All this patter about straight people was beginning to wear on Blindy's nerves.

"No! She meant it," cried Mrs. Sullivan defensively.

Blindy knew that discussing family could produce the most heated interchanges between people who have known each other for decades, let alone a few hours. She loosened her grasp on Mrs. Sullivan and the woman rolled away a little.

Mrs. Sullivan pulled Blindy's arms back around her, "Oh, don't do that. Stay."

Blindy entwined her fingers in Mrs. Sullivan's and asked, "Do you have to get going soon?" hoping the answer would be yes.

"No. I'd be returning to an empty apartment. I hate how that feels."

"I kind of like that feeling," said Blindy.

"If it's what you want, then it's fine. I haven't gotten used to it. I was thinking of getting a pet. Something to warm the place up."

Blindy made no reply to this. The idea of pet maintenance got on her nerves. Cats were all hairballs and smelly litter boxes. Dogs were breathing on you all the time and needed to be walked.

They lapsed into silence. Her hands wandered over Mrs. Sullivan's thighs and stomach. She wondered what to do next. She felt a bout of mania coming on and remembered why she hated casual sex. It made her feel lonely. It was an emotional experience devoid of emotional attachment.

Blindy needed to get back to her apartment. She felt Mrs. Sullivan's breathing move into the easy rhythm of sleep. If Blindy was going to escape, now was her opportunity.

Blindy didn't owe Mrs. Sullivan a thing. She felt odd sneaking out, but she didn't want to say goodbye. She just wanted to get home and be comforted by her books. She wanted to lie on the rug that had once been her grandmother's and had been the only housewarming gift from her mother that Blindy liked when she moved into her first apartment. She hated the way the hotel room smelled. She knew if she stayed the smell would be in her hair, stay on her skin, and give her bad dreams. She felt the panic of not being able to get out of the room fast enough.

Blindy edged her way off the bed, careful not to make a sound. She noted that she didn't have the energy to care about

Mrs. Sullivan. She used to feel a sense of guilt after sex, but she used to have a sense of expectation. Tonight she felt neither. She couldn't find anything to latch on to in Mrs. Sullivan. With some women it's the way they say your name or the way they look at you or the way they walk. There has to be something.

With Mrs. Sullivan there was no edge and certainly no hook. She was a confused woman who didn't have the guts to inform her family that she was a divorcée. None of this was any of Blindy's business.

Blindy scooped her clothes off the unused bed and went to the bathroom. After she peed she didn't flush but remained sitting on the toilet. She pulled her weekly planner out of her purse, tore the last page out, and wrote, "Sex between two women who don't know each other can be distinguished from sex between a man and a woman who don't know each other…" Blindy couldn't answer the riddle. She wanted to say, "Because it's just better, damn it!" and in her opinion it was.

She crumpled the piece of paper and stuffed it into her purse. She put on her skirt and buttoned two of the buttons on the blouse. She balled up her knee-highs, panties, and bra and threw them in her bag, alongside the crumpled note.

She flicked off the bathroom light and tiptoed to the door. Mrs. Sullivan snored gently. She carefully picked up the carry-on, as one of the wheels had a tendency to squeak. Even if Mrs. Sullivan did wake up and call out to her, by the time she had enough clothing on to give chase, Blindy could be down the hall and out the door of the main lobby if she took the stairs. It was only two flights. She placed the bag outside the door, and then, fearing drama, carefully pulled it shut. It closed noiselessly.

As a precaution she used the stairs. She hoped the clerk who worked the night shift wouldn't notice that her calves were now bare. As she turned the corner where the sliding doors came into view, she saw a cab waiting for a fare. She hurried toward it. The cool night air kissed the bare skin of her legs and gave her goose bumps. Her nipples hardened, and as she slid onto the vinyl seat she felt her anxiety begin to fade. She would be home in 20 minutes. She might be bored and alone, but at least she'd be alone.

What I Learned in Yeshiva
Raphaela Crown

*I*t's not like my family is super-religious or anything. Yes, our home was kosher ("for Grandma"), but we ate whatever we wanted at the Chinese restaurant we went to every Sunday night—except for spareribs, for some reason. I mean, I went to public school, plus twice-a-week Hebrew school, which was a real drag. But I must have talked about my friend Christopher a little too much, because the next thing I knew, it was goodbye freshman year at Barnard, hello yeshiva—in Jerusalem! Little did my parents know that I was hanging around Christopher because of his twin sister, Christina. But somehow I didn't think that piece of information would help distract them from the looming threat of intermarriage.

So here I am in yeshiva. Well, it's not exactly a yeshiva, since that's just for guys. I'm at "Midreshet Lippenschmuckler," which means…well, I'm not sure what it means, except that it's like a yeshiva, only for girls, and some people named Lippenschmuckler gave a shitload of money to have the place named after them. If my name was Lippenschmuckler I sure wouldn't go around advertising it. But everyone calls the place "Lipsmackers" anyway.

And speaking of names, I'm not Suzanne anymore—I'm Shoshana—and my frankly hot body is completely hidden in these stupid long skirts and long sleeves. Well, you're allowed to roll them up to your elbow. Big whoop. But suddenly I'm looking at elbows in a way I never did before.

The other girls are actually pretty nice, especially my roommate, Tzipporah, formerly known as Tiffany. She's kind of a Jewish Southern belle; she's from Atlanta and has the cutest accent. We look a little like Mutt and Jeff. She can't be more than 5 foot 3, this side of plump but not an ounce over, and with her firm, bouncy tits she actually looks sexy in these clothes. She's all pink and blond, while I'm 5 foot 9 and strongly resemble the illustration for "Rebecca the Jewess" from that book *Ivanhoe* we read in senior English. You know, olive skin, dark brown hair, green eyes, and what my mother claims is a Roman nose. It just looks long to me. Tzippy's, on the other hand—-she claims it's really hers—is so cute I want to… But that's definitely not on the program here. Instead we spend all morning reading *Chumash* (the first five books of the Bible) and the Prophets, who are always wailing about something or other, then all afternoon talking about modesty and "family purity" (that means sex) and which *bracha* (blessing) you're supposed to say before you eat which food.

I tell you, there's nothing like talking about modesty all day to make a person obsessed with sex. When we go out—careful to keep our elbows covered; you just know what a bare elbow can do to a susceptible man—I feel like a huge sign saying, SEX! SEX! BUT DON'T TOUCH! Tzippy's brother is in the guys' yeshiva (those Lipsmackers were definitely into putting their name in large letters on the outside of buildings) and says it's even worse for them. They're always getting hard-ons during the Talmud discussions.

Take "Practical *Halacha*"—religious rules and stuff—which we have in the afternoons. It can get pretty graphic. If Mom and Dad only knew. For instance, the *ketuba,* the marriage contract, not only guarantees a woman's right to have sexual relations but actually entitles her to sexual satisfaction! And it's a mitzvah—a really good deed—to have sex on Shabbat. So all those people who won't desecrate the Sabbath by turning a light on are actually screwing like rabbits. But according to Jewish law, a woman isn't supposed to have sex when she's having her period or for the seven days afterward. In the Bible the prohibition is just for the time that you're actually bleeding, but later the rabbis tacked on extra days. "Probably at the request of their wives," Tzippy leaned over and whispered to me.

Today we talked in excruciating detail about how a woman knows exactly when her period is over and it's time to go to the *mikvah* and get immersed so she can start having sex with her husband again. Sometimes a woman can't tell if she's "clean" or not, and she actually has to show her underpants to the rabbi for a ruling. Can you imagine? All of this stuff about underwear and cleanness and "discharge" and everything made me kind of sick but also excited, in a way.

"I'd check *your* undies, honeybunch," Tzippy whispered, wiggling her blond eyebrows like Groucho Marx.

"While I'm in them?" I wanted to say, but I lost my nerve. If I didn't know better, I'd swear the girl was flirting with me. She's always touching me when we talk. And when we have *havruta* (that's studying in pairs) she always looks at me with those big blue eyes of hers. "What do you think?" she asks. "I really want to know what you think." Or, "Oh, Shoshi, you're so smart! I never would have thought of *that.*"

It drives me crazy just to be near her. She's so delicious I want to nibble on her neck or suck her fingers, but of course I'd never do any of these things. At least during the day. Last night I had the most wonderful dream. Tzippy was in it, of course, whispering in my ear, like she always does, only this time she was saying, "Yes, do it, do it." Tzippy said I woke up with a huge grin on my face, but I refused to tell her what I'd been dreaming about.

Fortunately, since nobody takes girls' learning all that seriously, we can go out whenever we want to, provided we're with another girl, of course, to shops, cafés, even aerobics classes. Yesterday we went to the Arab market—the souk—in the Old City. "Come look, pretty American girls, it doesn't cost anything to look!" the shopkeepers kept saying. Tzippy was a huge hit. Several men offered to marry her on the spot.

"Yeah, your parents would really go for that," I said.

"I can think of something they'd like even less," she answered, looking right at me, "and it would definitely be more fun." I'm not sure what she meant, but I got a funny feeling somewhere in the midsection of my long denim skirt.

One word about those skirts: It's hard to walk without tripping over yourself. As we were wandering through the souk, I twisted my ankle and ended up falling right on top of Tzippy. I was mortified, of course, though despite my embarrassment I managed to register the fact that she felt pretty soft and wonderful. But the weird thing is that I could have sworn she pulled me tighter just as I was trying to scramble off her.

"You'd better take my arm," she said. "We can't have you falling for these Arab guys, now, can we?" But though I tried to tease her back, all I could think of was how deliciously plush she felt and how good she smelled and how my arm seemed to rub against the side of her breast with each step we took. She insisted on buying me some lavender-scented oil to rub into my twisted ankle.

Actually, my ankle is fine; it's my heart that feels like it has an Ace bandage wrapped around it. But I'd better recover in time for aerobics today. It's a women's-only club. We can't have men watching us prance around in next to nothing, now can we? I'm amazed, though, at what these *frum*—super-religious— ladies wear when there aren't any guys around. They come into the club in hats, long skirts, long sleeves, and high-necked blouses and then emerge from the dressing room wearing slinky Spandex cut all the way up the side. Tzippy has a cute two- piece number that holds her body tight and firm, and as she sweats, two perfect circles start to form around her breasts. And her butt is almost a perfect match: high and round, like a cou- ple of beach balls. I love the way the Lycra hugs the bottom of each cheek. Frankly, it's all I can do to follow the instructor and not Tzippy's ass. Fortunately, I'm pretty athletic. I ran track in high school, so I can keep up without too much effort. Sometimes Tzippy calls me "Legs."

Today, after "Funky Step," we decided the shower at the club looked kind of gross. So we headed back to the dorm with our sweaty workout clothes underneath our skirts, feeling very daring.

So get this. While we're in the shower, Tzippy asks me to scrub her back. That old line, I think to myself. Can the Georgia Peach really be that oblivious? But of course I'm delighted to help my fellow Jew, so I take the bar of soap and run it up and down her downy back. I wish I could soap the crack of her ass. Those globes are pretty much irresistible. Is it my imagination or can Tzippy actually be groaning as I drop the soap then slowly stand up? She does seem to be rinsing herself awfully carefully down there.

"Shall I do your back?" she asks.

"No," I say, embarrassed that my nipples are standing

straight up and that I have goose bumps all over even though the water is nice and warm.

"You could be a model," she says approvingly, "so trim and muscular. I've got myself a little belly. See?"

I groan silently. I can't look, or I'll be rubbing my hands all over the slight but delicious rise of her stomach. So we towel off and put on clean underwear, but somehow we don't get around to getting dressed. We agree it was a great workout, but Tzippy says she's kind of tight and would I mind rubbing her back with those big strong hands of mine? Again, I think, even a girl from Georgia can't be this naive, but of course I agree, using the lavender oil she bought me at the souk.

"Any place in particular?" I ask. At first I simply try to sit at the edge of her bed and lean over, but it's kind of awkward.

"Well, just sit on me, darlin'," says my delightful room-mate, which of course makes sense, so I start kneading her lovely back, still soft and warm from the shower. But her lacy white bra is in the way. I definitely don't want to get oil all over it, so I ask and Tzippy agrees, well, of course she should take off her bra. But the thing opens in the front, not the back. So I reach around to unsnap it, trying not to actually touch her breasts, though of course I want to.

I notice her delicious peachy tits seem to stand up as I brush against them—inadvertently, of course—and it's all I can do not to cup them in my hands. God, to put them in my mouth, to suck those nipples…I can't even think about it.

So like a good girl, I go back to her back. But I'm heading slowly but surely for her ass. She literally feels like putty in my hands. I can sense her muscles smoothing and lengthening underneath my fingers, and I'm getting closer and closer to her crack and the light brown hair between her legs. I slip my hands under her white lace panties, trying to push them down a bit. I mean, it would be a shame to soil such beautiful underwear, but I'm afraid if I actually ask if it's OK, Tzippy will come to and realize what's happening. So I gently slip my fingers under the lace and slowly slide the panties down her legs. As I pull them free of her feet I can't help giving the crotch a little sniff. I can smell her delicious peachy cunt, Tzippy's cunt.

My nose is wet. My God, her panties are soaked with peach juice. Does Tzippy know what's going on here? I can't help it, I've got to explore that delicious ass, so I scoot down to the end of the bed and part her cheeks, then push my Roman nose down between her lips and give a long, satisfying lick. She opens her legs for me—peach or not, she knows how to be eaten—and lifts her beautiful belly off the bed so I can put my fingers into her. First one, then two, she is groaning for me, coming against one hand and grabbing the other to pinch her pink nipples.

Suddenly she throws me off. *Oh, shit,* I think, *expulsion! exile! death! Well, it was worth it.* But instead Tzippy lies on her back and pulls me down onto her.

"I want to taste you," she says. Not bad for a beginner, I think. She moves so her lips are next to my sopping panties and pulls them aside so she can lick my clit. "Like this?" she asks, and I don't know if it's the question of a novice or a seasoned lover, but I'm so turned on I know I'll come if she just breathes on me. Besides, I haven't even gotten to kiss the girl. So I sit on top of her, slowly wiggling out of my sports bra, my brown skin and red-brown nipples an amazing contrast to Tzippy's golden pinkness. I lean my head down over hers. For a modest girl, she's one hell of a kisser. Suddenly she's running the show, pulling me down, biting my neck, then rolling over so she's on top of me, her hands gripping my wrists and holding me tight. She works her way down my body, giving little kisses and swirls with her tongue, till she makes it to my promised land. *"This* is manna," she says, sucking and licking.

As we lie there panting with huge grins on our faces, we have to interrogate each other. "When did you first know you wanted..." I start to ask, but trail off, embarrassed.

"I've been trying to get you into bed for weeks!" Tzippy complains. "The oil, the soap, the back rub...I couldn't tell if you weren't interested or just totally clueless."

I can't believe it. All my attempts not to even look at her glorious body and she's been trying to seduce *me*.

"Do you feel bad about this?" I ask, wondering how such a thing could be possible but knowing that Tzippy takes this religion business more seriously than I do.

"It's OK," she says confidently. "In *Vayikra*"—that's Leviticus—"it's written that a man shall not lie with another man as with a woman. But it doesn't say anything at all about two women!" Even so, it turns out the guys in the yeshiva are all busy giving each other hand jobs. I guess as long as you don't actually lie down together it's kosher.

"But actually there is one problem," she adds. Oh no, I think, my heart sinking. "How do we find out the right *bracha* for eating pussy?"

First Rites

Myriam Gurba

When you join a gang, it's kind of like getting baptized. At least that's how it was for me. It transforms you. Your homies become blood to you. They're your new family. You know they'd die for you, and in return you'd die for them. You've got to pledge your loyalty to your new *familia,* but instead of water being poured over your head, it's their rage and anger that makes you one of them. You come out of it a new you with a new name. Your *clicka,* the new family you've just joined, picks this name out for you. Bye-bye Jose, Johnny, or Fernando. Hello Puppet, Smiley, and Snoopy. Forget Lupe, Lorena, or Beatriz. Remember Shady, Shy Girl, and La Green Eyes. See, your homies watch you. They know you better than anyone else, better than your mom or even her old lady, *tu abuelita.* They watch you, and they give you a name for who you really are, for what your actions and the little things about you tell about your soul. You laugh all the time—*boom,* you're Giggles! You score things from the corner store without ever getting caught, hey, we know who you are—you're Bandit. And if you have a distant look in your eyes, like you're somewhere far away from the barrio and you ain't never coming back, they call you Dreamer. That's how it goes.

I knew who I was before I officially joined the *clicka*. My name had been picked out a long time ago 'cause what my true nature was showed through and through. Since I went to junior high, they'd been calling me La Payasa. Payasa means "clown" in Spanish. You might think I got this name 'cause I'm funny, some kinda joker. But that's not why they call me La Payasa. They call me Payasa for my drag, homes. How do you tell a clown apart from everyone else? They got that crazy costume that makes them stand out, that makes them different. I got my costume too. I'm always in drag. I call it my *loco* drag—khaki Dickies with sharp creases ironed into them, three sizes too big with a cotton belt holding them up high, my bright white wife beater with a blue Pendleton over it, one button buttoned at the very top, and old-school Nikes on my feet. Oh and my head's shaved completely bald, *puro pelon*. That's me, that's my outfit, my drag. I'm the Payasa. The only *loca* in the Latin Playboys.

That's the name of my *clicka*, Los Playboys Latinos. I was the first *loca* to ever join the Playboys. Usually, the way it works, if you're a guy, the Playboys jump you in. If you're a girl, the Playgirls take care of business. But not me, I'm a different kinda gangster. The Payasa is a straight-up *loco,* no doubt. The truth of that is what makes me La Payasa. My homies know me through and through. It's like they can see right through me, and they don't see the soul of a Playgirl— they know I got the soul of a *loco veterano*, an old school gangsta. That's why it was the *locos* who jumped me in, the *locos* who showered me with their rage and their violence and beat the shit out of me to prove that I was one tough macho, worthy of the *familia* Playboy.

It went down where it always does, under the bridge behind crazy Momo's house. It's dark back there, and Momo's shack covers the field up real good so the *jura* can't see nothing. And if they do wanna see anything, they gotta shine a bright light from their squad cars through all the bushes, and once we see that, we know to split. *Pinche* LAPD don't know this barrio like we do, and once we start running we can disappear into this neighborhood like hoodlum magicians into thin air.

We all met back there before midnight. All the *locos* were there. They were quiet. One of them, the one we call Azteca 'cause he's so dark, had a lead pipe in his hands. The field that we were in was totally still, and I could hear the traffic whizzing by on the freeway on the other side of the bridge. The moonlight bounced off Azteca's pipe like some kind of crazy magical glow, and I knew right then that it was gonna start. I didn't even see it. I just felt that cold lead crack against the back of my knees and my whole body gave out and I hit the ground. They beat me for a whole 15 minutes. I took every second of it, everything they had to give me. After a while they were all kicking me so hard that I started to puke up blood. Then someone got on top of me—I don't even know who it was, but he straddled my hips while I was on the ground and just started boxing the shit out of my face. I felt my cheek tear and blood came spilling out of it. One of my eyes was swelling up. The air smelled heavy, like blood, puke, spit, and sweat. And then it stopped. One of the *locos* reached out his hand and helped me up. That was it. I was in.

The next day I went to Sammy's house. Sammy does the best tattoos in all of East Los Angeles. He learned in prison. Sammy is an artist.

I gave myself my first one, three dots on my hand, on the

flesh between my thumb and my other finger, that soft part. I cut open the little holes with the sharp edge of a paper clip and filled them in with ink. When my mom saw them, she went crazy. "Do you know what you're getting yourself into, *mal crea-da!* Those three little dots are gonna get you killed!" My three green dots. *Mi Vida Loca.* "My Crazy Life," the original gangster motto that I wear proud and true. I'd write it on my body if I wanted to. Maybe that made me an evil girl, an evil creature like my mom said. I didn't care. All I knew was that the words made me feel branded, and I liked the way that felt.

Sammy was gonna ink my name across my stomach that day, Payasa curving over me across my hips, cut into me in Old English. I was so excited that I got to Sammy's pad hella early, but he didn't care. He was ready for me. He was up cleaning his needles and getting the ink ready when I got there.

"Sit down, Payasa. I gotta take care of some shit and I'll be right back."

I sat on his dirty couch, staring up at a velvet painting of a big puma. I heard his voice, and it sounded like he was arguing with someone. He came back after a minute. He had to tell me something. At first I was pissed, but then when he explained, everything was cool. See, he wasn't gonna ink me—his sister was.

"What the fuck, Sammy!" I yelled at him. "I didn't come here to get inked by no girl. What the fuck is wrong with you?"

Sammy looked at me, "*Calmate*, Payasa—take it easy. You don't understand. Heartbreaker knows what she's doing. Serious, dude. My sister has got the soul of an artist, man."

Sammy sat down to explain everything. He told me about how when he was locked up in *la pinta*, he got a letter from Heartbreaker every week, just like clockwork, and that those letters were what kept him alive and hoping for the next week to come around. She'd send him these envelopes with mad drawings all over them and pages of poetry with walls of roses climbing around the words. He pinned the scraps of paper to the walls of his cell like some kind of inspirational wallpaper that wrenched his heart each time he stared at it for too long. There were *virgenes* who looked down from the walls with eyes of redemption and bleeding *corazones sagrados* to make you cry and give you hope that maybe when our moms and *abuelitas* lit candles at church for us, there might be some greater thing out there that really was watching out for us. He quit fucking around while he was doing his time and decided to leave the gangster life behind him. He started going to the prison library and reading and working out. After a while all he did was study, lift weights, and practice his new hobby, tattooing. Most of the guys in the *pinta* have someone from their own *clicka* that does everyone's tattoos. But since he wasn't down for the life anymore, it was OK for him to work on anyone. Even the *puto* faggots from the Aryan Brotherhood got inked by Sammy. He perfected his art, and he knew that when he got out he would come home to his barrio and teach his little sister the art that could make her work live and breathe. He started her practicing on the skin of dead chickens. Their skin is best. All plucked and smooth, it's pale and tight. It doesn't jiggle around too much. When she was ready, Sammy let his sister work on his own arms.

He rolled up his sleeves to show me his biceps. I looked at his arms and couldn't believe what I saw. I couldn't believe that La Heartbreaker, the most beautiful *loca* in our barrio, was responsible for the ghetto art dancing across her brother's arms. His body featured drawings of Jesus with thorns piercing his head and blood pouring from them like you could taste it. Flowers surrounding the feet of *La Virgene,* and Christ's mother with a look on her face like she was so proud of all the beauty and pain created by her son. I reached out and traced the pictures with my finger, feeling the lines that were carved into his arms by the hands of his kid sister. When I looked up, Heartbreaker was standing in the doorway. When I saw her I knew I couldn't say no to Sammy's proposition.

La Heartbreaker was true to her name, like we all were. She was the finest *heine* in the barrio, the one all the homies wanted to get with and put a baby in. This girl had green eyes, big and glassy, like emerald obsidian or smoky glass. She had long, brown Mexican hair that hadn't been cut since she was 7 years old and looked red when it was in the L.A. sun. Long, lo-o-ong eyelashes. Fine-ass body. Tight smooth skin, stretched across her cheekbones. Pretty Latin freckles. Her body was long. Everything about her was long. And she had this voice. It was like the sound of crystal.

"Hey, Payasa. You don't mind that I'm gonna work on you, right?"

"No, no Heartbreaker, that's cool. Let's get on with it, then."

She sat down with her brother watching over her, master and apprentice on dirty old chairs, and she showed him the stenciled letters that would be etched into me.

"Nice job, Heartbreaker."

She applied the letters to me with Speed Stick then peeled off the stencil slowly. She turned on the power to the needle and then she touched me.

"Take a deep breath, Payasa. Don't forget to breathe."

I did like she told me and breathed. I saw her hair fall around her face as she came at me with the needle. It pierced my skin, but she stood her ground, her hand firm and steady, unmoved by my rippling skin, the thin layer of fat that sits on my belly. I tried to do like she told me, keep breathing, but it was hard. I bit my raw lip and drew blood from it. She never

stopped to comfort me, she was so into her work. I looked down
and saw blood mingle with black ink. Every once in a while
she'd turn and dip her needle for more paint and then get right
back to work on my skin. I felt some of my skin rising up to
form my name, burning and seared, torn into fancy scars. I
loved it. It was a pain that I owned. I couldn't believe I was
actually trusting La Heartbreaker with a tattoo as important as
this one, but with each stroke she proved herself.

When she got to the last "A" in my name, my T-shirt that I
had refused to take off was covered in blood and ink. She finished
up and stared at her own work. She was just as in awe as I was.

"Heartbreaker," Sammy said, "I'm gonna take off. I gotta go
meet Spooky at the park. You know how to show her how to
take care of it, right?"

"Yeah, Sammy."

"OK, *pues. Cuidate,* Payasa. Watch your back. I'll see
you later."

He left and we were alone. I lay back on the couch. My
body had this rush that I'd never felt before, like I was high.
There was just this rush, like when you get all fucked up on
whippets or meth. I feel stupid saying it, but I felt so fucking
happy, like I could do anything. It was like all the pain took me
somewhere else. That tattoo took up so much of my body; it
outlined my name, smooth and clean.

Heartbreaker got out a metal tube and squished some stuff
all over her fingers. She pulled up my shirt and told me she was
gonna rub it on me. It would keep me from getting infected. It
felt cool when she rubbed it on me, and then she asked me if
she could trace the lines of her work on my stomach.

"Sure." She followed each letter with her finger, tracing it
and then jumping to the next one, over and over like she could
hardly believe she'd done that to me. My tummy felt so tender.

first rites

Then she looked me in the eye and I knew something between us changed with that look. She kept her hand on my stomach, all lubed up, and slid it down to my belt buckle. At first I was scared, but when I saw the flash of green from her eyes, I knew it was OK. She worked her hand down my pants, through my boxers, and stroked my pubic hair. She squeezed me down there, getting that goo all over it. She rubbed it onto my thighs and got them all slick. They were hot and slippery. She started rubbing, slow then faster. Her arm kept coming down on my stomach and it would burn with pain, but it felt so good down there I didn't want her to stop. She pulled her hand out real quick, and I was worried for a second that she was gonna stop. Then she flipped me over real fast and pulled my pants down. I had my legs apart and I was on the floor, kneeling with my head on the couch. She took one of her wet slimy fingers and slipped it into my ass crack. She got it all wet and slippery like my stomach and started to play with my asshole. It felt so good. She played with the skin around the hole, teasing and pulling it, and then she slipped a finger inside and pumped it. I'd never had anything inside my asshole before. Then she put in another finger and then another. She had three fingers inside me, moving all crazy like she wanted to rip me open, and I was moving back and forth down there with her all crazy on my ass. I felt her middle finger jamming way up inside of me. I started to scream and breathe real hard, and she reached around and touched me in front. She rubbed on my thing up there, and it got hard like a dick. She was touching me on both ends, and I started to shake all crazy. I felt like I was losing control, and for a quick second I got scared again and thought of my cousin, the one who shook all the time, but then it was like I just ate her hand right up inside me and I was just an extension of her and her art and her beauty.

She took her hand out of me and bit me on the neck and collapsed against me. She kept rubbing my ass, dirty from the lube stuff and my shit and some blood. She kept biting me until my shoulders were marked from her teeth and they were like tattoos from her mouth.

She breathed real softly in my ear. I hadn't touched her once. She was the girl all the *locos* wanted.

She whispered in my ear, "How did you like it, *mijo,* eh, lil boy? How did you like your first time?" My first time.

On the Spanish Main
Catherine Lundoff

T he *Revenge* cut slowly through the warm Caribbean waters, a slight breeze barely filling the great white sails. It was fortunate that there had been few other ships in sight all day. With the wind as unfriendly as it was, the ship stood little chance against even the lumbering Spanish galleons. Still, it also meant there had been no prize, no Spanish or French gold to buy a few days' joy in Spittlefields or the other island ports.

It was a thought that filled many a pirate's head as they went below at the end of the day's work. They left the night watch and the captain's woman behind to pace the deck under the newly risen moon. Let the watch fret under the eye of "Captain Bonney," as most of them called her when Calico Jack was not in hearing range. Not they. There was plenty of rum and salt pork below. Aye, and good company too, away from the brooding amber stare of the woman on the foredeck.

The warm wind picked up slightly, sweeping around Tortuga to whip the big woman's hair out from her bandanna and toss it behind her like a bright orange banner. She tilted her face up to the full moon, closing her eyes against the wind and the flag with its skull and crossbones that flew above her. The wooden deck rocked beneath her feet in the gentle push of the current that drove them slowly toward Hispaniola, and she braced her feet easily against the sway of the waves.

Harney, the midshipman on watch, gave her a wide berth. He'd felt the power of those big fists before and was unwilling to try her mood when he was sober. Their captain was less wise.

"Aw, Annie, come to bed!" Calico Jack appeared on deck to weave an unsteady path to her side. He caught her arm and got an elbow to the jaw for his trouble, a blow that made him stagger backward until he caught himself on the rail. She cast an angry look over her shoulder at him, one hand slipping to the dirk stuck through the thick silk sash at her waist.

He leaned against the rail rubbing his chin gingerly and looked at this woman who stood near his own size and weight. He could try to carry her off, but angry as she was, she was as likely to stick that shiv into him as to let him join her in the bed that she'd driven him out of a fortnight before. Captain he was, and no coward, but no fool either. He turned and lurched back along the deck, the woman behind him forgotten for the time being. There'd be a warmer welcome awaiting him in the purser's bunk, and a smile creased his thick brown beard at the thought of that muscular young man.

Anne Bonney watched him with a jaundiced eye. Her nights had been more pleasant since she drove him from the cabin they had shared, but, truth to tell, she was bored. There'd been no prize in a week, and not a man jack among the crew would dare to lie with her. They were a rum lot, she thought, watching Harney carefully avoid her as he made his rounds of the deck.

It had been better in Tortuga. A wry smile touched the corners of her broad lips. She could almost feel the round, soft breasts of the black-haired whore at Mother Mary's. Feel them spilling out of the woman's open dress and into her palms, her callused hands pinching the hardened nipples until the woman's fat body writhed against her. She remembered the brown thighs opening before her questing hand, the other woman's groans, the scent of her sex. Oh, it had been sweet! She could feel the wetness flow between her own legs at the memory.

Her nostrils flared, sucking down the warm salt air like she could smell the port before them, though it was still several days ahead. There was still not a sail in sight on the calm waves. She sighed. Nothing for it then but a lonely cabin and the hope that their luck would change soon. She finished looking around and spun with a curse to go back below.

The English boy stood leaning against the rail studying her when she turned around. The impudent little bastard had watched her for the past moon since they'd pulled him from the English frigate and gave him the choice of joining the crew or taking his chances on the islands. His shipmates picked the islands, but he'd stayed on, watching her. She'd had enough of it. Since he found her so bloody interesting, he could have a closer look. She snarled at the thought as she crossed the deck in two of her long strides. Harney, watching, bolted behind the mast.

She towered over the Englishman when she stood before him and examined him closely for the first time. He seemed naught but a boy, thin, beardless yet, though old enough to have been picked up by the press-gang. Cool gray eyes looked up into her gold ones, and the thin lips quirked in an amused grin. It made him look older at the same time that it enraged her.

She'd soon have that look wiped off his cheeky little face. Her broad hand anchored his chin as she pressed her lips hard against his. Her tongue pushed its way inside his mouth, savoring the taste of salt pork and rum for a moment. Then she pulled back, sinking her teeth into his lower lip, biting just enough to draw blood before she pulled away, laughing.

He watched her lick his blood from her lips for all the world like a lioness. She smiled savagely as he wiped the back of one hand over his bleeding lip. The gray eyes were cold as a winter sea now, no more mirth to be found swimming in their depths. She dropped unconsciously into a fighting stance, her hand finding the hilt of her knife, though she grinned all the while.

When he moved, he was faster than anything she'd ever seen—swinging forward under her arm, one foot striking out at the back of her knee as he darted past. She staggered back, barely avoiding the kick, but lost her footing. He stuck a firm hand against her ribs in a quick shove. She slashed out quickly as she slipped sideways, but her stroke missed, throwing her further off-balance. He pressed the advantage, sweeping her feet out from under her with a sudden motion of his feet.

Suddenly she was down, her knife kicked free and his own at her throat. She flailed a moment, trying to get purchase on the deck, but it was slick beneath her, rubbed smooth by salt and scrubbing and wet with spray. With a curse and the beginning of a laugh, she raised her bare hands in a mocking gesture of surrender. This one would do. She'd get her own back later.

He grinned, making himself look even younger for all that he was a sturdy brute. She appreciated his body more now that it rested upon her stomach, giving her a better view. Still, there was something about him...he watched her a moment, the lines of his face softening. Then he pulled the knife back to the buttons on his shirt, hesitating a moment. Anne realized the truth at the same moment that he, with a single slashing motion, cut open his shirt to expose his—no, her—bound breasts. Better and better.

Anne let out a roar of astonished laughter, yanking her erstwhile foe down to her for a fierce kiss. She drank deep of pork and rum, with just the slightest tang of blood, running her tongue into the other woman's mouth. She slid a hand up the other woman's ribs and over her bound breasts, pinching a nipple to rock-hardness under the tight cloth.

The other pulled back with a sharp breath. Her hand found Anne's and held it away from her breast for a moment. The gray eyes looked wary. Ignoring the other woman's gaze, Anne shifted her backward as she pushed herself up from the deck, bending her face so her sharp teeth could find the hardened nipple under the cloth. Glancing upward, she watched with approval as the short-cropped head tilted back, red scarf slipping off first to expose dark hair, then landing on the deck behind the other's arching back. Pulling away, she reached out, grasping the woman's chin in her meaty hand. "What's your name, girl?"

"Mary...Mary Read," the other gasped in reply. A quick hand yanked loose the ties on Anne's rough tunic as the sea-gray eyes met golden ones, caution ebbing away. Anne wordlessly tilted her head toward the stairs that led down to the captain's quarters.

Then she could feel Mary drop a knee between her thighs as if by accident, shoving it upward. The sharp pang of her own hardened nipple rolling suddenly between Mary's fingers made her flush, heat flowing from her cunny down her thighs and up over her stomach and breasts. A ragged groan tore from her throat as Mary's thin lips pressed down hard and hot on her own.

The hiss of breath and a creaking board reminded her of Harney's presence, and she pulled away again, climbed to her feet, and tugged Mary with her. "Come on, luv," she crooned softly, "I've just the place for you." She caught Mary's unresisting hand and grinned down into the feral smile that met her own.

Mary's other hand found the dirk she had stuck back in her belt, and she pulled it loose. Seconds later it shuddered deep into the mast, a whisker from Harney's watchful face. With a strangled yell he fell backward, sliding and rolling as far as he could away from it.

Anne roared with laughter and leaned down to kiss Mary once more. On a whim she bent her knees, reaching out to pull the other woman over her shoulder to carry her below. A rough hand thrust against her chest, pushing her away, and the gray eyes burned into hers. Anne froze, puzzled. None of the other women she'd bedded before had objected. Hell, from time to time, she'd even let Calico Jack stagger beneath her weight down the companionway to his cabin. She had always thought it was funny.

Mary's free hand pulled her shirt closed, and she dropped her other hand so that she no longer held Anne at bay. She walked backward to the mast to tug her knife loose and stuck it back in her belt, watching Anne all the while. Her gray eyes grew cool, and the flush on her cheeks died away while Anne met her gaze.

Anne stood still, raising her palms slowly to show that they were empty, held carefully away from her own knife. It was a cautious, puzzled gesture. What did the wench want, then? "No harm meant," she offered awkwardly into the silence that had been broken only by their own harsh breathing. Mary's thin lips twisted in a grimace.

"No harm! I'm not a prize to be hauled below for you and your mates," she spat out the words, the Bristol accent getting thicker as she spoke.

Anne cursed softly. "Lass, I want you for no bunk but my

own. Will you join me?" The words rolled out before she thought about how they sounded. Why should she have to ask anyone to bed her? Mary's kiss still burned on her lips, but with an effort she stilled her breathing. Better to lie alone and command than to have company she had to plead for. She met Mary's mocking gaze and felt the answering flare of fury in her own eyes.

"To the devil with you!" Anne snarled, her big fists clenching. She stomped toward the other woman, thinking she would have to fight her way past. It was no way to end a night that had had such promise, and she cursed the impulse that let her treat Mary like she would any other wench. At that moment Mary stepped aside and sheathed her knife so that Anne had a clear path to go below.

"After you," she gestured toward the companionway. Surprised, Anne looked deep into the gray eyes, which still bore little of comfort and much of the winter sea. She paused a moment before she walked within knife range. It went sore with her to turn her back on the knife, but there was nothing for it but a dignified exit if she didn't want to fight on-deck. The skin prickling between her shoulders, she passed in front of Mary, moving faster now as she walked forward into the passage.

She sped down the narrow stairs, heading toward her cabin and the bottle of rum that she knew was still hidden there. Mary sauntered down after her, lips curled slightly in a sardonic smile. As she approached the last step, she raised her hands to show that she didn't hold a knife, mimicking Anne's gesture on the deck.

Anne flushed, pausing a moment to wrestle with rising fury and ebbing desire before she strode toward the cabin. Mary's hand caught her arm, but she shook it off. Mary ducked swiftly around her, planting herself in the cabin's narrow doorway. Anne could barely see her in the gloom below the deck, just the glow of her pale-brown skin and the flash of white teeth. "You're quick to anger, lass. I've a mind yet to see what feeds the fires of the captain's wench," Mary growled in a throaty whisper.

Anne reached out, shoving the door open behind her so that the other woman stumbled back, losing her balance. She grabbed the tatters of Mary's open shirt as she fell back and tossed her into the hammock that rocked between its posts in the middle of the small cabin. Kicking the door closed, she stalked to the hammock. "Don't ever call me that again," she hissed softly, one hand holding Mary's face in a bruising grip so their eyes met.

"Prove it." The words hung in the stale air of the cabin. By the dim light of the moon shining through the porthole, Mary could see the golden eyes almost blazing. Her breath quickened as Anne's mouth came down roughly against her own and the long, callused fingers tore at the bindings that held her breasts flat. She reached down to pull at the ties of Anne's sash, tugging at the knot until it loosened.

Anne straightened, reaching down to catch her knife as the cloth fell to the floor. She paused a moment to meet Mary's eyes, her fury changing to desperate desire. With a deft motion she slid the gleaming blade beneath the wrappings that covered Mary's small breasts, slicing the gray cotton open to expose her white skin.

She heard the breath hiss from the other woman's lips as she ran the cold flat of the blade over her breasts, teasing her freed nipples into brown pebbles. Her gestures were teasing rather than threatening, but she could feel the smaller woman stiffen. Mary raised a hand to catch her wrist, but Anne was already reaching across her to drive it into one of the beams that supported the hammock.

Then Mary's hands slid under her tunic, dragging the loose leather breeches down until Anne's legs were momentarily trapped. She pulled up the rough tunic to expose Anne's large breasts hanging loose beneath it.

The smell of sweat and salt filled the cabin as she reached up to bite the round nipples before her, sinking her teeth in until she tore a groan from Anne's throat. Her tongue eagerly swept Anne's breasts, almost clumsily lapping up the taste of the sea, until the thump of boots being kicked to the floor made her look up as Anne pulled back. The leather breeches followed the boots, and she tugged the tunic off to stand naked before Mary.

Red-gold hair gleamed between her muscular white thighs and beneath burly arms, but paled in comparison to the glorious red mane that poured over her broad shoulders and down onto round breasts and solid belly. Her pale skin glowed in the moonlight, the sight drawing a low whistle of admiration from Mary. The captain had been a lucky bastard to get his hands on her, she thought, but she'd be damned if she wouldn't keep what he couldn't. She reached down to pull her own boots off and grinned invitingly up at Anne.

Anne caught the belt that still held Mary's leather breeches, yanking it open with a single abrupt tug. The breeches she pulled down over slim hips and sturdy legs, pausing to breathe in the warm scent of Mary's sex. She reached out to part the black curls with a single finger, rubbing against her slit until Mary's legs parted with a groan, feet busily kicking breeches off and onto the cabin floor. A second finger joined the first, rolling in the wet curls, slipping inside her, her thighs tensing and parting before the insistence of Anne's hand.

She bent to take Mary's breast in her mouth, tongue, then teeth, tasting each hardened nipple as a third finger slid in to join the others. Mary groaned, back arching against the hard knots of the hammock as she twisted to reach the glorious nest of red-gold hair between Anne's thighs. She stretched out a work-roughened hand, pushing into the red-gold bush as Anne closed her legs, trapping Mary's hand before it could begin to work its way upward.

Anne's fingers thrust their way inside Mary, whose hips rolled against them like they had a will of their own. Throwing her legs open wide, her feet searched for, then found purchase on, the ropes to rock her hips against the unaccustomed pressure that filled her. She yielded in spite of herself, surrendering a little to the other's touch.

Anne leaned down, bending her face to lick Mary's slit. Her tongue teased at the sour, salty taste, savoring it, dragging growls and moans from Mary, her ragged breathing filling the cabin with sound as she pushed up against Anne's demanding mouth. She felt herself open, welcoming Anne's fingers into the sea cave of her cunny, her hips riding Anne's tongue like a ship on stormy waves, heat rising to warm her legs, her belly, flushing over her breasts. Taut legs locked, she succumbed to the mouth that drank her in until the cup of fire inside her broke open, spilling itself along her skin as she rolled against the ropes, her sharp cry filling the cabin.

Anne's tongue stroked upward, trying to pull more from her body, but Mary reached down to pull her up for a kiss. Their lips met, and Mary could taste herself on Anne's lips. Her tongue probed the other's mouth a moment as she wrapped her legs around Anne's hips.

Then, with a swift gesture, she pulled back and twisted out from under Anne. She flipped out of the hammock, tilting it to land in a crouch on the cabin floor at Anne's feet as the big woman stood up in surprise. She lunged gracefully upward, her momentum pushing Anne down onto the hammock, making her golden eyes wide at the suddenness of the movement. In a moment she had swept Anne's feet up and out onto either side of the ropes, spreading her legs so that Mary could see her sex shining wetly in the moonlight.

Standing alongside the hammock, she ran a rough hand over Anne's leg, stroking upward along her thigh, up over the solid curve of belly to the soft curves of her breasts. She closed her eyes as she slowly stroked first one palm then the other against Anne's breasts, worshipfully rubbing her hands, hardened from rope and oars, over the soft skin. Anne reached out for Mary's right hand, sending it down between her thighs to the empty cave that waited there, the saltwater waves lapping its sides.

Mary resisted, grasping Anne's wrists in her hands to pull them over her head, holding them there a moment while she leaned down to kiss her. She felt the other woman's muscles clench in protest and quickly released the big hands to let them stroke their way along her ribs and breasts. Then she swung her leg over the hammock so she straddled Anne's body, almost sitting on her. Rocking her hips forward, she ground herself into Anne, driving against her, wet curls entwined.

A strangled groan greeted her as Anne rolled her hips upward to meet hers. Mary slid backward and swung her leg over Anne's body to stand beside the hammock. She slipped her hand into the red-gold nest, feeling her way into Anne's cunny as she thrust hard, opening her with her hand, breath harsh and fast at the feel of soft, wet flesh riding her fist. The golden eyes were closed now as the other woman turned her head from side to side, the motion tearing groans from her throat.

Mary bent her head to bite a solid thigh, her teeth closing hard on Anne's pale skin, moving inch by inch up her leg, hand driving in all the while, now fast and now slow. Anne bucked against her, knuckles turning white now from clutching the sides of the hammock, nails digging into the rope. Mary's tongue found Anne's slit, and her back arched like a bow, legs shaking, closing fast around the fist inside her. The coaxing tongue lapped slowly up and down until Anne went limp, shaking and panting. It continued sliding, teasing until her back arched again and she wrapped herself once more around Mary's fist with a sharp cry.

She collapsed back on the hammock, shuddering, and Mary slipped her hand out with an impish grin, climbing up onto her lover's body. There they lay, damp with sweat, the salty tang of it filling the cabin as the hammock rocked gently to the ship's motion and their own. Anne ran her fingers through Mary's wet hair, pulling her face up so she could kiss her. It was a gentler kiss than the first one that Anne gave her on deck but none the less fierce for that. Mary held on tight, arms wrapped around Anne's neck.

"Stay the night." Anne's whisper fell somewhere between a request and a command.

Mary tilted her head to look at her, the golden eyes slitted in the moonlight, red mane spread out around her face and dripping through the ropes of the hammock to swing below them. She kissed Anne fiercely, her leg sliding between Anne's thighs to rub against her sex once more. "I chose to stay on board when I saw you," she offered, pulling away from Anne's lips to whisper softly against her ear.

Anne knew the confession for what it was. Reaching up, she buried her hands in Mary's cropped hair, pulling her face down where she could see her in the dim light from the porthole. For the first time the feral face looked wary, the whites of her eyes showing a little, like a horse ready to bolt. She met Anne's silent gaze almost calmly, but her pulse beat against

Anne's fingertips, racing heart telling what gray eyes would not. Anne watched her a moment longer. "Good," she declared simply, a slow smile splitting her lips as she leaned up to kiss Mary again. In answer, Mary rocked her knee forward, grinding into Anne's wet sex. Her lips and tongue caressed Anne's neck, kissing and biting her way along her shoulder. It would be enough for now. She bent to her task, rejoicing in the deepening timbre of Anne's breath as it quickened at her touch.

Storytime

J.L. Belrose

*T*here's nothing sweeter, in my opinion, than hearing a butch choke back and say, "Yes, sir." And, as soon as I saw the faggy dyke up at the Red Spot's mike, that's the sound I wanted to hear come out of her mouth.

She sure looked fine. Her pin-striped suit fitting just right, sleeves showing the correct amount of white shirt cuff, and pant legs the perfect length above her wing tips. All pressed and polished. I would've bet 50 bucks she was wearing boxers, probably silk, and that they were fresh pressed too. I'd also have bet there was a tank top under her shirt, snug enough to flatten her breasts, and that even the tank was pressed.

I imagined how, prepping herself for the night's performance, she'd stood in front of her bathroom mirror, her hand following her comb as she slicked back her smooth dark hair. How she'd fingered it into place at the back where it curled slightly longer over her collar. And how she'd teased those few loose strands to fall casually across her forehead.

She finished reading her first piece and smiled in a satisfied way, flushing with obvious pleasure as she got her applause. She loosened her tie, unbuttoned her shirt collar, and stood there, sexy and rakish, as the audience resettled. She was playing the crowd like a pro, making everyone wait a few suspenseful moments while she shuffled a careful disarray of papers, like she didn't know what to read next.

I'm not much into literature myself. Just haven't had the time. It was mostly by accident that I'd stumbled onto book launches and readings as great places to cruise. The added bonus was that, even if I came up empty, the events themselves were pleasant deviations from my work-oriented, almost monastic existence.

I scanned the crowd. Everyone's eyes were linked to the stage. Most of the femmes had tight secret smiles on their enraptured faces as they absorbed her words, while butches, posed around the bar at the back, stood stone-faced and quietly assessed her. She was so hot even the fags in the crowd looked respectful. I was very soon focused on her again myself.

Her indulgent half-smile, when she looked up from her paper, provoked a tug from my groin. Again I pictured her preening at her bathroom mirror, and fantasized myself behind her, pressing my pelvis into her ass, pushing her forward over her sink, butt-fucking her into star-blasting oblivion.

I couldn't concentrate much on her story, which was about a miscued tangle of polyamorous friends. All I could think about was the subtext of hunger I heard in her voice and saw in her eyes. Despite all her polish and posturing, I began to see her as someone who was perhaps innately lonely, maybe needy. I wondered if she ever jerked off with fantasies of strong butch hands and hard dyke cock slamming her into submission.

I left the seat I'd found near the wall and eased my way past tables and people to the back of the room as she finished her reading. She grinned from the stage, lingering there to accept her applause, while I stood, ready and mobile, watching for where she'd sit and who she was with. I couldn't believe my luck when she curved through the crowd toward me and placed her papers on the bar not three feet away from where I was standing. And, even more fortuitous, she appeared to be solo.

I edged over and said, "I love your work."

My baritone startled her.

I pulled my wallet from an inside pocket and pretended I hadn't noticed her reaction. I said, "I hope you'll let me buy you a beer." I extracted a 20 and laid it on the counter.

She looked me over, from my flattop down to my scuffed brown oxfords and back up again. I'm not a small person, and I prefer casual clothes, oversize shirts and jackets, and baggy pants. I knew she'd taken in every disorderly detail and that she wasn't overly impressed. She raised her eyebrows. Like a challenge more than a question.

I ignored her little display. "I'd like to read more of your work," I said. "Where can I find it?" I knew writers can't resist vaunting where they've been published. It's usually places I've never heard of, but I always nod as if I'm suitably impressed.

Our beer appeared. Her eyes strayed and stuck a moment too long on the bartender who, white T-shirt rolled up to the shoulders, was decidedly a big bad butch. I smiled, and lifted my bottle. "Here's to your future bestsellers," I toasted, drawing her attention back to me.

She clicked her bottle to mine. I smiled again as she said, "Thank you." I adore faggy dykes who are reflexively polite, who say "please" and "thank you."

Using a few names I remembered from other readings, I kept her talking, while my mind worked on how I could get her out of the place before the night's socializing began and someone snatched her away from me. I dragged in a nearby stool, planted a foot on one of the rungs, and nonchalantly adjusted my crotch. Her gaze was drawn down, as I'd hoped it would be, to my hand. I saw her eyes fixate and knew she'd focused on the bulge I was exposing on the inside of my raised leg.

Suddenly she looked up again, slicing through my stare with one of her own. I expected her to spin on her heels and stride away, but she didn't. An arrogant little smirk twitched the side of her mouth. If my lust for her needed more fuel, that expression alone was more than enough. It ignited me from my toenails right up to my tonsils. More than anything else on earth, I wanted her on her knees, being Daddy's good little angel boy, sucking Daddy's cock.

But I knew I had to bring her in slow. In the same tone of voice I might use to discuss the weather, I said, "I was wondering, do you write about stuff that really happens? If you met someone like me, for instance, and we ended up back at your place, would you write about that?"

Again, I was given the raised eyebrows. Again, I ignored them. I waited patiently for her reply. Eventually she shrugged, then relaxed and leaned back against the bar, arms folded, legs crossed. "Yeah, it's possible. Almost everything ends up in fantasy or fiction sooner or later."

"We don't have to be just a fantasy," I told her.

She tilted her bottle up to her mouth and drained it. I was sure I'd lost her. Sure she'd finished her beer so she could dump me. Politely, of course, because that was her style. But instead she set the bottle down on the bar and spun it around a few times, staring at it, as if she wasn't quite sure what she wanted to do.

My desire was blistering me deep inside, but I waited, giving her all the time and space she needed. Then suddenly everyone was applauding. The last reader had finished and was leaving the stage. People were on the move, migrating toward the stairs, the bar, the washrooms.

A blond with a bare, lean midriff streaked toward us like a heat-seeking missile and scooped my writer from behind, wrapping arms around her waist, nuzzling into her neck. My writer jerked and giggled, struggling out of the clutch and turning to convert it into a mutual face-to-face hug.

"This is Cassie," she said to me as they disentangled. I knew by how she laughed, and by the way her eyes glinted against mine as she draped an arm around the girl's shoulders, that she was relieved Cassie had appeared to pull her away from the edge I'd presented.

I hung around a while, had another beer, offhandedly keeping tabs on them in the crowd. She must have been tracking me too because she looked my way several times, but each time, as I caught and returned her gaze, she averted her eyes, flustered.

There's nothing as exciting or endearing as a butch on tenterhooks, jousting her need against her pride. But I've learned when to press and when to fold, and it was time to fold. I made my exit when she was distracted and wouldn't see me leave. I hoped she would look for me again and not find me. I hoped it would gnaw at her while she made her love to Cassie. I wanted her to roll off Cassie and lie awake, thinking about me and realizing she harbored an ache only someone like me could satisfy.

I checked the event listings in *Word,* the postings in Glad Day and other bookstores, and eventually saw her included among readers for a magazine launch at the Lava Lounge. As it turned out, I couldn't make it that night. One of my teaching assistants had screwed up and I spent the evening regrading a pile of essays. But a few weeks later the Red Spot had another *storytime*

Clit Lit night. It was where I'd first seen her, and I figured there was a good chance she'd be there again.

I was late arriving. I couldn't spot any empty seats so, guided by the permanent Christmas lights tacked to the wall, I eased my bulk down the side of the room and edged in at the bar. I scanned the crowd and didn't see her. But then, after two others had done their stuff, she was introduced as the next reader.

She rose from a place at the front where she'd been sitting on the floor. I felt familiar tugs of desire radiate up from my groin as she loped with choreographed gangly grace across the stage, shoved her papers under her arm, and used both hands to adjust the mike to her height. She was wearing jeans, fag-boy tight, and a black leather vest over a maroon silk shirt, its cuffs folded back, the neck casually open. And, like before, a few strands of dark hair were arranged to fall raffishly across her forehead.

Her smug grin as she assessed her audience made me want to haul her down and fasten her against a wall. I wanted to see sweat sheen her skin. Wanted to hear her moan and whimper and beg. But I wasn't prepared for the story she read. One character sounded a lot like me, physically at least, and something clicked about the dialogue too, except it was twisted around, but what unnerved me was the violence. I can be assertive, and I maybe look big and tough, but beneath the facade I'm a mushball. Blood and pain, and kidnapping and rape, and ties being used to bind people's wrists and mouths, and whipping with belts, just isn't my thing. Not even in fiction.

When she loped off the stage, back to her place in the audience, a girl stood and hugged her before they disappeared onto the floor together, still half-embraced. It wasn't the same girl as the first night, but a longhaired blond type just like her.

241

It wasn't my intention to intrude on them. I'm not into disrupting anyone's life. But I did want to talk to her again. I held my spot at the bar, hoping she'd eventually make her way back for a beer. And she did.

She flushed when she saw me, her chest and neck blossoming a red brighter than her shirt. "You have it all wrong," I told her.

Despite her unease, her eyebrows lifted. "How so?"

"Well, all that pain and violence. That's not what it's about. At least not with me."

Regaining her composure, she pursed her lips, slid flat hands into her front jean pockets, spread her legs for balance and, braced, faced me off. "Everything's not about you," she informed me.

"Well, if it *was* about me, it wouldn't happen anything like in your story."

She looked away, located her girlfriend in a group near the stage, and watched her for a moment before turning back to me. "What would it be like with you?" she asked.

I smiled. I heard the raw yearning in her voice. I could almost taste her hunger. "I don't want to tell you. I want to show you," I said, making my voice soft.

Her only response was a silent, rather shrewd, appraisal of my person. I added, "There wouldn't be any rough stuff. Nothing you didn't want. I'm a professor at U of T. Check me out if you want to."

"Which department?"

"Physics."

If I'd been hoping to impress her, I'd have been disappointed. All I got was a noncommittal nod. Then she said she had to get back to her friends. I didn't try to delay her.

She was halfway to them when she stopped and turned.

My heart went squishy for a beat or two. I thought she was coming back to me. But, of course, she wasn't. She detoured wide around me, went to the far end of the bar to order, and then, with the drinks, took the same roundabout route back to her group.

We didn't connect again until the following month. I'd been too pressed at work to track her down sooner. The reading was at Chello's. It was a calm warmish night for late fall so I walked from campus, taking side streets to avoid the jostle and panhandling of the downtown strip. Even after stopping at a tiny Thai restaurant on the way, I still arrived early enough to squeeze into a seat near the front. I wanted her to see me, to know I was there, before she read.

When they announced her, she made a delayed entrance from the back. She was all natty again in her pin-striped suit. She scanned her audience during her adjustment routine with the microphone, saw me, and moved quickly on, her expression inscrutable. The mike attended to, she shuffled through her papers. Her smile, when she looked up again, was coy.

Before she was halfway through her story, sweat was slicking my palms and sticking my shirt to my back. I shifted around in my seat, crossing and uncrossing my legs, until people each side of me scrunched away. It was about a faggy dyke, not unlike herself, coming on to a dyke daddy, not unlike me, all of it culminating in an incredibly hot scene of pounding jackhammer butt-fucking, all of it so graphic it had to be heard to be believed.

The room was dead silent for a breathless moment after she finished. When I applauded, others joined me. Then more. She grinned triumphantly, bowed, and bounced from the stage. I heaved from my seat in time to see her exit the door at the back, leading to the patio. I followed.

The patio was closed for the season but, on such a warm, velvety evening, a few people had elected to sit outside. The sweet aroma lingering on the still night air indicated they were having their own kind of party, but she hadn't joined them. She was standing against a wall, shielded from them by a lattice draped in withered vines which partitioned off a servers' workstation when the patio was operating. She was waiting for me. I took a deep breath and strolled over.

She allowed me to take her hand and guide it toward my crotch. I positioned her fingers so she could palpate the shaft strapped to the inside of my right thigh. "See how hard you've made Daddy?" I said.

She raised her eyebrows. Like an invitation and, at the same time, a challenge. Her smile was impish, provocative. She opened her mouth and ran the tip of her tongue slowly across her top lip, from one side to the other, and back. An involuntary spasm forked through my pelvis. The tremor might even have run down my cock and into her hand.

I took another deep breath. I wanted to place a hand on her shoulder, and on her head, urging her down, piloting her into servicing me. My arm flexed, but I restrained myself. My voice, I think, was fairly even when I said, "If this was your story, you'd invite me back to your place now. You'd have a room nearby, and no jealous girlfriend or interfering roommates."

"Since this isn't fiction, my place is miles away. Out in the Beaches."

"Well, we'll need a cab then. What about roommates?"

"No roomies."

I stood aside and extended an arm, indicating she should lead the way. She did. In fact, she seemed pretty damn sure of herself. She even flagged down the cab. I let her. I'm relaxed in public about who's in control, and if she wanted to take charge until we got to her place, it was OK with me. I sat back in the cab too. Didn't make any moves. She chatted, maybe a bit too animatedly, about tribulations she was having with a publisher. When she dug into her pocket, I thought she was going for money, but it turned out to be keys. She let me pay.

Her place was basically one room with a kitchen nook and bathroom in a shambly old frame house that had a sign on the lawn announcing it as Beachview Apartments. There wasn't a dirty dish in sight, not even a coffee cup, and the bed was made up like a magazine picture, with a fitted slipcover and an arrangement of cushions. I'm more at ease in rumpled, lived-in places like my own, so I just kind of stood there, not knowing quite where to put myself.

She removed her tie, opened her closet, and placed the tie neatly on a small tie rack attached to the back of the door. Then she took off her jacket, positioned it just-so on a padded coat hanger, and inserted it carefully into the closet. It was all done with such detached intensity it seemed like a ritual. Then, with equal precision, she rolled up her shirtsleeves. "I'll make us coffee," she announced.

I didn't answer. I was hoping she wasn't just a tease.

"Or would you rather have tea?" she asked.

I turned my back to her and looked out the window, past shrubbery, into the quiet street. "There was a joke years ago, but it was about airline personnel, not writers, so it maybe doesn't apply here. And maybe you're not old enough to remember. It went, 'Coffee, tea or me?'"

"Does one necessarily cancel out the other?" she asked.

I heard water gurgle from the tap, and turned to see her filling a kettle. Even as I approached her from behind, she gave the appearance of remaining totally concentrated on her task. It was only when I placed my hands on her hips and she didn't flinch that I knew for sure she'd been waiting for it. Her coyness puzzled me, but then I figured it was only that she had trouble asking for what she wanted. And that's probably what attracts me to some butches. Their stubborn pride.

I massaged her hips and pulled her back into me as I pushed my pelvis into her ass. Jamming her against the counter, I kissed her neck and whispered into her ear. I told her she could be Daddy's queer boy that night, if she wanted.

She turned her head and opened her mouth as if she was going to say something to me over her shoulder. Maybe she was going to protest, but her legs spread wider instead. I slipped the fingers of my left hand into the back of her belt and pulled her away from the counter so I had enough space to push my right hand down her front, between her legs. Her soft, throaty moan betrayed her arousal. I pressed my fingers into her cunt and, groping her through her trousers, told her how many different ways I could fuck her. Then I let her go.

I stepped back, unzipped, reached in through the loose folds of my pants and boxers, pulled at the Velcro strap holding my cock down against my leg, and hauled it out. It's a realistic model, thick and ridged and veined, flesh-toned. She gasped when she turned and saw me cradling the shaft in my hand. "It's too big," she said, biting at her lip as she watched me fondle it.

I smiled. If her wide-eyed act was intended to excite me, it was working. I wrapped my free hand around the back of her neck. "Does Daddy get a kiss?" I asked her.

"Damn you," she murmured as she fastened her lips into mine. I nudged my cock head into her crotch. She responded by plunging her tongue into my mouth. We sucked each other's lips and tongues until she was grinding herself against me, hunting with her clit for any contact point that could satisfy her.

I moved my hand from her neck to her shoulder, applying slight downward pressure. She slid down my body until she was kneeling at my feet.

She steadied herself with one hand grasping my leg, her other on top of the hand I was using to anchor my dick, as she kissed and licked the cock head, teasing its molded slit with the tip of her tongue. Her eyes turned upward to mine, and a thrill, like no other feeling on earth, rippled through me. I felt a release like precome leak into where the cock connected to my body. I stroked her soft, dark hair and smiled down at her. "You're a very good boy," I told her as she swallowed both my dick and her pride, tears streaming down the sides of her face as she took it deeper.

I was overwhelmed by a surge of tenderness for her as she tried so desperately not to gag from it penetrating the back of her throat. "It's OK," I said, easing away. I helped her to her feet and, with my thumbs, gently wiped the tears from her flushed cheeks. I smoothed the hair back from her forehead and kissed where it had been. Then I took her hand and led her toward the bed.

She stood in mute submission as I unbuttoned her shirt and slipped it off her shoulders. I tossed it over against the wall. I let her keep her tank on. Left it as a token of my respect for her butchness. I want submission from my boys, but I don't humiliate them.

She fumbled with her belt buckle and zipper, then sat on the edge of the bed to remove her shoes. She stood again to take off her trousers. I smiled when I saw her silk boxers, smooth-pressed just like I'd imagined, decorated with blue teddy bears. She hesitated a moment, holding her trousers. She started to fold them, but then, like a painful decision had been made, tossed them to join the shirt in a crumpled pile on the floor. Lowering her eyes, she said, "There's lube in that drawer," and pointed to the bedside table.

I guided her to turn around, climb onto the bed, and lie face down. She silently obeyed. All her posturing and arrogance had vaporized. I hooked my fingers into the band of her boxers. She lifted and shifted so I could ease them off down her legs. I ran my fingertips over the smooth exposed flesh, marveling at the vulnerability of it, the trembling trust. I slid my hands under her hips, and she responded immediately, raising her ass invitingly into the air.

I kissed both her ass cheeks and stroked them lovingly, massaging in toward her ass crack, spreading her. Her breathing merged into moans. I ran my tongue up and down her crack until she groaned, swaying into my touch. I slicked my thumb with juice from her cunt and rimmed her tightly puckered asshole, pressing into it, testing it. "I'll need lube," she whimpered.

"I have it here. You can tell me when you're ready."

She pulled a cushion in under her face. Her voice was muffled when she said, "It's too big. I've never done this before." She sounded like a child, like a frightened child trying to be brave.

I froze as full comprehension of the situation and her fear clobbered me. And I knew then that there had been signs. I didn't know how I'd missed reading them.

"I'm sorry," she mumbled into the cushion.

"It's OK. I wish you'd told me. Your story gave me the impression you were more…you know…but that's OK. It's OK." Making my voice soft as powder I said, "Tell me what you want."

I could barely make out the words, but was sure I heard her say, "Fuck me."

"You want a cunt fuck?"

She sniffled, "Yes."

I could see, within its veil of dark curls, the pink of her cunt was slick with juice. I knew I could make her say again what she wanted, say it louder. "You have to tell me. I want to hear it."

"I want a cunt fuck," she whispered.

"Louder. Ask nice for it." I knew I could make her beg.

There *is* one sound sweeter than a butch saying, "Yes, sir." It's when they say, "Please, sir. Please fuck me." I made her repeat it again and again, louder and louder, until she was ready to scream it at me. When finally I centered my cock head on her creamy opening and entered her, she sobbed with relief. And when I pulled back out, she cursed me. "Damn you," she howled, rocking back and forth on her knees, groaning her need.

When I thrust into her again, she pushed back to meet me and took me in deep, clenching on my shaft, grunting and weeping her release, riding back into me until I too came, taking my pleasure from hers.

But that's not the end of this story. It's really just the beginning. We've had many nights together since then and she's written about them all, and had the collection published. So if you want to know more, pick up a copy of her book. She's out promoting it right now. Maybe even at a club or bookstore near you. Just look for a tall faggy dyke who works the room like a pro, who knows what she wants and isn't afraid to ask for it. Be careful, though. You could end up in one of her stories.

Lock Bend Exodus

Julie Lieber

1 suppose we done the old lady wrong by taking her teeth. Others might say we done more wrong in stealing all her cash. The way we see it, she had no more claim to the money than we had. At least that's what Angie says, though she won't talk about the teeth. I suspect that part of the caper leans on her conscience.

My grandmother's sister Ida raised me. My mother dropped me off at Aunt Ida's house when I was a baby and ran off with some good-time Charlie from up in Virginia. People at church always told me to pray on it, and Mama might come back for me. She never did, but I never prayed for it either. As long as I minded Aunt Ida and went to church, we got along just fine.

Then I grew up. When I turned 17 I got a bit restless and took to staying out late at night with young people who weren't from the church. Aunt Ida called them no-accounts. I had to sneak around a lot. Then last year, when I was 19, I got caught for shoplifting, and there wasn't any sneaking around that. Aunt Ida screamed and cried, said I'd better straighten up or she'd turn me out of the house for good. So I didn't have much choice about joining her Prison Ministry for Ladies.

Aunt Ida had been ministering at the Women's Prison in Lock Bend for as long as I could remember. She preached to small groups of inmates. She taught the illiterate how to read and gave away booklets about Jesus. Once a month she hosted a warden-approved gospel party in the prison mess hall. Aunt Ida sang gospel songs, and the warden provided refreshments. All the inmates were invited, and about half of them usually showed up.

My part was in helping with the gospel parties. A lot of inmates came to the parties because the warden let their families come too, and those poor lonely women wanted more than anything to see their kin. The families were so grateful, they testified and praised the Lord and gave generously when Aunt Ida passed around the offering basket.

That's how I met Angie. She turned up at a gospel party a few months ago. I noticed she was staring at me, but she never opened her mouth, not even to say amen. I thought maybe I had spilled something on my bosom, and then it dawned on me that she was taking notice of my shape, which I'm very satisfied with, and which Aunt Ida has always warned me about, telling me I should cover myself to avoid wantonness with men.

She never said anything about women. I felt sorry for Angie at first, not having any family to visit with her for the gospel, so I sat next to her one evening to chat. It was partly the way she made me laugh but more the way she looked at me that made me warm to her. Pretty soon I was visiting her at the prison without Aunt Ida's knowing about it. I lied and told the guards it was for the ministry. Angie couldn't touch me through the prison windows when I visited her alone. She could only gaze at me and smile, and it was a wicked smile, with mischief in her eyes, like she had her hand under my skirt, and sometimes her smile and her eyes gave me the same feeling as if her hands were on me, and I felt hot.

Of course by then I knew Angie had no interest in redemption. She just wanted to get out. It was at a gospel party, where we could talk without guards listening in, that she asked me to help her escape.

"I'm here to give hope to your soul," I said. "I'm no jailbreaker."

"Tracy," she said, "you're here to give me wet dreams, and you know it. You want me too. I can tell. So you just drop the angel act and do like I say."

We sat close so that our legs touched, and she leaned in and whispered in my ear and hid her hand behind my back and slid her fingers under the seat of my skirt. I felt her breath on my neck as she talked in my ear, and her voice fell in a whisper. "Are you gonna help me, Tracy?" Her lips brushed against my ear, and I glanced nervously around the mess hall. Everybody was singing praises as Aunt Ida preached. "Don't be scared, baby. Nobody's watching us. We're just chatting." She pinched my bottom over the fabric of my dress. "When you break me out I want you to show more skin. Clothes are like another kind of wall, and I want to take yours down, sugar."

I didn't dare breathe, for I knew if I did I would let go a moan. I parted my legs slightly so she could slide her hand closer to my crotch.

She shuddered, her lips still grazing my ear. "You're wet. I can feel it through your skirt. I can't even kiss you. I'll carry your scent back to my cell tonight and lay awake in misery for wanting you so much. If you don't get me out of here, I'll do something desperate, Tracy. You've got to help me."

My whole body broke out in sweat. "Anything," I mumbled.

"What?"

"I said I'll do anything."

She glanced over her shoulders to make sure nobody was watching. Her voice was low and steady. "I'm on a work crew near the south field. You don't know where that is, so listen up." She gave clear directions on where to go and what to do, and made me repeat after her.

I said, "I don't have a car."

"How the hell do you visit here alone?"

"That's the ministry car. Ida's Cadillac. She thinks I take it for shopping."

"They'll recognize that," she said. She looked deep in thought.

"My cousin Vern has a truck," I said on a sudden thought. "I can take it."

She smiled. "Do it. Only don't let on like it was you. Make like it gets stolen. Even if it gets spotted, we can fix it so they don't trace it to him."

Now there are those who would judge me for spiriting a jailed convict away in a truck stolen from my own cousin. No doubt those same people would question why we flipped the truck in a ravine and set it afire. Angie said Cousin Vern could justly claim it stolen and collect the insurance money in good conscience. Besides, she said, it was a piece of shit.

Nobody saw her leave the penal farm. She figured they never even missed her till head count. She was a trusty from a minimum-security wing on work detail. A prison break was as easy as a smoke break, she said. And that's when she took off: At the very instant a guard turned his back to light a cigarette, she bolted down a hill and hopped over a creek bank, rolling down stream to the south field, where I was waiting in the truck.

She jumped in and told me to floor it. I spun the wheels

and kicked back gravel. She told me where to drive, and I stopped the truck when she said so, in an old mining yard with rocky ravines. She grabbed the change of clothes I'd brought her and told me to get out and help her tip the truck down a ravine.

After we set fire to it, I asked, "What are we gonna do now?"

She was looking at the fire and breathing heavy from her labors. She turned to me and smiled. She pulled her straight black ponytail out and threw the rubber band on the ground. She walked toward me as she unbuttoned her shirt, streaks of perspiration gleaming against her brown chest. I started to pick up her new clothes, but her eyes stopped me. They were narrow, black eyes like an Indian's, full of warmth and mystery. She stepped out of the orange-and-yellow glow of the fire below like an otherworldly spirit. She took my hand and led me into an oak grove behind the mining yard.

I fell into her embrace and lost all feeling for a few seconds, but her kiss electrified me. It was like all my nerve endings were exposed, and she had her hands on all of them. She held me tight by my buttocks and the small of my back, and then took her hand up under my skirt. "You bare-assed?" she asked, grinning.

"You said you didn't want no walls."

She laid me down on the moist, smooth carpet of moss and stroked the insides of my thighs. She pulled my legs apart, took her hand inside me, and covered my mouth with hers. It didn't hurt like I thought it might, but I was burning up inside and so wet she couldn't hurt me no matter how deeply she penetrated. I split my legs as far wide as I could and pushed her face into my bosom. All my senses rolled up to one spot laid bare between my legs, and I pitched a fit. She turned me over. I was shaking and breathing heavily into the moss. I heard her unzip her pants and pull them off, and then felt her hand slide back inside me. She pulled my bottom up and rubbed my hip between her legs. She pushed back and forth along a slick track of my hip until she let go a husky cry and unloosed a flood down my leg. I came right along with her, digging my fingernails in the moss and sticking my legs straight out, stiff as line-dried cotton.

She lay down next to me. She was smiling, a sweaty strand of black hair stuck to her lip. I got my breathing steady and asked, "What are we gonna do now?"

"I need to hide out," she said. "I figure I can stay with you."

"I live with Aunt Ida."

"The preacher lady?"

"I thought you knew that."

"Shit."

"It's a big old farmhouse. It might work."

She looked troubled. Then it dawned on me that I didn't just want to help her—I had to. I was an accomplice to escape, and for all I knew she was a killer, a drug dealer, a thief. I didn't know what and I didn't care. "She never looks in on me," I said.

"How's that?"

"Her knees and joints are bad with arthritis, and she can't climb steps. So I stay upstairs. She never knows what I'm up to."

A thick black cloud of smoke billowed up from the ravine. She raised up and said, "We best get out of here."

"How? We just burned up the truck."

"Of course we burned it. We can't be caught in a stolen truck. You ready to hike?" I lay there half naked wondering where my shoes had gone. She rubbed my belly and winked, telling me to sit up. She pulled my dress all the way off and looked at my naked body with something like love in her eyes. I thought she would never take her eyes off me, so lost was she in the sight of my flesh. There was a sudden boom, and she looked over my shoulder. "That fire's gonna attract attention. We best get out of here."

She put on the new clothes I had brought her while I got dressed and wiped my legs clean with her old prison shirt. Drenched in the embers of fire and sex, we walked about two miles out to the state highway and hitched a big old trailer rig. The fellow was real nice and said he was passing through to North Carolina, but he didn't mind dropping two pretty young ladies off at the county line, which was a 10-mile hike to Aunt Ida's.

A waxing moon hung in the sky above us, but it was dark as pitch under the shade of oak trees as we straggled up a hill to the house. Ida was in bed, so sneaking Angie upstairs wasn't a chore. We got to know each other pretty good once we got home, but not the way you're thinking, not at first. We lay in bed and stared at the shadows of willows sweeping across the ceiling as Angie explained how she ended up in prison.

Angie said there was a law against shooting in an occupied dwelling, but she got in trouble for what she called shooting in an occupied person. The law called it attempted murder. What happened was she caught her lover in bed with another woman.

"I snapped. I went for the shotgun and took care to aim for the right one."

"How come you shot the one you loved and let be the one you didn't even know?"

"She hadn't betrayed me." She let go a heavy sigh. "I figured there was somebody else to deal with her, or not to. It weren't my business."

The jury called it aggravated assault. She got five years, and after two years she came up for parole.

"They denied me. Well, I figured I'd learned my lesson whether they thought so or not. For weeks I pondered how I'd get out, without much in the way of a good idea. Then I heard about the gospel parties, and how there was a mix of family and friends among the inmates. Figured I'd lay my hooks in somebody on the outside."

"So you laid your hooks in me," I said, but she just smiled in that way that made me want to please her.

She raised up on one arm and faced me in the moonlight. "Naw. It was the other way around," she said low and easy. She tugged at the hem of my nightshirt. "What are you doin' in that thing?"

"You've got one on too."

She sat up and pulled hers off. She had a strong build and a finer bosom than mine. I let her open my nightshirt, as I lay still and watched her run her fingers along my skin, and she smiled at me sweetly, without any meanness in her eyes. She leaned over me and tenderly caressed my belly and my stiffening breasts. I turned over on my stomach, almost by instinct, for I knew she wanted to taste my whole body, and I wanted her to. She touched me all over with her hands and lips and tongue, like she was consuming my flesh and spirit all at once. I felt as if I were adrift on some warm south sea.

She whispered, "Sugar, you won't be getting much sleep for a while." She turned me over on my back and parted my legs. She kissed the inside of one thigh as she went down. She parted my lips with her tongue and bore inside, licking me inside and out. She swept her tongue along my clit, long and slow at first, then shorter and quicker as she zoned in on my spot. When she found it, I gasped and rose up on my elbows, wild-eyed. She winked at me and played with it, teasing me by moving away from it and descending inside again, then coming back and sliding all around it. I fell down on my back and writhed while she toyed with me, flicking her tongue closer,

closer, until she touched down and drew a tide of rapture.

I brought a pillow to my face. Angie's breath and low groaning rose with the quickness of her tongue, and she gasped mightily when my little rivulet let loose upon her cheeks. I arched my back with the rising swell beneath her tongue, until a white-hot wave of ecstasy rolled over me and I screamed into my pillow like I was going mad.

"Hellfire!" she whispered. "What was that?"

"My muffled screams."

"Damn. You act like you was the one locked up."

"We best not do this in Aunt Ida's house again."

She shimmied up next to me and stroked my cheek. "Yeah, you'll need to keep me scarce around here. That'll be tricky."

It wasn't easy keeping Angie shy of Aunt Ida's notice, except at night. By the mornings, Aunt Ida went on errands and to Bible meetings, and witnessed at the nursing home. I rested after breakfast, though Angie waited till afternoon, when Aunt Ida got home. She whiled away the lonesome hours as best she could without calling attention to herself, but she grew restless.

After Aunt Ida went to bed at sundown, we sneaked outside and ran down to the old barn. It was risky running down there, but Angie said she needed the air. It hadn't been used in years, except for the hay Aunt Ida's farmhands stored in it. I made a little living spot in there for me and Angie. The first few hours of each evening were largely spent in the throes of passion, which seemed to grow with each passing night, though always a bit one-sided.

I felt like there wasn't a square-inch patch of my flesh that Angie hadn't tasted and touched several times over. She made love to me with such fever she wouldn't stop until I came dry. When she came she wanted me facing down away from her, but one night I turned over and pulled her down and thrust my hand between her legs. Her eyes went ablaze. She pushed me off her and looked at me so fiercely I thought she might slap me. My heart pained and my eyes welled up. I started crying.

"What the hell are you crying for?" she demanded. "Stop it, now."

"That was hateful," I said, trying in vain to stifle my sobs.

"I don't want you to fuck me. Besides, you don't know what you're doing."

That broke my heart. I lay down in the hay and felt more sorrowful than I had in all my life. "You're cold-blooded," I said. "I just want to make love to you."

She put her hand on my shoulder. "Aw, baby. I just ain't ready."

"How come?"

"I don't know. I feel like if a girl does that too soon in a romance, I'm liable to lose respect for her."

"Well, you did it right off the bat. I still respect you."

"That's different. Anyway, stop talking about it. It's hard to explain."

"You just don't want to feel beholden to me. That's what it is."

She turned me over and gave me that dark look of hers. "Beholden? You broke me out, so I've been beholden from the get-go. I said I don't want to explain it. Don't act like you know me, little girl. You don't know shit." She kissed my forehead and lay down. "Hey, you still want to go to Canada with me?"

I would have gone anywhere with her. "Yes."

As we lay on old quilts by the light of oil lanterns, it crossed my mind that she didn't love me, and I grew ever sadder. And the more she talked, the deeper my heart sank. All Angie wanted to talk about was plotting her run to Canada. She would need a car and then a switch down the road to keep the law off her trail. And getting all the way to Canada would cost. She needed money.

I knew where she could find money, though I didn't tell her at first. Aunt Ida hid the money from her gospel parties under the floorboards beneath her bed. She never banked the money and never paid taxes on it. She always said, "Render unto Caesar that which can be traced" and called the money God's own mercy.

I figured there was no sense in it going to waste. I thought Angie could use some of it to get to Canada, and I waited till Aunt Ida went out on her morning errands one day and sneaked into her bedroom. I moved her bed to one side and lifted the loose pine slabs in the floor. The money was kept in freezer bags, and I grabbed a fat one. I stuffed it in my pocketbook, fitted the pine slabs back in place, and pushed the bed to its centered spot above the secret trove of cash.

That night, after Aunt Ida was in bed, I washed the dishes, which was my regular chore, and warmed up the leftovers from what I had cooked. This was my habit now that Angie was living upstairs. She liked having a cold beer with her supper, and that was tricky, since Aunt Ida forbade alcohol. I crept down to the basement, where I kept a cooler full of ice, and snatched a beer for the tray. When I had the plate and the beer ready, I took the freezer bag out of my pocketbook and put it on the tray. Then I took Angie her supper.

I put the tray by her bedside, and she squinted as her eyes became adjusted to the dull lamplight. Then her eyes grew wider, and she got a hungrier look staring at the forest green and ivory tones of those treasury notes.

"How much is there?" she asked.

"A thousand in 20s and some small bills."

"You counted?"

"I sure did."

She tore open the bag and flipped through the bills. "Where'd you get it?"

"Out from under the floor of her bedroom, under the bed."
She looked agape at me. "How much has she got?"

"I don't know," I shrugged. "She's been collecting it for years. I'd say thousands."

"You never counted it?"

"What for?"

"What the hell do you mean what for? All that cash rotting away under her bed and you ain't even curious?"

"It ain't my money."

"It ain't hers, either. This is that money she ripped off from all them poor families at the gospel parties, huh?"

I explained that it was charitable contributions for Aunt Ida's ministry, and Angie had no call to accuse her of thieving. Angie laughed real sarcastically and called Aunt Ida a hypocrite.

She leaned in close to me and said, "Tracy, honey, there's two kinds of people. Them that dwells in the flesh of this world, which is me, and them that dwells in the kingdom of heaven, which is not you, and is not the old lady." That's what she called Aunt Ida, the old lady.

"Which one am I?"

"You're in the flesh, sugar, whether you like to admit it or not."

"And Aunt Ida?"

She grinned savagely. "You have to lay claim to the life of sinner or saint, Tracy. That old lady has herself a cush spot somewheres in between, which is the life of a hypocrite. If there's a Judgment Day, I'll have better shot at eternal life than that deceiving old bag."

"Don't call my Aunt Ida names."

"I call it like I see it, sugar." She dropped the bag next to her on the bed. "Come here, curly head." She pulled me down on the bed and fixed her black eyes on mine. "You're prettiest thing I've ever seen. Go on down to the barn and light the lamp.

I'll be down directly." She rose up over me and seized me with a deep kiss. "Mmm. I want to turn you inside out. Go on before I do something here that'll wake the old lady up for sure."

Of course, all the while I was keeping Angie company, preparing her meals and plotting her escape, there was a hefty bounty on her head. It was all over the news in nine counties. It troubled Aunt Ida that one of the unsaved souls of the Women's Prison had broken loose of the just hand of the law, but she only spoke of it once or twice. After a week or so I had grown used to my secret life with a fugitive, right under the nose of my dear old aunt. The only worry troubling my head was the thought of Angie taking off to Canada and leaving me behind. I hadn't a shade of concern that Aunt Ida would find us out, as careful as I was. But the old lady turned out to be anything but a fool.

"There's trouble afoot!" Aunt Ida hollered one morning as I fired up the gas for her fried eggs and bacon.

My spine went all rubbery, and devil's fingers tickled the base of my neck. I turned to see her glaring at me through the doorway of the kitchen. "What's the matter, Aunt Ida?" I asked feebly.

She cast me a suspicious eye. "There's been money taken from up under my bed."

I was flush from head to toe, but I played like it was on account of concern over her predicament. "Whatever happened?"

"Don't act to me like you don't know! You've thieved before, though I never thought I'd see the day you'd thieve from your own flesh and blood!"

I couldn't believe she noticed one missing freezer bag among dozens stashed away. I played dumb, still and serene as a lamb. "What are you talking about?"

Her brow sagged. "You've done pilfered God's money from my mercy bank, is what I'm talking about."

By now I was upright and indignant. "I never bother your room and you know it! What's got into you?"

Her features took on a softer look, like she was confused, and she shook her head. She began to cry, and I almost pitied her. "Maybe my mind's going," she sobbed. "But I know how much I had in there. Oh, Lord, I do hope I haven't gone to misplacing things! I do take it out on occasion for a count. Maybe I left a bag in some odd place. Oh, Tracy, child, promise me you didn't take it."

I rushed to her side and took her in my arms, and I comforted her as best I could, telling her not to worry about losing her mind, which was her greatest fear. I felt tempted to tell her she needn't worry, that she was sharp as a tack and had me plum figured out. But I couldn't. For as strong as my feeling was for absolving the agony of Aunt Ida, my desire to please the fugitive lurking upstairs was even greater. Loyalty to the old lady was treachery to Angie, and I had already staked my claim.

Angie says you can't know a person by what they say or how they think. You only really know a person by their gut reactions, when there isn't time to sort things out by word or thought. She knew what she was going to do the minute I told her about Aunt Ida's missing cash.

"I'm leaving tomorrow and that's that," she told me as we lay on the bush-hogged field below the barn. She sat up, leaning into her arms outstretched behind her. "What about you?"

I looked up at the near perfect orb of the moon in a clear autumn sky and recalled the night almost two weeks before, when we had trudged exhausted under its waxing glow to home. The promise of its fullness gave me the idea that we were blessed in some way, that I was meant to leave with Angie when the time came. I said, "I want to go where you go, if you'll have me."

She had her back to me, like she was letting me know the choice was mine. She said, "I'll need your help."

"What do you want me to do?"

"I want you to make the old lady scarce tomorrow. All day long, until suppertime. Can you figure out a way to do that?"

"Yeah."

"At sundown, we'll leave."

"What are you gonna do?"

"Never you mind. Just keep her away, like I said."

It dawned on me that she meant to rob that money. "Don't take all of it," I whispered. "That'd be mean."

She didn't look at me. "It ain't hers."

"It ain't yours either."

"I've learned my lesson," she said, almost prayerfully, like she was talking to that moon. "Now it's time that old lady learned hers. I got the idea when I was inside, after one or two of those gospel parties, that she had a deal with the warden. Ain't no doubt in my mind now. Some old preacher lady running through the pockets of wretches, and a happy warden standing by for his cut. Why the hell else would he let her run a scam like that right under his nose? I've toured the house, Tracy, while she was away, and you was resting upstairs. I got real familiar with where y'all keep things about. Especially under the floorboards. You never counted that pile of cash. Well, sugar, it's nigh on 30 grand. Fifty-odd freezer bags packed with donations. After the warden's kickbacks." She snorted. "To hell with them, Tracy. To everlasting hell with them."

She turned and leaned over me. "You still want to go with me?"

"Yes, Angie. I don't care where you end up. I'd follow you clear to jail."

Her dark features looked soft in the scant light. "Let's sleep out here tonight."

"It's getting cold."

"We've got quilts and sleeping bags."

She made us a bed under the moon, and I laid her down to rest. We were warm and naked on top of old sleeping bags laden with quilts. I climbed on top of her and felt snug between her flesh and the weight of the covers.

I felt her legs part underneath mine. "I want you, little doll." She held my hand and moved it between her legs. "Touch me." She gave me a sly look and stroked my hair.

She was warm and wet to my touch. I kissed her desperately, but I was nervous about doing much else, and my ignorance embarrassed me. "I love you, Angie."

She nudged me after a little while and said, "Sugar, just do whatever comes over you. Whatever fuels your need. Shoot. I could come at the sight of you and not much else." I rested my head on her breasts and moved my hand back and forth between her legs. She drew her legs farther apart and gave a sigh. "That's good, baby. No, no. Don't put it in. I'm not so crazy about that. I want you to kiss it."

"You mean your vagina?"

"Pussy, honey. This ain't the doctor's office," she giggled.

Not knowing what I was doing, I surprised myself that it came rather natural to me. I lay down between her legs and felt aflame inside my own skin as I took her into my mouth. I swept about the folds of her tender flesh with my tongue, not trying to imitate how she made love to me, but according to my own whim. I parted her lips and found her clit, as firm and full as a huckleberry. I was rapt in her wetness, spellbound by her sex. I heard her breath grow heavy and her voice give out a low moan, and by its pitch I could tell she was smiling. She told me how good I made her feel. Then all of a sudden she stopped me and grasped me by the hair of my head.

I looked up at her. "What?" I asked fretfully. She had barely begun to show signs of pleasure, and now she was staring at me with that old fire in her eyes.

"Come on up here."

I felt uneasy, for her look was stern, and she held fast to my hair, though it didn't hurt. She pulled me up to her and cupped my face firmly in her hands. Her grip was strong, and her breath was heavy.

"Don't be mad," I said. "A girl can't learn everything all at once."

"I can't let you go on till you make me a promise."

I nodded.

"You won't let me down tomorrow."

"No way."

"You'll stay with me to the end. Never leave me, not even after we've made it."

"I'll never leave you."

"I love you, Tracy, and I will love you till the death of one of us." It sounded almost like a threat. Whichever way I looked at it, my fate was sealed.

The next day I cooked a real fine breakfast for Aunt Ida. Biscuits with gravy and sausage and fluffy scrambled eggs and boiled apples. She acted solemn, though, like it didn't even please her a little bit. She stared at me while she poked at her food, and I got a bad feeling she knew something. Like I said, she was no fool.

"Why are you going to the home with me all of a sudden?" she asked.

"I want to minister to the sick," I said.

She dropped her fork and leaned back in her chair. "Is that a fact? That's a might Christian of you, Tracy, child!"

I noticed she wasn't altogether convinced of what she was saying, so I kept my mouth shut, with bated breath.

She scooted back and pushed herself to her feet. She disappeared into the hallway, and I heard her walk into her bedroom. Then she came barreling back to the kitchen—shuffling along as quickly as her arthritic legs would carry her—and she burst through the swinging door shaking an empty beer bottle at me. She was a little woman with a little voice, but she could be fearsome. "How long have you been spiriting the devil's poison in my house?" she hollered in a high pitch that chilled me.

It wasn't deceit but curiosity that made me ask, "Where did you get that?"

She clutched that bottle like she was wringing a neck. "I went looking for my money, like I do every day since I lost it—or you stole it, you foul little sinner—but I'd looked everywhere I could think of except the trash cans up yonder. Don't act like you don't know it! I found half a dozen of these empty bottles. You've been a-drinkin', and I told you back when you ran afoul of the law that I'd not put up with vice in this household."

She pitched the bottle into the wastebasket and said calmly, "I'll not be toting you to no ministry of the sick today, child. You get your things packed, and then we'll spend the morning in prayer before I take you to the shelter for wayward women."

I was shaking from head to toe, though not from fear of a shelter. I feared what Angie would do now, for I knew she was listening. I climbed the stairs to pack my things in accordance with Aunt Ida's wishes and, as fate had it, my own plans for later that day.

Angie was waiting. "I've already packed our stuff," she hissed, her eyes black conniving slits. "I got all your little vanity items and whatnots." She handed me my suitcase. "Go on downstairs and do what I say." Then she told me what to do.

I walked slowly down the steps and looked for Aunt Ida. I spotted her through the doorway to the kitchen. "Aunt Ida? Is that you in the kitchen?" I asked loudly.

"Course it's me!" she hollered. "Now come in here and sit down to pray."

I had one task ahead of me after the prayer, before Angie took over. I always drove Aunt Ida when we traveled together, on account of her stiff hands, so it was my habit to ask for the key, which I did. She picked slowly through her pocketbook for the key and handed it to me. "This will be the last time you drive me, unless you fall to the floor and beg for forgiveness."

I felt weak. I took a deep breath and said as loud as I could without shouting, "Let's go, Aunt Ida!"

"Child, I ain't deaf! What's got into you?"

Angie had the stealth of a cat. She came up fast behind Aunt Ida from the shadow of the hallway and wrestled the old lady's arms behind the chair.

"Lord God!" Aunt Ida screamed. "Who's that?"

"Be still, Sister Ida," Angie said low. "Tracy tells me you got a strong heart." She stayed behind Aunt Ida so as not to show her face.

"Go easy on her," I said. "Don't break her arms. Remember the arthritis."

"What?" Aunt Ida gasped. She was hyperventilating. "Tracy! Child! You know this woman?" She looked dreadfully afraid.

Angie was gentle, under the circumstances. She held Aunt Ida's arms back and directed me to tie each one separate to the arms of her chair with leather straps she had found in the barn. I did as I was told and whispered to Aunt Ida not to worry, that we didn't mean to hurt her.

lock bend exodus

Then she got her fire back. "You evil varmint!" she hollered, looking at me with dagger eyes. "You fiendish harlot!"

Angie had told me not to talk to her, no matter what she said. It was hard to ignore her calling me a harlot and a demon. Still, I worried about Aunt Ida. I told Angie, "Her arthritis is bad. She won't be able to free herself without help. She'll die up here alone."

Angie scowled at the back of Aunt Ida's head, but more in the way you'd scowl at a flat tire or a busted water main. "How else are we gonna keep her down?"

"She can't put up much of a chase. And you've already cut the phone line."

All the while, Aunt Ida was screaming and crying in rage. "You foul devil! You ungrateful whore! I'll not have you in my house after this!"

"Get me a rag," Angie said. "She's fraying my nerves."

I handed her a dishcloth off the counter. She held the old lady's head tight and whispered in her ear, "OK, Sister Ida. Spit 'em out." She meant the dentures, and that gave me an idea.

Aunt Ida hollered, "Let go of my head, Satan. Stay thee behind me!"

"I said spit 'em out," Angie repeated, gritting her teeth. "I'm liable to snap your neck, the way you keep on."

Aunt Ida froze up, and her eyes welled with tears. She slowly worked her teeth loose and gently spit them into my hand. She sure gave me a spiteful look, though.

"She can't talk at all without her teeth in," I said, while Angie stuffed the rag in Ida's mouth.

"Get me that duct tape you keep in your tool drawer yonder."

I got the tape and handed it to her, but I appealed to Angie as she taped over the cloth. "So if we undo the straps and let her loose, she ain't got no way to call for help, not for a while.

269

No phone, bad knees and joints. Even when she reaches somebody, she won't be able to talk. Nobody understands a word she says when she don't have her teeth in. And she can't write a word with her hands the way they are. Well, she can, but it takes forever."

Angie took off her belt and wrapped it around Aunt Ida's chest and buckled it tight in back of the chair. "Watch her," she said, and ran into Aunt Ida's bedroom.

Aunt Ida's eyes bulged as the realization came to her what Angie was in there doing. She tried to shout, but the cloth and tape stifled her, and she began to cough and choke against her rage. She struggled against her binds with such fury that I wondered whether God hadn't miraculously cured her of arthritis. "Hurry!" I shouted, careful not to call Angie by name.

"Let's go," she said at last as she breezed into the kitchen. "Get the car started."

So that's why we took her teeth. Not out of meanness like everybody on the news has been making out. We weren't evil, just desperate. We took pity on the old lady and left her untied, though she seemed wore out by the time we had packed her Cadillac with our belongings and her money. I daresay it was hours before she made her way to a neighbor's house, and by the time she made any sense I'd surmise we had already ditched the Cadillac and picked up that Honda we found in a Wal-Mart parking lot. I doubt anybody knew Angie had a thing to do with it before we crossed the state line into Kentucky and caught a bus to Chicago. They know now, though. We saw it in a national newspaper this morning. That's why we're lighting out of here today, Canada bound. Angie says that's where we'll find some peace, and I guess I believe her.

Contributors

J.L. Belrose's stories have appeared in the anthologies *Queer View Mirror, Pillow Talk II, Skin Deep, Best Women's Erotica, Uniform Sex, Set in Stone, Body Check, Herotica 7*, and *Hot and Bothered 3*. She lives in Ontario, Canada.

Patrick Califia is the author of three erotica collections (*Macho Sluts, Melting Point*, and *No Mercy*) and several nonfiction books. Califia's most recent book is *Sensuous Magic: A Guide to S/M for Adventurous Couples*, available from Cleis Press.

Wendy Caster is the author of *The Lesbian Sex Book*. Her short stories have appeared in *Bedroom Eyes, Lesbian Bedtime Stories 2, Heatwave*, and *Lip Service*. Her published work also includes opinion columns, articles, reviews, and interviews. She lives in New York City.

Raphaela Crown has published erotica on cleansheets.com and has had a short story published in *Best Women's Erotica 2002*. Her work has also appeared in *The Paris Review, The New Republic, The Massachusetts Review, University of Pennsylvania Law Review*, and *Seventeen* magazine. A lawyer and teacher, she lives in Jerusalem.

Linnea Due is the author of three novels and *Joining the Tribe: Growing up Gay and Lesbian in the '90s*. She is also the editor of the erotic anthologies *Uniform Sex* and *Hot Ticket* and coeditor of *Dagger: On Butch Women*.

While earning a doctorate in English literature, **Margaret Granite** wrote erotica to prevent desiccation of her creative organ. She now teaches college writing, indulges a screenplay-writing habit, and authors a column for the 'zine *Domestic Queer*.

Sacchi Green has had work published in *Best Lesbian Erotica* (1999, 2000, and 2001), *Zaftig, Set in Stone, Best Women's Erotica* (2001 and 2002), *Best Transgender Erotica*, and *More Technosex*.

Myriam Gurba is a Chicana femme dyke born and raised in semirural California. She works as an editorial assistant for *On Our Backs*. Her nonfiction has appeared in *On Our Backs, Girlfriends*, and *Inside Pride 2001*.

Renee Hawkins is a disc jockey living in Atlanta, Georgia. Her fiction has also appeared in *Pillow Talk II* and *Best Lesbian Love Stories 2003*.

Ilsa Jule lives in New York City, where she spends some of her time writing. She dedicates "Mrs. Sullivan Takes Off" to Elizabeth Grainger and Leah Devun.

Julie Lieber has published short stories in *Love Shook My Heart II* and *Bedroom Eyes*.

Rosalind Christine Lloyd identifies as a "womyn of color, native New Yorker, and Harlem resident." She has had work published in *Pillow Talk II, Hot & Bothered II, Best American Erotica 2001, Skin Deep, Set in Stone,* and *Faster Pussycats.* She is working on her first novel.

Computer geek by day and writer by night, **Catherine Lundoff** lives in Minneapolis with her fabulous girlfriend. Her short stories have appeared in anthologies such as *Best Lesbian Erotica 1999* and *2001, Electric, Zaftig!,* and *Set in Stone: Butch-on-Butch Erotica.*

Lesléa Newman has edited several anthologies, including *Pillow Talk: Stories of Lesbians Between the Covers* (volumes I and II) and *Bedroom Eyes: Stories of Lesbians in the Boudoir.* A fiction writer and poet, she has published many volumes of her own work, including the short story collections *Girls Will Be Girls, A Letter to Harvey Milk, She Loves Me, She Loves Me Not,* and the forthcoming *The Best Short Stories of Lesléa Newman.* Visit her Web site at www.lesleanewman.com.

Thomas S. Roche's fiction has appeared in publications such as the Best American Erotica series, the Mammoth Book of Erotica series, and the Best Gay Erotica series. He has also written or edited 10 books, including four volumes of the Noirotica series and his own short story collection, *Dark Matter.*

Anne Seale is a creator of lesbian songs and stories who has performed on many gay stages, including the Lesbian National Conference, singing tunes from her tape *Sex For Breakfast.* Her stories have appeared in *Set in Stone, Dykes With Baggage, Pillow Talk I* and *II, Lip Service, Love Shook My Heart, Hot and Bothered, The Ghost of Carmen Miranda, Wilma Loves Betty,*

Best Lesbian Love Stories 2003, *Harrington Lesbian Fiction Quarterly*, and other journals and anthologies.

Carol Queen has a doctorate in sexology, which she uses to impart realistic detail to her smut. She is the author of *Exhibitionism for the Shy*, *Real Live Nude Girl*, and *The Leather Daddy and the Femme*, and coeditor of *PoMoSexuals*, *Switch Hitters*, *Sex Spoken Here*, and *Best Bisexual Erotica*. She lives in San Francisco.

Jackie Strano is the lead singer of the band the Hail Marys. Along with her partner, Shar Rednour, she runs S.I.R. Productions, creators of the best-selling Bend Over Boyfriend series and the dyke erotic video duo *Hard Love & How to Fuck in High Heels*. Check out www.thehailmarys.com and www.sirvideo.com.

Renette Toliver is an African-American writer living in Dallas, Texas.

Trixi is the editor of the anthology *Faster Pussycats*. Her work also appears in *Body Check: Erotic Lesbian Sports Stories*.